A HUNDRED BILLION GHOSTS GONE

By D.M. Sinclair

First published by DMS Print 2020

This novel is entirely a work of fiction. The names,
characters and incidents portrayed in it are the work
of the author's imagination. Any resemblance to actual
persons, living or dead, events or localities is entirely
coincidental.

First edition
ISBN: 978-1-7752034-6-9

Book 2.
Only 99,999,999,998 to go.

1

All the lights went out, and the theater sank into darkness.

True darkness anywhere in the world was a rarity since the ghosts had returned. A hundred billion luminous souls was more than enough to keep even the deepest parts of night from ever being truly black. Even with all the lights off, any large space like the Orpheum Theatre in Boston would still be illuminated by the silvery-blue glow radiating from hundreds of ghosts in the room.

But not this time.

When this new blackout struck, the whole theater—and the entire Western hemisphere—went absolutely dark. It was an enveloping darkness the likes of which had not been seen in years. Everyone knew that this kind of dark could only mean one thing.

The ghosts were gone. All of them.

It drew from the living people in the auditorium a collective gasp of incredulity. The sound had a pressure to it that rippled through the space, a rolling shock wave of surprise.

It lasted for nine seconds. Nine full seconds of gasping blackness.

And then it was over.

The house lights snapped on, then blinked off, then blasted back on again and stayed that way. The light shouldered the dark aside, heaved it forcibly back into corners. And the ghosts, as quickly as they had vanished, faded up out of emptiness like fog breathed onto glass. In seconds, everything seemed to be as it had been. There was another collective sound, a sigh of relief.

But seconds later, there was a cry of alarm from someone at the front near the stage. Soon, other voices joined that cry. And gradually, mutterings of concern rippled through the crowd. There was an unmistakable rising sense that things had not gone completely back to normal. Something remained very, very wrong.

Ryan Matney was there. But he missed most of what happened because he was in the men's bathroom buying a box of cereal.

2

It was called Hubert.

It was named for the character on the box, a spherical caveman clad only in woolly hair, sneakers, and an upbeat attitude. It was produced for a single year, between 1974 and 1975, and even then only in extremely limited test markets. The manufacturer obviously knew that the name "Hubert" was woefully uninformative for a breakfast cereal, because the slogan in its magazine ad admitted "The name is a shame, but the taste is insane!" It boasted six essential vitamins along with a staggering smorgasbord of ingredients that were decidedly non-essential, at least in a dietary sense.

But by far the most significant thing about it was this:

It was butter-flavored.

Butter-flavored breakfast cereal. To Ryan, the words themselves were tantalizing. As a connoisseur of cereals, he prided himself on having tried literally every one. And yet he had never imagined that somebody might make a cereal that tasted like butter. Now that he knew about it, he could think of nothing in the world more enticing.

It took him years to find. He knew it existed thanks to clues and hints in the dark corners of the internet. But months of painstaking research turned up nothing. As far as Ryan could tell there were no intact boxes of Hubert anywhere in the world. He couldn't even find a whole picture of one. Hubert seemed to have faded away, forgotten, without ever having made the impact on the world that butter-flavored cereal surely deserved to.

And then, a glimmer of hope.

A man from Fort Collins, Colorado named Irvin Curry, who identified himself as a 1970s nostalgia collector, finally replied to one of Ryan's online posts. He claimed to possess, somewhere deep in his collection, a mint condition, unopened box of Hubert. Perhaps the only such box left in the world. It had been kept on a clean shelf in a cool, dry, ventilated space, so the cardboard was in good shape. It was reasonable to assume that there would be a standard liner bag inside providing moisture barrier and guarding against mineral oil migration, so it was likely that the contents were in decent shape. And Ryan had a strong intuition that after some cajoling, Irvin Curry might be willing to sell. He certainly had no need for the cereal. He was, after all, a collector specifically of nostalgia. And nobody on Earth, living or dead, was nostalgic for Hubert cereal.

As a precaution, Ryan didn't reveal that he planned to eat it.

He was worried, first, that Irvin Curry was a purist and would want the box kept intact. If Ryan revealed his true intention to open it and devour its contents, it could sour the deal.

And second, he was equally worried that Curry would try to tell him that eating cereal nearly fifty years old was not a good idea. Given that it was butter-flavored, even in 1975 eating it was something that most people would probably not have recommended.

Still, it existed, it was exceedingly rare, and it was something Ryan simply had to be a part of. He had found his Holy Grail. If he now happened to find the *actual* Grail as well, it would serve only as something to eat Hubert Cereal out of.

His mind was made up. He was going to offer two thousand dollars for it, more than had ever in history been paid for a box of cereal. It would surely outbid any other buyers sniffing around. And then, because he didn't trust couriers with so precious an object, he was going make the 30-hour drive to Colorado to get it. This seemed to him like a bargain. An archaeologist, after all, might fly halfway around the world and invest millions in recovering a broken hunk of Mesopotamian pottery. And an intact box of Hubert was certainly more valuable than that. For one thing, it was butter-flavored.

Margie was somewhat less enthusiastic about the idea. Or, at least, Ryan assumed she would be when he told her, which he hadn't yet.

He hadn't quite gotten used to the fact that, after living together for nearly thirteen months, they were sharing finances now. But he did understand that if he wanted to spend that much on something, he needed to tell her about it. And if he was going to disappear on a road trip across the country for several days, that was probably something she needed to know about in advance as well.

But he delayed. For days. Margie was a cereal-phile too but her interest tended to wane quickly outside suggested retail prices. And this cereal was significantly outside them. Even offering her a taste of the cereal would likely do little to mollify her. And he understood, in a small and thickly walled room near the very back of his brain, that buying the cereal was wasteful and frivolous beyond all reason.

But he still wanted to do it. Barely more than a year ago he had come perilously close to total existential obliteration, and that experience had given him the impetus to savor every moment of life to the utmost. And he expected to get quite a few such moments from Hubert. Butter-flavored ones.

He made up his mind on Monday morning. And then he resolved to tell Margie about it before the day was done. They were going to the theater that night for an event that Margie was excited about, so he knew he'd need to get it done before then.

He waited all day. But work, as it frequently did, got in the way. The Post-Mortal Services Clinic was busy and Margie was its Manager and Chief Specialist. As such, she always seemed to have a packed schedule. Even when she wasn't performing specific procedures, she did lengthy consultations both with ghosts and with their living relatives. That meant long hours. And Ryan was her "Lab Assistant", tasked with lab-assisting her in everything she did. That meant he had to do long hours too. He did it because it was better than his old job, and because it meant he could be around Margie all the time. But it was tedious, it was rarely fun, and it was almost never enriched with six essential vitamins.

It got to be late afternoon and the final scheduled appointment of the day before he determined that he could wait no longer. Irvin Curry's direct messages had started to sound impatient. So Ryan was forced to stop waiting for the perfect moment and just go for it.

He waited until she finished a consultation. The clients—a ghost in his 50s with a persistent cough and his exhausted-looking wife carrying an autographed football that, presumably, her dead husband was haunting—trudged out of her office. Ryan chose his moment to knock softly on Margie's door and push it open a crack.

Margie was behind her desk, typing notes, with her glasses halfway down her nose the way she always did when she worked at her computer. She didn't look up at him. "Wait outside, please. I'll call you in."

"Uh, it's me," Ryan said. He stepped through the door and closed it behind him.

She still didn't look up. "Are we ready downstairs? Mr. Tinsley is next."

He had studiously set up everything in the exam room in the basement because he knew she would ask exactly that question. And he wanted to put her in a good mood by having a good answer. "Yep. All set."

She nodded and kept typing.

It was time. He began simply. "Um..." Maybe *too* simply.

She glanced at him, but continued typing.

He tried again. "There's..." He prided himself that he had actually managed a word this time. But he was still far from getting his point across.

Before he could attempt the next word and whatever words would come after it, there was a rapid, hard knock at the office door. "Come in, Mr. Tinsley," Margie said.

The door was thrown open and the gaunt, spindly ghost of the Clinic's former owner, Roger Foster, unfolded into the office. "...always lovely to see you, Mr. Tinsley," Roger was saying. "You're looking well on such a trying day."

Ryan shifted aside as Mr. Tinsley strode in behind Roger. Mr. Tinsley was eighty-seven. The many years of mortal life had whittled away at his body like a paring knife gradually reducing an apple to its core. He was left with little more than brittle bones shrink-wrapped in papery flesh stretched to the utter limit. What remained of his body had to be near death, so he had begun preparations for his post-mortal ghostly existence. And he had decided—for reasons entirely his own—that he wanted to spend eternity dressed as Batman. His first plan was simply to wear the costume all the time and hope that he'd be wearing it when he happened to die of natural causes, thereby ensuring that his ghost would be wearing it forever. But despite all his knocking at death's door, death still hadn't gotten off the couch to answer. So he eventually elected instead to have his ghost manually extracted at a scheduled time wearing the costume of his choice. And the place to do that was here at the Post-Mortal Services Clinic.

So here he was, shuffling into Margie's office in a child's superhero costume he had evidently purchased at a Halloween store. He stopped just inside the door, puffed out his chest, and put his fists heroically on his hips while his cape settled around him like a curtain. "Let's get this done," he said. "I don't have all day."

Roger clasped his hands together and smiled benevolently at Mr. Tinsley. "I will of course do all I can to accommodate your schedule—"

Margie stopped typing and gave Roger a hard look. "Leave him alone, Roger."

Roger winced and closed his eyes, fighting whatever combative urges were welling up within him. "I apologize that your appointment today is not with me, Mr. Tinsley, but rather with this... person."

"You don't work here anymore, Roger," Margie said frostily.

Roger had been forcibly ousted from both his position in charge of the Clinic and from his body at the same time, on account of his being unspeakably corrupt and evil. But they had so far not managed to get him to leave. He wasn't haunting the place, or anything in it.

He just didn't want to give it up. So they had resorted to tolerating his pretense of still being in charge. Even Ryan, whose entire existence had been almost wiped out by Roger's scheming a year ago, now felt a little sorry for him.

Roger opened his eyes to offer Mr. Tinsley one more sympathetic look. "Oh dear, how awful that someone should behave this way on such an important—"

"Out, Roger," Margie said.

Roger compressed his long stick-insect limbs around him and slid out the door in a huff. Ryan could see his ghostly jaw muscles clenching as he went.

Margie pushed back from her desk and came around to meet her client. "How are we today, Mr. Tinsley? All ready?"

"I decided I'm going to be one of those ghosts that makes things move. Watch!" He swept one hand across the desk and knocked over a cup full of Margie's pens. "See? I've been practicing! Knocked them all over."

Margie gathered up the pens and put them back into the cup. "Well, it will likely be more difficult when you're a ghost."

"Mah!" Tinsley said with a hand wave. "It's all the same."

Margie seemed eager to get Mr. Tinsley out of her office before he could find something else to demonstrate on. "If you'll follow me downstairs, sir, we'll start the procedure. Thank you."

Tinsley whirled his cape dramatically and swept out the door.

Ryan felt his opportunity to talk to Margie slipping away. He took her arm gently as she moved to leave. "Margie, I need to—"

"It will have to wait. I need you downstairs."

"Yeah, but I need to—"

Margie studied Ryan as if he was a complex, multi-tiered street parking sign she was trying to decipher. "Need to what?"

Ryan's phone chirped, and he whipped it out.

A message. From Irvin Curry.

He didn't read every word, because there were lots of them he didn't care about. The ones he cared about said this: Curry was selling his entire collection as a single unit to another interested party. He was receiving a small fortune for it, which he intended to spend on a child's medical bills or something blah blah blah. But... he was willing to take the Hubert cereal out of the collection and ship it to Ryan separately. He would pack it in such a way that the courier couldn't possibly destroy it. He would send it immediately. If Ryan sent him the cash. Today.

Which Ryan couldn't do until he talked to Margie. And when he looked up from his phone, trembling with fresh excitement, Margie had already given up and followed Mr. Tinsley downstairs.

Ryan took one more look at the image Curry had sent of the cereal box. The illustration of Hubert the caveman up to now had always seemed cheerful to Ryan. But now, the same expression appeared annoyed. Hubert was losing patience with him. *Do it, you fool.*

I will, Hubert. I will.

3

Mr. Tinsley lay sprawled on the padded table in the exam room in the basement of the Clinic, fighting with tight spandex bat-shorts that had clearly been designed for a child. He adjusted them vigorously and then resumed his splayed-on-his-back pose. "Let's do this!" he demanded.

Ryan stood next to the Box and watched, wringing his hands the same way anxiety was wringing the softest parts of his digestive system.

Margie prodded at Mr. Tinsley's skull with a long metal instrument that was equal parts pointy, serrated, and electrified. That meant at least three possible ugly consequences if Ryan distracted her, so he stayed quiet and danced from foot to foot.

She finished with the prodding and deposited her instrument beside the Box on its cart. She picked up the "spider", a metal device with long spindly legs designed for delivering a precisely targeted electric charge into the client's brain. That was its intended function, but what it did most effectively was terrify clients. Mr. Tinsley had protested earlier when she insisted that they'd have to cut a hole in his Batman mask in order for the charge to reach his brain. And it was perfectly understandable why he was upset. What dramatic effect his costume managed to conjure up would be mostly negated as soon as he turned around and revealed his bald patch, exposed through a neatly cut round hole between his pointy bat-ears. But there was simply no other way to make the procedure work, and Margie's calm insistence eventually won him over. She affixed the spider to his head and adjusted its legs so they wouldn't puncture the old man's already distressed skin.

Mr. Tinsley watched Ryan skeptically. "What's he for?"

"I don't think even he's sure about that, Mr. Tinsley," Margie replied. "But I do need him. Ryan, charge please," she said. "Ninety percent. Two-stage."

This was the most important part of Ryan's job: operating the Box during Margie's procedures. The Box wasn't as complicated as, say, a respirator or an electron microscope. Not that he had ever used either of those, but he imagined they'd have more buttons. The Box, freshly modified and perfected by Margie, had only an on/off switch, a couple of dials for adjusting various aspects of the charge distribution, and a few other toggles and controls that Margie had told him to never, ever touch. Yet Ryan's indifference to the whole thing meant that it had taken him months to perfect even what few controls he needed to. Still, he was confident and competent now. And he was still determined to keep Margie happy so she'd respond well when he inevitably had to bring up the subject of Hubert Cereal again.

With practiced ease he clicked the switch to "on" and adjusted the dial for a ninety percent charge. As electricity flowed into the Box it began to hum, a slow and steady ascent through every octave from vibrating rumble to ear-stabbing shriek. Ryan always wished at these times that he had some kind of hearing protection, because by the time the Box was fully charged it could be genuinely painful to stand next to.

"What's that sound?" Mr. Tinsley said. He tried to shift his head so he could see the Box behind him.

"Don't move, Mr. Tinsley," Margie said. Her voice was level but layered with an urgency that forced Mr. Tinsley to hold still and shut up. She grabbed two paddles off the cart and held their flat surfaces against Mr. Tinsley's chest. She had already checked his bat-suit to make sure it would allow the charge through at that spot.

Waiting for the Box to charge was always the most agonizing part of the process. It had been so when Ryan was a patient, and it was nearly as much so now that he was an employee. It took a solid minute at least, and all he could do during that minute was stare at the Box in a way that made him appear to be expertly monitoring it. He did that now, letting his eyes drift over all the dials and readouts without knowing what they meant, and occasionally checking the little charge meter to make sure it was still climbing.

And as his eyes drifted, his mind did too. Like a leaf afloat on a trickling stream it drifted, bobbing languidly, uncaring. The stream, it so happened, flowed gently all the way to Fort Collins, Colorado. And his mind found its way along that stream to a single box on a single empty shelf, upon which a sneaker-clad caveman beckoned him with a bowl of cereal nuggets in one hand and a stick of butter in the other. He wondered if the nuggets of cereal would be moist from the butter, or if the butter flavor was just a powder dusted on them. And he wondered which of those two great options was better. He wondered how crunchy they were. He wondered what color the milk would turn after the nuggets had been marinating in it for two or three minutes. He wondered if, after eating the only box in existence, he would be forever depressed at the prospect of never, ever being able to eat it again. He wondered if—

"Ryan!"

Her sharp tone whipped Ryan's wandering mind back to the exam room, back to the Box, and back to Mr. Tinsley, whose costume was on fire.

He quickly pieced together that the fire was probably the reason Margie was upset.

Margie threw the paddles down and slapped the flames, which had rapidly blackened part of the chest and were now working on melting the bat logo into an unrecognizable blob. "Ryan! How much charge was that?"

Ryan's intellect got a grip on the moment and he checked the charge meter on the Box. He was surprised to find that it was at zero. No charge whatsoever.

The situation penetrated his brain like a hot railroad spike. She had asked for a "two-stage" charge. Ryan had learned during his training that a "two-stage" charge meant that Margie planned to discharge the Box twice. The capacitor could only hold so much power, so for a ninety-percent two-stage procedure Ryan was supposed to have charged it to sixty percent first, then immediately back to thirty percent after the first discharge. He hadn't done that, though. He had gone all the way to ninety on a single charge. He'd been distracted because his mind was doing that leaf-floating-on-a-stream thing, which had been a nice vacation at the time but now seemed like a bad idea.

"It's... I don't... ninety..." Ryan couldn't get sentences out. He also couldn't decide exactly how much of a problem this was. It seemed like maybe a lot.

Margie got the flames out so that the costume was only smoking. But the logo was completely melted and there was a ragged black hole in its place, exposing a small section of Mr. Tinsley's pale, bony chest and exactly four hairs of various whitish shades with burnt ends.

Mr. Tinsley lay absolutely still, and Margie stepped back to survey the damage.

"Is it bad?" Ryan said. "How bad is it?"

She didn't answer. So it was bad.

A bluish glow rose in and around Mr. Tinsley, surrounding his entire body like a second skin, and getting brighter fast. Ryan had seen this many times before. Mr. Tinsley's ghost, torn free by the jolt of electricity, was emerging.

The ghost, formless for now, lifted free of its body and floated there, serene, like a dry cleaning bag on an updraft. Then it seemed to roll over in the air, as though shifting sleeping positions in a bed. Ryan remembered this moment from when he had gone through this same procedure. The old man was looking down at his own body. Remembering who he was and what he looked like.

And while Ryan and Margie watched, tense and transfixed, the ghost started to take shape. They could see the suit, the rippling abdominals painted onto the torso, the cape, the gloves. The exposed lower jaw slowly became recognizable, with a look of astonishment rendered in increasing detail. And after perhaps thirty seconds of all that, pointy bat-ears popped out of the top of the head on either side of the exposed bald patch.

And also, dead center on the ghost's chest were the melted plastic bat, the scorched hole, and Mr. Tinsley's four burnt chest hairs.

Ryan and Margie, side by side, kept watching in silence. Ryan was afraid of saying anything at all, because that would open the door to Margie being upset with him for screwing up. He thought it best to keep that door closed for now.

Mr. Tinsley's ghost studied his body. Then looked at himself. "I'm Batman!" he said in a barely recognizable voice. It was a thrilling realization that he would get to have every day from now until, presumably, the heat death of the universe. Then he noticed the hole in the chest, which was another realization he'd get to have every day forever. He looked at his chest, his body's chest, then his ghost chest again. Both were smoking, and the ghost one would keep smoking literally for eternity. "What's that?" He frowned and poked at his exposed chest.

Ryan thought he should probably be the one to make the admission. He stepped forward, tense, afraid of being attacked by an elderly ghost Batman. But Margie started for him. "Mr. Tinsley, there was a small—"

Mr. Tinsley's scowl expanded smoothly into a grin. "Badass!" he said. He thrust out his chest proudly and pounded it with one fist.

Ryan almost collapsed onto the Box in relief.

He risked a sideways look at Margie to see if she was thinking about saying something to him. He feared what it might be, but he wanted to be ready for it when it came.

It came now. "Ryan," she said, "can I talk to you in the hall?"

◊

"I need to know," Margie said, quietly and far enough away from the door that there was no chance Mr. Tinsley would hear them, "are you here?"

"Yeah. I'm here," he said with a note of puzzlement. "Where else would I be?" He recognized right after, though, that this wasn't what she was asking at all. "Are you? Because it doesn't seem like you are. What we do in there affects people forever. You understand that, right?"

"I understand that," Ryan said. He did. She had hammered this point home to him numerous times in the year he had been working with her at the Clinic. They were there to make people's lives better. To help them achieve happiness in their post-mortal lives. Working at the Clinic meant significantly improving the eternal existence of everyone who came in.

On the other hand, Hubert was butter-flavored, so...

Margie jabbed him with a finger. "Did you hear what I just said?"

"Did you say something after 'what we do affects people forever'?"

"Yes!"

"Then no, I didn't." Ryan cringed. He wished he had heard what she said. He wished he could tell her that he promised he'd pay attention and do his job. But he knew for a fact that, until the little buttery caveman Hubert was no longer dancing in the corners of his mind, he was not going to be able to pay attention at all.

So he blurted it out. All of it. Hubert and his seductive smile. Butter. Irvin Curry. Two thousand dollars. The whole thing. In about fifteen seconds.

Margie crinkled up one corner of her mouth in a way that made him certain she was about to point out how stupid the whole idea was. And he did not have any kind of rebuttal prepared, because she was right. It *was* stupid. Which made it particularly surprising when all she said was: "Okay."

For a long moment, Ryan assumed he had heard her wrong, but couldn't figure out how. "No" sounds nothing like "okay", and laughing in his face sounds even less so. Both would have been reasonable responses. He had to verify. "Okay?"

"You're experiencing a surge in impulsive behavior. I've noticed it increasing over the past thirteen weeks especially."

"I am? And you have?"

"It's fine. I take some responsibility for it. When we first met, your prefrontal cortex had near complete dominance over your brain stem. Impulsive responses were being quashed almost immediately. It's been interesting to see how, with the power of suggestion and some practice, you've allowed your control over your impulses to diminish, and I think you've experienced more enjoyment as a result. With the unfortunate side effect being that occasionally you'll spend two thousand dollars on a box of cereal that sounds, I have to say, truly awful."

"So... you're okay if I buy it?"

She shrugged. "Do what you have to do. Just make sure you're ready to go by six thirty. We have to be at the theater by seven."

"Of course! Yes! I will!" It sank in that she was going to let him do it, and not try to stop him at all. This was an impossible scenario that he hadn't planned for, and he was thrilled. He thought if he turned to go, he might skip.

He turned to go, and skipped.

Inside of five minutes, he had composed a reply to Irvin Curry requesting details for transfer of the cash. He felt good. He felt jazzed. He felt *lucky*.

By the time 6:30 rolled around and they had to leave for the theater, he felt less of all three. Because Irvin Curry still had not replied.

4

Ryan had never been to the Orpheum Theatre before, but he liked that it appeared to be the kind of place where an opera or a symphony would feel right at home. He didn't like operas or symphonies, but liked feeling classy just for being there.

But the auditorium was suffocatingly crowded. Ever since the Blackout, theaters like the Orpheum had started double- or even triple-selling their seats for big events. As long as there was only one *living* person in the seat, that material occupant could share the space with any number of ghosts all overlapping each other. With the ghosts being mostly transparent and entirely immaterial, you could usually shift around until you found a position where their fog wasn't in your eyes. Then you could try to forget that they were there except for the occasional overlap of their emotions with yours. It only became problematic when one or more of the ghosts had a radically different opinion of the show than the others sharing the space. If you were a thirty-year fan of, say, Bon Jovi, but one of your seatmates was only there for the opening act, you could find yourself dealing with the uncomfortably dissonant feeling that *Livin' on a Prayer* simultaneously both rocked and did not rock. Fortunately it would pass when you left the seat, and you could return to your usual opinion on the subject of rocking. But still, an event could be effectively ruined with the wrong ghostly seatmates.

Ryan did his best to ignore the two ghosts he was forced to share his seat with. They were an elderly couple from, he guessed, the mid-19th century, and they seemed nice enough. There was also a third ghost crammed halfway between Ryan's seat and Margie's with the armrest jutting through his abdomen. Ryan had introduced himself to all three of them when he arrived, which seemed polite given that they were going to have their immaterial souls mixing and mingling for the next couple of hours. And the ghosts had told him their names in return. But now, twenty minutes later, he had already forgotten them. The one with the armrest through him was clad in furs and appeared to be a neanderthal, and yet Ryan was pretty sure he had said his name was Steve. The names of the other two were possibly Dutch and he had lost them entirely, but that was fine. He had more important things to attend to.

Curry still had not responded. This was more than just worrying. It was all-consuming.

He didn't even react when Neanderthal Steve started hitting on Margie by inviting her to see a cave painting he had done in France 30,000 years ago that was still there today. Ryan used the distraction to check his phone again. No messages.

"You're not going to be doing that all night, are you?" Margie said. She used the line to effectively shut down Neanderthal Steve, who went into a sulk.

"I probably am," Ryan admitted. "I can do it in the lobby if you want."

Margie looked at him sideways, one eyebrow curved up in a way obviously calculated to express her incredulity. "You would really miss this..." She nodded towards the stage. "...for a box of cereal?"

Yes, Ryan thought, *I would*. But he deemed it wise not to say that part out loud. What he did say out loud, though, was arguably worse. "To be fair, it's butter-flavored."

"Okay, so let's say you get it, and you eat it. What happens when the box is empty?"

"I wouldn't eat it all at once. I'd make it last."

"Uh huh. So let's say it takes a week. Then the box is empty. Then what?"

A week? Her definition of "making it last" was clearly quite different from his. There was no way it was going to take him a week to eat one box of cereal. Breakfast, lunch, and dinner for two days at the absolute maximum. *That* was "making it last".

But before he could offer—or even think up—a reply, the house lights faded and an anticipatory hush descended over the auditorium.

Margie reached across the armrest (and through Caveman-Steve's midsection) to grip Ryan's hand. She had bought tickets to this event fully a year ago. That it was now about to start was clearly of overwhelming significance to her. He could feel a rare tremble in her fingers. Both ghosts in his seat, too, tingled with a sense of excitement so powerful that he could almost believe it was his own.

He was tingling about something else entirely, though. Maybe the ghosts wouldn't know the difference.

He checked his phone again with his free hand. No messages.

There was no spotlight on the stage. When the speaker or performer was a ghost, a bright spotlight served only to make them harder to see. So instead, the stage lights glowed only dimly, created a soft wash of amber-orange that would contrast nicely with the shimmering bluish tint of a ghostly figure. There was no background, no set dressing at all. Just an ancient wood podium at center stage, half-invisible in the faint amber light. There was no announcement, no introduction. This speaker needed none.

The audience went utterly silent. Not a whisper.

Ryan didn't see the speaker walk onto the stage, because he was checking his phone again. No messages.

A sudden explosion of applause and cheers forced him to look up. And there on the stage, at last, was the reason why everybody but Ryan was here.

He was thinner than Ryan had imagined. He strode with a long, awkward gait, as though he had never quite figured out how to make all six-feet-four-inches of him move in perfect sync. Nevertheless, he looked remarkably spry for a man 200 years old. With no backdrop behind him and with the dramatic stage lighting, it was easy to forget he was a ghost. He was just a man lifted out of 1865 right into the twenty-first century, walking to a podium with a modest wave to the crowd and a slightly embarrassed half-smile. The only mildly disappointing thing was that he was not wearing his iconic stovepipe hat. He hadn't been wearing it when he was shot so he didn't have a choice in the matter. Ryan wondered if the event planners had asked him to enter from stage left so that the bullet wound in his head would be turned away from the audience as he crossed the stage.

But still, it was Abraham Lincoln. The actual, for real Abraham Lincoln. Right here. And he was about to impart some of his legendary wisdom to a rapt crowd. It was sure to be unmissable. The applause went on for more than a minute as the former president took his place behind the podium and humbly accepted the audience's adulation. And then the auditorium fell back into a hush. It was time for Lincoln to speak.

Ryan checked his phone again. One message.

One message.

With the subject line "Re: re: re: re: re: re: Hubert".

Ryan yelped.

It earned him immediate pointed looks from everyone in the theater. He was pretty sure he even saw Lincoln's eyes shift his way. He felt flashes of anger and embarrassment from both of the old ghosts in his seat, and they shifted away to find somewhere else to sit. Margie elbowed him in the arm.

Ryan sank as far back in his seat as he corporeally could and slipped his phone into the inside pocket of his blazer. He almost apologized, but decided it would be better to say nothing.

Lincoln, who still hadn't said a word, chuckled and shook his head, bemused. It gave Ryan a strange sense of pride that Abraham Lincoln now knew he existed, even if it was for being an idiot.

Right up until the moment Lincoln finally spoke, all Ryan could think was that he should have taken the opportunity to read at least the first line of the message before he put his phone away. But he hadn't. And now everything he wanted to know in the world was in his jacket pocket, and there was no way he could look at it.

He basted in steaming sweat.

And then Lincoln sunk his hands deep into the pockets of his pantaloons, and spoke.

"Is anyone here in the market for a major appliance?"

It wasn't the kind of opener one might have expected from the likes of Abraham Lincoln.

But this crowd was prepared for it. In other stops on his speaking tour, Lincoln had shown little shame about promoting his chain of used appliance warehouses.

Four Score and Seven Appliances had launched a few years earlier in Dorchester to modest success, with Lincoln as its chief spokesperson and mascot. It had expanded to six other locations across the country. And he rarely shut up about it. Some of his audience in Chicago famously asked for their money back because he had spent fully half his hour on stage informing them that his stores sold only appliances that were one hundred percent not haunted. Given that he had started the chain more than 150 years after his death, there was no possible way he could ever have actually used a microwave or a dryer himself. Yet still, based on the other achievements of his life, people were willing to put up with a little product placement. They knew that he always got past that part of the speech and into the important stuff: recalling anecdotes from his time as President, extolling the virtues of freedom and democracy, and only occasionally mentioning dishwasher rinse cycles.

As Lincoln went on about exactly how much love went into expertly testing every gasket on every clothes washer, Ryan started to think that if he and Margie were going to have a conversation about this speech later, they'd probably skim right over the appliance section. So if he was going to read the message on his phone, it was now or never.

Moving as imperceptibly as he could, he slid his hand into his jacket pocket. He risked a glance over at Margie, but he needn't have worried. She was completely engrossed in the President's infomercial. So he dared to pull the phone out all the way and surreptitiously lower it next to his thigh on the side opposite Margie. He kept it facing downwards so she wouldn't see the screen come on. And he ran his finger over the fingerprint scanner. The light from the screen cast a hazy rectangle on Ryan's leg and part of his seat, but he was pretty sure only he could see it.

When Lincoln made a joke about stackable washer/dryer combos and everybody else focused on pretending to find it amusing, Ryan made his move. He flipped the phone over and skimmed the message.

What it said was: "Send me the cash in the next 30 mins and we have a deal." And there were details for a wire transfer.

Ryan stopped breathing altogether. His sweat boiled.

He clicked the phone off and stood. His knees almost gave out. "Bathroom," he muttered apologetically as he pushed around Caveman-Steve, then Margie. "Right back," he muttered. Then he added "I'll be" to give it some context. He didn't stop to see Margie's reaction, but he could imagine it in great detail.

The trip up the aisle and out into the lobby was a blur. Once he got there, he found the bathroom nearly empty. A few ghosts were in there but only as a spot to watch Lincoln from. They had their heads crammed through the wall into the auditorium, only their legs and half their torsos on this side. He didn't know why they chose this vantage point. Perhaps it afforded them a better view.

Ryan stumbled into the closest stall, tapping clumsily on his phone as he went. He struggled to remember his banking password. He sat down on the toilet lid, dress shoes tapping on the floor as he danced them nervously. *Come on, come on, come on.* The app was taking forever to load. Why did it always take so long when he was in a hurry?

Something at the top of the phone display caught his eye.

He froze.

"No service."

He shook his phone. "No no no no no!" *Why now? Why right now this actual minute?!*

And then, for no reason he was aware of, all the lights in the bathroom went out.

The glowing rectangle of Ryan's phone display was suddenly blinding, and he had to look away. He staggered forward and yanked the stall door open.

The collective gasp from the main auditorium filtered through the bathroom wall. Ryan stood rooted in the stall doorway, gripping his phone, struggling to process what was happening. *Blackout*, he realized. *It's another blackout.*

He had barely registered the thought when some invisible force seized him and tried to rip his ghost from his body.

He clawed at his chest with both hands, as though he could grab hold of his ghost there and keep it from escaping. The world spun horizontal around him and the floor came hurtling sideways at his face. He wondered for a moment if he'd have time to check his phone again before the tiles hit him.

◇

The men's room lights flickered on, and Ryan felt cold tile and warm liquid against his cheek. He sincerely hoped it was his own drool, because all the other bathroom possibilities were scary.

He pushed himself off the floor, but couldn't quite get himself vertical. He wasn't even entirely sure which way vertical was. Everything felt tilted like the deck of a sinking ship. He clutched at the bottom of a stall to keep from sliding down the floor and maybe falling into a boat propeller.

Through the walls he could hear commotion. Shouts and screams and lots of loud talking trying to be heard above the shouts and screams. He couldn't tell what any of it was about. Perhaps everyone was as worried as he was about the theater seeming to be sinking beneath the waves. Perhaps everyone also felt like they were going to vomit. He certainly did.

The bathroom door flung open and Ryan was enormously grateful to see Margie there. If nothing else, her verticality gave him some sense of which way he should be pushing himself.

"Ryan?" She dropped to her knees and slid over to him. As soon as she reached him she slid one arm under his shoulders and helped him sit up with his back against a stall. "What happened to you? Describe everything in detail."

Ryan could see the shadows of feet flitting back and forth in the crack of light under the door. There was a constant chaos of them, accompanied by a rising clamor of voices. He would have called it pandemonium, except that his mind couldn't presently handle all five syllables. "What's going on?" he managed to choke out.

Margie felt his forehead with the back of her hand. "He's gone. I don't know what happened, but he's gone."

"Who?"

"Lincoln. All the others came back but he didn't. He's gone."

5

Even before the lights went out, the night had not been going well for Lowell Mahaffey.

Most nights tended to go poorly when he had to do detective-ish, detective-y, or even detective-esque work. But even by his standards, this night had been a chore.

The cool part, though, was that he had borrowed a camera.

It was a good camera. One of those extremely expensive digital SLR deals with the beefy metal body and the lenses that screwed on and off. It was most often used for taking evidence photos at crime scenes. Not by Lowell, of course. Despite claiming to be a detective, Lowell studiously avoided crime scenes. But he had borrowed the camera from his police friend Detective Blair whose job it was to go to those scenes and do things like take pictures and talk to people and solve the crimes. As a condition of loaning the camera, he had made Lowell explicitly promise not to break it. It seemed like a dumb promise to have to make. Nobody *plans* to break a camera and then decides against it just because they were told not to. But Lowell had agreed to the promise. And so far, in contrast to almost every other promise he had ever made to Detective Blair—or indeed to anyone— Lowell had kept it. The camera was still in the proper number of pieces: by Lowell's count, one.

But then, despite his every instinct screaming at him not to, he was forced to climb a tree.

◇

Nearly a month before the camera and the tree, Lowell sat in his office at the Post-Mortal Services Clinic and tried his best to look indignant. "This is about the office, isn't it?" he asked.

Margie's eyebrows went through a range of shapes he hadn't ever seen them make before. They finally settled on bending close together between her eyes as though whispering secretly to each other about how confused they were. "What office?" she said.

Lowell waved his hand around at their surroundings, the office that Lowell had claimed immediately upon accepting his job at the Clinic. It was by far the biggest office in the building. It had formerly belonged to the previous director of the Clinic, Roger Foster. Lowell knew that it would make far more sense for Margie, as the new director of the Clinic, to take the big office. But then again, it wasn't his fault she had decided to take that vacation to Myrtle Beach with Ryan and leave the office door unlocked. So the office was his now, and over the months he had made it uniquely his own by hardly using it and changing almost nothing in it. All of Roger's stuff was still there, and only the re-purposed dentist chair in the corner gave any hint of Lowell's presence at all. Nevertheless, he was fully prepared to fight for the space. He liked it. It was big, and he didn't have to pay for it. "You want me out of here so you can have the office," he said, injecting his voice with a note of defiance. "I can't believe you'd be so petty."

"I don't care about the office, Lowell. This isn't about that."

"Fine then, take it. I'll use the supply closet. I'll use a stall in the bathroom. You want me to seem unprofessional, that's fine. Let's see what all my clients think of that." He stood up and made a show of packing up his things on the desk. None of the things on the desk were his, but he pretended to pack them up anyway.

"That's the thing," Margie said. Her calm unnerved him. His stomach started to tighten. "How many client cases have you solved since you started here? Precisely?"

Lowell discerned that this discussion was not actually about making him switch to one of the smaller offices. Because the answer to her question was zero. He had solved zero cases. Cases just made his job harder, requiring him to do unpleasant things like show up, and think. But he couldn't say any of that out loud, especially not to the person who signed his paychecks. And *especially* not when it seemed like she was about to say she would stop signing them. "I don't have my files here," was the feeble excuse he came up with on the spot. He hoped she would overlook the fact that this office was the place where such files would almost certainly be kept. If they existed, which they didn't.

"You've solved no cases at all?"

"That's not true. I've had lots of client cases."

"How many missing ghosts have you found?"

Lowell gave up packing the stuff on his desk. It was time for another angle of attack. "I'll take the loading dock," he pleaded. "I'll work from home." That was impossible, because he didn't have a home. But it sounded good.

Margie sighed and sat into the chair across the desk from him. "Lowell, I hired you because I thought the Clinic's clients might need the services of a ghost-finding detective. It seemed to make sense to have one in-house."

"Totally," Lowell said, nodding. "That was good thinking. Still is."

"But a requirement of being the in-house ghost-finding detective is that you sometimes have to actually find ghosts."

"I'll start now. I've got cases. I'll do one. I'll finish it."

"Six," Margie said.

Lowell was about to get outraged, but was distracted by a detail. "Why six? Why not, like, five? Or ten?"

"Six, Lowell."

Lowell let the number go, and unleashed his outrage. "Six?! In a year?!"

"No, in a month. Close six cases in the next thirty days, and you can stay on."

Lowell was about to complain that her request was impossible. But it really wasn't. Most cases were, in fact, very easy to solve. Missing ghosts usually weren't missing on purpose. They just weren't where their families and friends expected them to be. Finding them typically didn't take very long, though he usually tried to drag it out for weeks or months so that he could inflate the bill and appear to possess heroic perseverance.

So if he was uncharacteristically honest with himself, six cases in a month didn't seem that bad. It would require only a minimal amount of effort, and virtually no mental exertion. And the result would be that he had earned his place in the Clinic and the respect of his employer. He might even feel good about solving the cases. Maybe he would restore broken families, save lost loves, *help* people. He found himself infused with an unfamiliar sensation: drive. Determination. He could do it. He would serve the purpose for which he genuinely believed he was placed on this Earth.

Six cases in a month. He was going to do it.

"You got yourself a deal," he said. And then he and Margie stood and emphatically shook hands across the desk. She seemed nearly as confident in him as he felt in himself. This was a new Lowell, and they both sensed it. Things were going to be different. Twenty-eight days later, he hadn't solved even one case yet and was forced to climb a tree.

◇

The lower branches were fine. They were broad, and bent almost to the ground. Two of them curved right over the top of the chain link fence like the arms of a giant neighbor making casual inter-yard barbecue conversation. Lowell was able to hoist himself onto the top beam of the fence, and from there onto one of the big branches.

So far so good. A few ghosts milling near some dumpsters down the alley glanced his way, but just as quickly looked away again. Two more passed by on the property behind him, apparently out for a jog despite exercise being utterly useless to a spirit without a body. It seemed nobody was interested in why he was climbing the tree, and so nobody was going to bother him.

Nobody but the tree itself, that is. The tree had an apparent beef with being climbed on. One more branch up it snagged his raincoat, forcing him to yank his arms out and abandon the coat among the leaves. He was, so far, unconcerned. Surely he'd be able to grab his coat on the way back down.

And then, pulling himself up to the next higher branch in a clumsy, fat, middle-aged imitation of parallel bar gymnastics, he caught the hem of his pants on a bent twig. The strongest twig of all time, as it turned out. A giant among twigs. A twig hell-bent on making a name for itself. Because no matter how many times he pulled, it would neither break nor release its grip on his pants.

He balanced himself carefully on the branch, which bent alarmingly beneath his weight, and crouched sideways in a way that his body was clearly not designed to bend. Rolls of himself folded into each other uncomfortably, and he worried that if he listened close enough, those rolls might be making squishing noises. But he bent further. Maybe if he could just reach his pant leg, he could unhook it manually.

But bending like that created the exact angle the camera strap needed to slip off his shoulder. He didn't bother trying to grab for it, instead resigning himself instantly to just how badly things were now going.

Seconds later he heard his promise to Detective Blair break loudly on the asphalt below.

Lowell would have cursed out loud. Except it wasn't his camera, so no big loss really. But now he wasn't sure how to proceed. His every instinct roared at him to give up, climb down, and come back tomorrow night with another of Blair's cameras and another promise. But that would be another day lost, and a virtual guarantee that he wouldn't finish his six cases in time. So he went with his second choice, which was to hang there stupidly in the tree having no idea what to do.

The dumpster ghosts, drawn by the noise of the shattering camera, approached the base of the tree now, peering up at him and muttering to each other. They weren't speaking English, but "idiot" was apparently a word in their language too. Their commotion was loud enough that he started to worry it would draw the attention of his mark inside the building.

"Shhh!" he tried, without optimism.

The ghosts shushed him back. One of them called up to him at full yell. Lowell didn't know what the ghost was saying, but he imagined it to be "Get down from there before you kill yourself", which he couldn't disagree with.

He was going to have to hurry this up. He still had his phone, and his phone had a camera. It was a terrible camera and it had virtually no ability to zoom, which was why he had gone to Blair for help. But maybe if he tried he could persuade it to take a usable picture. He propped himself against as many branches as possible and distributed his weight in a way approximating balance. Then he found a way he could hold his head that let him see through the leaves all the way to the back wall of the building and the window where he expected to see a ghost. A ghost that he needed a picture of, to prove that he had found it.

And there the target was. Framed so perfectly in the window that he might as well have been posing for the pictures. His name was Lester Massey. About two years ago he had come in to the Post-Mortal Services Clinic to have his ghost extracted from his body. Fifty-six years of almost constant smoking had produced the unexpected complication of rendering him seriously ill. And rather than wait for the inevitable decline, he had borrowed money from his daughter and booked an appointment at the Clinic to leave his body behind while he could still function. The procedure, according to Clinic records, had gone perfectly. But Lester Massey's ghost had disappeared. According to his thirty-year-old daughter he had just up and left, never to be seen again. Now she wanted him found. She had come to the Clinic, weeping and pleading, devastated that her father wasn't home where she expected him to be. She insisted that he loved her. And that he loved his other children, and his wife, and that they missed him. Their familial bond warmed Lowell's heart. Finding him was a chance for Lowell to do good, to help a family clearly in need.

He left the case file in his bottom drawer for nine weeks and got three different kinds of condiment on it. He vaguely recalled caring about it, but couldn't remember why. But now, thanks to Margie's bargain, here he was, solving it.

It had taken roughly forty minutes.

In life Lester Massey had loved his family, but he had also loved the poker room above a dive bar in Southie called Robbie-and-Bobbie's. The bar had closed three years ago following a fire that had burned either Robbie or Bobbie, and a fraudulent profit skimming scheme that had burned the other. Six months later the space was filled by Classy Happy Nails & Waxing, which despite its name seemed to be not at all classy, and possibly not happy either. And the poker room above it was now somebody's terrible-looking apartment. But Lester Massey didn't seem to have noticed, because he still spent every day up there, sitting at the kitchen table of the apartment's current residents and waiting for his poker buddies to arrive. He had been there for more than a year now, which was fine because, being a ghost, he had literally all the time in the world. And then some.

Lowell had found all this out through the deep-dive detective work of asking one of Massey's friends. Nicely.

Lowell could see Massey now, reclining with his feet up on the table, smoking an invisible cigarette because he hadn't had the foresight to bring one with him when his ghost was pulled out. He was framed dead-center in the window, which suited Lowell's picture-taking needs perfectly. It was now or never.

Closer to never, as it turned out. Because in trying to balance himself to frame the picture, Lowell grabbed a branch hard with his left hand, and a sharp and violently ambitious twig stabbed into the soft part of his palm.

He cursed. An original, profoundly emphatic curse that he made a mental note to remember for use later. And the ghost of Lester Massey heard it. The ghost pulled his feet off the table and turned to look out the window, curious.

Lowell pressed himself backwards into the trunk of the tree and hunted for a pose that would obscure him behind the maximum number of leaves. And then he wondered why he was hiding. It might actually work in his favor if Massey saw him. If Massey came over to the window it might give Lowell a clearer shot.

Massey did indeed get up and move towards the window. He seemed to have assumed that the sound had come from ground level, because he was looking only downwards. Lowell steadied his phone, pressing it forward through the leaves of the tree—

And then the lights went out. All of them.

Buried in the branches of the tree, Lowell heard the collective gasp of the city's ghosts rippling through the night. Puzzled and disoriented for a moment, Lowell risked a look through the leaves up and down the alley. All the street lamps were black, and the ghosts stood out starkly in the darkness, a rippling river of translucent, moving bodies. Beyond them, the usual amber wash of the city's night sky had turned pale blue, the light of tens of millions of ghosts unchallenged by the city's electric grid. Above the city he could see stars. More of them than he had ever seen from within the city bounds.

Lowell twisted his head back to the business at hand. Lester Massey was still framed in the window, peering out into the night, trying like everyone else to discern what was happening. The room around him was dark, as was the outside wall of the building. With no light to wash out his details, he stood out brilliantly. He was more recognizable than before, and would likely render perfectly even with the terrible camera on Lowell's phone. Lowell thought that the blackout might actually have worked in his favor. He was going to get the perfect evidence.

He dared to release his hold on branches with both hands, and raised the phone. He pinch-zoomed the image as far as he could and let the camera's auto exposure adjust. There was the window. There was the ghost of Lester Massey. It was perfect.

And then the screen on his phone went black.

At first he thought his phone had died. He shook it, which he knew to be the universal method of repairing technology. But then he noticed that all the icons and text around the image were still there. Including the warning at the top that now said "No service". He lowered the phone.

The phone hadn't died at all. The window was actually dark. Because Lester Massey was gone. Lowell would have naturally assumed that the old man had merely moved out of sight, and would reappear in a few moments. Except that Lowell could faintly see the living residents of the apartment circling around inside, pointing and talking animatedly. They seemed pleased that this invader in their home had vanished.

The old man was gone. Not just moved out of sight, not just left the room. Gone.

Then the city lights exploded back on.

The grey leaves around Lowell turned sharply green, startling him and almost making him lose what little balance he had. The alley lit up starkly, and the amber glow in the sky bloomed like a stove burner heating up. The stars faded and vanished into the blank murk of the nighttime city sky. The ghosts in the alley blinked back into existence. In a matter of seconds, everything was exactly as it had been.

Except that Lester Massey's ghost was still gone from the window. The people inside were still looking for him. He had not reappeared like the ones in the alley. Lester Massey was gone.

Lowell felt his chance at closing this case slipping away, even more than he felt his feet slipping off the branch. And the only thing that went right for him the whole night was that he managed to grab his raincoat and drag it with him on his way through the branches to the ground.

6

After leaving the Orpheum, Ryan and Margie rushed home to check on all the ghosts haunting their place. The old couple, Sye and Sye's Wife (whose name they had never figured out due to the couple's still-unbroken silence) sat gazing at each other across the table, Benny the Poltergeist was busy trying unsuccessfully to make a hanging light swing eerily, and the name-unknown Algonquian tribesman nodded to them from behind a rising crust pizza box in the freezer. All seemed fine there, but Margie was still worried about Ryan and insisted that they go to the Clinic and run some tests.

The Clinic was quiet and empty, closed for the night. Trudy, the ghostly and decapitated receptionist, was behind the reception desk because that's where she always was. Even at night she sat there with her hands resting on either side of the phone, as though expecting clients to arrive any moment. But Ethan and Ewan, the Clinic's gigantic and largely interchangeable twin orderlies (one alive and one dead), had left for the night and Lowell was reliably never there. There were only the usual scant few meandering spirits minding their own business in the former funeral chapels and flitting past the windows. Ryan always thought the silence at night made the place feel haunted and spooky. Of course, literally everywhere on Earth was haunted these days, so the term was largely meaningless. But the Clinic felt particularly so, maybe because it had so *few* ghosts in it. He always wondered if there were some that he couldn't see, watching him. Invisible ghosts that probably weren't there seemed much scarier than visible ghosts that were. Ryan wanted to go back home.

Margie made Ryan lie down on the exam table so she could run some kind of scanner over him. Then she made him stand up so she could run it over him again.

"What are you looking for?" he asked her, more to fill the silence than anything else.

"I don't know. You clearly suffered some kind of episode because of the power incident. I just want to be sure that your ghost is intact. You know it's more prone to instability than most people's."

He did know that. He knew it because she had told him, and she was the expert in such things. Having his ghost removed (voluntarily), then attached (involuntarily) to a snow globe, then ripped (voluntarily) off of that snow globe, then assaulted (involuntarily) with enough voltage to power a Las Vegas city block, had left it understandably delicate. He had even been told—again, by Margie—that the next time his ghost left his body for any reason it would almost certainly fall apart completely within minutes, rendering him unpleasantly non-existent. Which is why they were both so alarmed by what had happened tonight.

He wrung his hands and made nervous fists with his toes inside his shoes, and tried to think about other things. "Is that my stud finder?" he asked as she swept the scanner over him. He had used it just a couple of weeks ago at home to find structural beams to hang their new TV from. The TV had fallen down and broken the next day, which suggested that the stud finder was unreliable at best, malicious at worst. Now she had what appeared to be most of a fondue fork welded to the front of it and the whole assembly had become inexplicable and frightening.

"No more questions until the scans are completed, thank you," she said in the tone she normally reserved for the irritating families of clients.

He obeyed. When she used that tone, it was impossible not to.

Once she was done with the forked stud finder, he thought the tests were finished. But instead, without a word, she picked up another handheld device. This one gave her a shock when she touched it, but she didn't seem bothered and jammed the device against his chest anyway. He found it increasingly useful to let his mind wander.

Oh God, he thought. *Hubert*. His message to Irvin Curry had never gotten through, and cell data service still hadn't been fully restored after the short blackout. He feared he had missed the window. Hubert was slipping through his fingers, and at present there wasn't anything he could do about it. Despair was like a little cartoon storm cloud raining only on him. So he focused on Margie instead.

Watching her face as she moved around him with genuine concern and care, Ryan ran mentally through his entire relationship history prior to her. It didn't take nearly as long as he thought an adult person's relationship history should take. So he ran through it again. He was disappointed to find that it went even faster on the second pass. It started to depress him.

Yet here was Margie. She had stuck around for more than a year now. And here she was, worrying about him, fawning over him, jolting his nervous system with dangerous levels of high voltage and radiation because she cared. And between electrically-induced muscle spasms and applications of topical burn cream, he felt enormously fortunate for her continued presence in his life. He even almost told her so.

But oh God. Hubert. Just when he was starting to feel better, the thought brought him down again. Hubert was butter-flavored, and it was gone, gone, gone.

Margie finished. "Well, I can't find any new damage. Your ghost is exactly the same resolution as before the incident."

Ryan let the tension drain out of him. He unclenched his toes. "Okay. So. I'm all good."

"Oh, far from it. Your ghost is a complete mess. The slightest disruption could reduce its cohesion to nothing. The day your body dies, you may last a few minutes at most outside of it, but then you're *gone*. Entirely."

Ryan's toes re-dug themselves so deep into his insoles that he could feel the cool floor through the rubber. "But it's the same as it's been. Nothing changed tonight?"

She ran her finger over one of her scanning devices, and it gave her another small electric jolt. Which seemed to be what she wanted from it. "No, I don't think so." She hooked her stool with one foot and rolled it over to her. She sat straight on it, not a trace of slouch, like it had an invisible backrest. He had never figured out how she did that. She closed her eyes and tapped the middle of her forehead with one finger, perhaps giving the thoughts inside a rhythm to dance to. "My assumption would be that you were affected by the incident tonight because of your ghost's instability. But the connection to your body is still strong enough that it shielded you. I think you're fine."

"What about Lincoln?"

"I don't know. I've never analysed him. But if his structure was unstable like yours, without a body to protect him even a relatively small burst of energy could have torn him apart. It's unfortunate."

"But I'm okay."

"Yes, you're okay."

Ryan allowed himself to be relieved again. "So, we can go home?"

Margie opened her eyes and picked up the forked stud detector. "I want to do the tests again. All of them, plus a few new ones. I'm going to need you to swallow half a liter of barium. Well, it's *mostly* barium."

"What else is it?"

"It's better if you don't ask."

Ryan cringed and involuntarily shrank away from the fondue fork. But before she could complain that he wasn't being cooperative, they were interrupted by a low-pitched *ploink* from Margie's phone. Her phone was configured to make a wide variety of noises with specific purposes, and Ryan could recognize certain ones. So he always knew the *ping* when she got an email, the *boop* when she had an appointment, or the *be-deep* when she had earned some diamonds in what-ever candy-matching game she was currently obsessed with. The *ploink* he recognized as meaning somebody was at the door.

Margie shifted the forked sensor to her left hand so she could grab the phone with her right. The fork swung perilously close to various parts of Ryan, prompting him to take a step back.

Margie checked her phone display. "It's the back door," she said. There was big chrome button next to the Clinic's loading dock door, meant for alerting staffers inside to come unlock the door when there was a delivery or somebody needing to come in the back. Ryan used it a lot to avoid having to go through the reception area, which often had clients in it. And he suspected that his over-use of the button was one of the reasons the orderlies, Ethan and Ewan, had mostly stopped bothering to answer it, and disliked him. At this time of night, somebody pressing the button went beyond unusual and well into the realm of alarming.

"Don't answer it," Ryan said. It couldn't possibly be anything good, and therefore should be ignored. He felt strongly that only good things should be paid attention to, especially right now.

Margie immediately strode from the exam room and went to answer the bell. So Ryan was forced to chase her all the way up the stairs and to the loading dock door.

"Don't open it," he said, right before she opened it.

Ryan braced himself to be murdered. But the only thing that surged in was a waft of cool, dumpster-scented night air. There was a man there, starkly blasted by the motion-activated floodlight over the loading dock. He took a step back, maybe to make clear that he had no murder plans, or at least that any such plans weren't urgent.

"Oh, you're here!" he said. He was an olive-skinned, middle-aged man with wide-set, pleading eyes. Based on the sweat pants and T-shirt he was wearing, and the mussed state of his thinning hair, he appeared to have been roused out of bed.

"Mr. Garza?" Margie said.

The name was faintly familiar to Ryan, which meant that Mr. Garza had most likely been a client of the Clinic at some point, or family of a client. But the fact that Margie could recognize every client she'd ever had, and name them immediately, never failed to amaze him.

"Yeah!" Mr. Garza said with a hint of surprise. "You guys did a thing for my mother a while back. You remember that?"

"Of course. How is she? Does she still knit?"

"She tries. You woulda thought she'd stop after it killed her. Who knew those knitting needles were strong enough to go right through a skull like that?" Ryan remembered the case now. And also remembered why he had tried so hard to forget it.

"She died doing what she loved," Margie said. "It's nice. In a way."

Garza wrung his hands and glanced back at the ghosts in the parking lot behind him. They were paying no attention to him, but seemed to be gathered in tight clusters, discussing something gravely among themselves. "I'm sorry to bother you so late," he said.

"Does she need something else done? Is that why you're here?" Margie leaned against the door frame, immediately suggesting with merely her pose that she wasn't troubled at all and was happy to help. Ryan became keenly aware of how he was lingering behind her looking tense and annoyed. Because he was tense and annoyed.

"No no, it's my father. Now he needs one of your services."

"Your father's dead?"

"Yeah. And he's not real happy about it, you know? He just sits in his car and yells at people out the window. He did that when he was alive too, but we used to be able to roll the window up. Now it's busted. And he never gets out of that car. It's like he's haunting it, you know?"

Ryan stepped up next to Margie, still hoping to coast on past this and, ideally, go to bed. "Give us a call in the morning," he said with as much cheer as he could muster. "We'll be happy to help him when we've all had a good night's—"

"No no," Garza said, wringing his hands tighter. "I can't bring him in. The car won't start. It's a Buick Riviera. None of them have started since the 80s."

Ryan gently tried to urge the door out of Margie's hand and shut it. "Then we can book a house call. We do that too sometimes. Okay? Good. Have a good—"

"No no, it's just with everything that's going on, we don't wanna wait, you know?"

Margie's forehead crinkled. "Everything that's going on?"

Garza motioned back at one of the small crowds of ghosts clustered under a lamppost in a kind of huddle. "You know, with the lights going out tonight. The ghosts disappearing. They said on the news it's going to happen again. Everybody's worried. They think maybe next time, they'll disappear and not come back. So natch, he wants to get this done while he still can, you know."

Margie nodded, but it didn't seem to be just a nod of understanding. She nodded as if Garza had altered her world view in some profound way. Ryan had no idea what she had realized. All he had gotten from Garza's words was that he should try saying "natch" occasionally and see if it worked for him.

"We'll meet you there," Margie said, nodding more vigorously.

"We will?" Ryan said. He had just had a brush with annihilation and didn't want to be anywhere but home right now. He certainly didn't want to go across town in the middle of the night to detach some ghost from a Buick.

"Thank you," Garza said, his hands pressed together prayer-like. "Thank you so much. Thank you."

"Go home," Margie said. "Get him ready. We'll be there."

"Thank you," Garza said again, backing away as Margie pressed the door closed.

Ryan was incredulous. It was after midnight and they were working? But he was afraid to complain, at least out loud. His face was apparently doing his complaining for him, though, because Margie gave him a disapproving look.

"You have more important things to do?" she said. "Get the keys. We're taking the House Call Wagon."

Ryan sighed. "Natch," he said.

It didn't work for him.

7

The House Call Wagon had been Ryan's idea—possibly Ryan's only idea of any value since joining the Clinic staff. He had found himself often taking calls from potential clients wanting to have unhauntings done in remote locations. Not all ghosts wanted to be detached from objects that were easily portable and could be brought in to the Clinic. Ghosts haunting immovable things or even specific locations were common, and when they called he would have to disappoint them by telling them they couldn't be helped. If they couldn't bring the haunted object into the Clinic, they couldn't be unhaunted from it. One day over lunch Ryan had idly mentioned, without any expectation that it was possible, that it would be nice if they could take their equipment on the road. Margie's face immediately lit up.

Thus the House Call Wagon was born. Ryan still claimed credit for the idea, despite Margie having done most of the actual work.

It was a 2005 Chevrolet Express cargo van that Lowell had bought or stolen from a friend or enemy of his.

Ryan wasn't clear on the specifics of where it came from, and didn't want to be. It was partially crushed in on one side as though it had been T-boned by a very slow-moving train. One of the headlights flickered in a way that was surely illegal, so they mostly tried not to drive it at night. Inside the cargo area, Margie had spent a crazy percentage of the Clinic's budget installing two client beds. They hung like hammocks so they were somewhat insulated from the bouncing of the van. And when someone was in them, they wrapped around the occupant so it was all but impossible to fall out.

Most impressively, Margie had rewired the van so that it could handle the considerable power needed to operate a portable version of the Box. The Box, with its collection of paddles and attachments, was obviously their most crucial piece of equipment. And she had invented and built it herself. So it wasn't surprising that she also made its younger cousin and all the modifications to the van, including all the necessary welding and soldering and, for a while, sledge hammering. And once she was done, the new Box did indeed work on the road, and could be powered by a fat, 20-foot cable that unspooled out the back and connected to the van's battery. But since it required staggering amounts of power, it consumed the battery's entire capacity after only one use, possibly two if you were lucky. More than once while making house calls they had been forced to call Lowell to come and jump start them. That was in itself a risky proposition given that the battery in Lowell's car leaked both fluids and powders, and had chunks caked on its terminals that looked like charred flesh. Lowell simultaneously denied that it was flesh and insisted the flesh wasn't his.

It was close to 2 A.M. when Ryan and Margie risked being pulled over for the headlight issue and headed across town down the ghost-infested streets. The address Garza had given them was in Waltham, at least twenty minutes away. Ryan let Margie drive because he didn't want to be doing this and he worried that, given the opportunity, he'd turn around and take them home. The drive gave them time to catch up on news about the mini blackout on the radio. The media, in their relentless need for shorthand, had already invented a name for it. They didn't want to call it a blackout for fear of confusing it with the capital-B Blackout that had made the ghosts appear nearly a decade ago. So they gave it its own equally unimaginative capital-B name: the Blink. And everyone on Earth was already calling it that. No doubt cable news networks had already prepared dramatic graphics built around the word, probably with lots of lens flares.

NASA had been consulted by the media to do two things: explain the Blink, and give everyone reason not to worry about it. They had so far failed to do either. The best that the radio NASA expert could offer was that the sun had hocked another stellar loogie at the Earth, which had caused a minor disruption in the power grid. Given that he used words like "loogie" he was clearly the space agency's B-list media guy and therefore didn't inspire a lot of trust. He did, however, offer the vague yet dire warning that the sun probably wasn't finished, and that they could expect more globs of solar mucus and therefore more Blinks in the very near future. The interviewer, going for the scoop, asked him if they could expect a bigger blast and a more protracted power failure—another capital-B Blackout—and what that might mean for the world's ghosts. But the NASA guy refused to speculate. It was unclear whether that was because he was only a media guy and didn't know science, or because there was something he wasn't allowed to say.

By the time they got to Garza's house they still hadn't gotten any information that was particularly informative. So they turned the radio off and, despite how tired Ryan was, got down to the task at hand.

Detaching Garza Sr.'s ghost from his car was a simple matter of parking the House Call Wagon at the end of the driveway, carrying the Box on the end of its cable up to the garage, and then Margie doing her expert best to position the paddles on both the ghost and his car. Mr. Garza Sr. didn't seem able to figure out any good insults to hurl at her, instead spending the whole time making fun of her glasses. Margie was unaffected by the abuse, and focused only on the procedure.

Once she got the paddles in place, Ryan stepped on the pedal to activate the Box, the House Call Wagon's battery briefly caught fire, Ryan blasted it with Garza's garden hose, and the job was done. The Garza car was no longer haunted, and the father himself was no longer required to stay with it. He still seemed inclined to, but from that point on it would be by inexplicable choice. Garza thanked them profusely and Margie promised to send a bill, which Ryan knew from the look on her face that she wouldn't. He would have sent one with overtime for the trouble, but he wasn't her.

Then they drove back to the Clinic via an extended and less-haunted route to give the battery a chance to charge up. They listened to the news again, and by this time the radio stations had found better experts willing to talk to them at such a ridiculous hour. Browsing around the dial, Ryan came upon one in mid-sentence.

"—tonight was just a precursor, like a foreshock that precedes a major earthquake," the scientist said. Her voice glowed with expertise.

"So there's a bigger one coming?" The interviewer obviously existed on an entirely different intellectual plane from her, and demonstrated it clearly. "It's big? Like, *freaking* big?"

"One of the biggest we've ever seen," the scientist said. "Bigger than the one seven years ago that brought the ghosts back. Significantly bigger."

The interviewer searched for a reply that would convey the gravity of the scientist's warning. "Whoa."

"Yes," the scientist said. "I agree."

"So... when is that happening?"

"It already happened. We observed the eruption on the surface of the sun last night. There may be some other 'foreshocks' or 'Blinks' like tonight's in the interim, but based on the force of the ejection and the speed the solar material is travelling through space, we expect the bulk of its effect to hit Earth on Friday. At approximately 10:17 PM Eastern time."

"Ooh," the interviewer said.

"Yes. Ooh. This is going to be serious," the scientist said flatly. "We can expect power grids to experience interruptions worldwide. Here on the East Coast, we'll be in the dark possibly for hours or even days."

The interviewer finally got to the question Ryan wanted to hear. "And the ghosts? What can the ghosts expect?"

The scientist was prepared for the question, in a way. Prepared, at least, to be unprepared. "That is not my area of expertise," she said.

"But you can speculate?"

"That is not my area of expertise. Frankly, given how little we know, I'm not sure that's *anyone's* area of expertise."

"Could the ghosts be *gone*? Is that what could happen?"

She sounded like his prodding was getting to her, forcing her to answer. "It's certainly possible. To be specific, they wouldn't be 'gone' per se. They'd still be here.

But the atmosphere could be charged in such a way that they are rendered invisible again. As they were for millennia before the original Blackout. It could happen. But I don't want to speculate on whether it *will* happen."

"Whoa," the interviewer said again.

"Yes," the scientist agreed. "Whoa."

The interviewer decided to lighten things up again by going to a PSA about heart disease, and Ryan turned the volume almost all the way down. The interview had pushed away his tiredness and replaced it with a fresh surge of worry. He looked over at Margie. She was watching the road, studiously avoiding looking in his direction. "What do you think?"

Margie twisted her head a little, but not to look at him. Instead she looked out her side window at the ghosts along the side of the street. She watched them silently.

And for the first time Ryan noticed how truly different things were. On an ordinary night the ghosts milled casually, indifferent to the street and to traffic even when cars passed right through them. Often you would see them dancing, or playing whatever games they could manage with what ghostly equipment they had, or strolling. Ordinary nights were alive with the dead. But this night was different. Just as in the Clinic parking lot, the ghosts were clustered in small groups along the sides of the road, talking animatedly to each other. There was no dancing, no play. There was a general anxiety that bled off them and filled the world with a sense of impending doom.

He looked back at Margie. "What do you think?" he asked.

She went quiet again for a long while, watching the ghosts pass outside her window.

Then she finally answered. "I think we're going to be busy."

8

Lowell returned to his office at the Post-Mortal Services Clinic around 10 A.M. Tuesday, still bruised from falling out of the tree the night before. He had an overstuffed steak burrito pleasantly warming his hand through a thin layer of foil wrap. The burrito had been planned days in advance. It was supposed to be a kind of celebration for closing the Lester Massey case and thereby getting one sixth of the way to saving his job. But now he had failed to close the case thanks to its subject vanishing out of existence when the lights went out. It had taken some of the joy out of his celebration.

He decided to eat the burrito anyway. The night had been disappointing enough without adding that into the mix.

He spent the whole walk between the burrito place and the Clinic focused on one thing: how to close the Lester Massey case with no evidence at all and with the subject having apparently been completely annihilated. Lowell knew very well it was the wrong thing to focus on, but he focused on it anyway. Because focusing on the right thing—being fired by Margie—hurt his head.

All of that went away, though, when he arrived at his office and found that there was a client waiting for him. This was the last thing he wanted. He already had plenty of cases he had successfully backlogged and ignored for months. More than enough to complete Margie's challenge. He didn't need another. Yet here a client was, sitting in the leather guest chair in front of Lowell's desk doing client things.

Lowell regretfully slid the burrito into his raincoat pocket, hoping the insulation in there would partner with the foil to keep it fresh. He gave it five minutes, tops, before it would become uselessly lukewarm.

Lowell cleared his throat, affixed his winning smile to its usual spot on the front of his face, and asked the obvious question. "May I help you?" He hoped faintly that the answer would be "no".

The man shot out of his chair and spun around as though Lowell had just jabbed him in the back of the head with a pencil. "I'm sorry!" he yelped immediately. "I didn't know if I was allowed to come in. The lady pointed at your door, but she's got no head so..."

"It's fine, it's fine," Lowell said, although it wasn't. He didn't like people going into his office when he wasn't there. And he liked them even less coming in when he *was* there, because then they'd talk to him. He sank into his chair, leaned back and interlaced his fingers behind his head. "What can I do for you?" *Please say 'nothing'. Please say 'nothing'.*

The client sank back into his own chair. Lowell took the moment of pause to size the man up. As far as obvious facts went, the client appeared to be a human in his 30s, male, shaven-headed, and alive. Learning anything beyond that would require perception and deduction, two skills that Lowell had belatedly accepted that he generally lacked. So he just noted the few things he had observed that were obvious and indisputable. And he even allowed himself to doubt those a little.

"You find ghosts, right?" the client asked hopefully.

"That's what it says on my business cards," Lowell said as jovially as he could. It had been his standard reply for years. He was happy that now, thanks to Margie, he actually did have business cards again. They didn't have "I find ghosts" written on them, though. He had requested it, but Margie had refused. Still, his standard reply was now comfortably half-true instead of all-false.

"Great. I'm looking for my great-grandmother," the client said.

"Awesome," Lowell said. He picked up the closest notepad and clicked a pen. He knew for a fact that the pen was dry, but it didn't matter because he didn't plan to actually write anything down. His handwriting was terrible anyway, and any notes he took would be illegible. So the whole note-taking thing was kind of pointless from the start. But he had found historically that the mere implication of note-taking reassured his clients, so he made a good show of it. "What's your name?"

"Derrick Quinn. R-r-i-c-k. Like the oil wells. Not r-e-k like Derek."

Lowell pretended to write that down. The pen made a rough scratching noise that he feared would give away that it was dry. "And your great-grandmother's name?"

"Paulette Quinn."

Lowell avoided the scratching noise by "writing" with the tip of the pen not quite touching the paper, hoping that the motion on its own would look realistic. "And how old is she?"

"A hundred and nine."

"No, I mean how old was she when she died?"

"Oh, sorry! She didn't."

Lowell looked up from the pad and eyed Derrick skeptically. "You said she was a ghost."

Derrick seemed not to notice Lowell's look, or his question. Instead he pointed into the corner. "Is that, like, a dentist chair?"

"It's temporary," Lowell replied. He had found that to be the answer that generally led to the fewest follow-up questions. "Sorry, you said your great—" He couldn't remember how many "greats" there had been, so he fudged it. "—ish grandmother didn't die?"

Derrick looked troubled. He shifted in his seat. "You should know that. It'd be in her file."

"Her file? Here? She was a client of the Clinic?"

"Yeah, she came in here a couple of years back. You guys did that thing where you make someone into a ghost."

That didn't seem to Lowell like an entirely accurate description of the process. But if he pointed that out then he'd have to give an accurate one, which he was ill-equipped to do. So he let it slide. "Okay. So, then what happened?"

"Last night the lights went out and... boom, she's gone. Just, like, disappeared."

Lowell looked up from his pad, reluctantly intrigued. "Disappeared? During the Blink?"

"The what?"

Evidently Derrick didn't watch the news and hadn't caught up with the hip terminology. Lowell ignored it. "She disappeared when the lights went out last night? Just disappeared?"

"Yeah! She was there before the lights went out. We were playing Chinese Checkers. I have to make all her moves for her, you know, but she still likes it. We've played it almost every night since I was, like, ten. Then the lights went off, and when they came back on, she was gone."

Lowell, despite his usual insistence on never getting interested in anything, was interested. This man's great-ish grandmother had vanished at the same moment as Lester Massey. And if the news reports were accurate, they had both also disappeared at the exact same moment as the ghost of Abraham Lincoln. Could there be a connection between them? Lowell was hopeless at spotting connections, but this really, really felt like it probably had one.

Derrick was still talking. "I told you all this in my voice mail message. Didn't you get it?"

Lowell blinked at him for a second, genuinely surprised. Not that Derrick had left him a message, but that he might have the capacity to receive phone messages at all. He studied his desk phone, remembering now that he had put a piece of electrical tape over the display on its face about a year ago to prevent it ever distracting him. He peeled the tape partway off now, exposing a little flashing green LED. Lowell tapped the light. "Is that a message light?"

"Maybe," Derrick said, shrugging.

"One second," Lowell said. He picked up the receiver and pressed the flashing button. It toggled to a steady glow, looking enormously relieved. Lowell held the receiver to his ear.

"New message," a digital voice said. "Yesterday. 11:43 A.M."

A man's voice followed. It was decidedly not Derrick Quinn's, but sounded like an older man with a nasal voice made even more nasal by the addition of a whole lot of angry. "This is Lucas Burns! You people need to bring my wife back! She disappeared when the lights went off a couple hours ago! This is Lucas Burns."

"What's happening?" Derrick asked. "Are you doing detective stuff?"

"Very complicated. Hard to explain," Lowell said. He skipped to the next message.

A woman's voice came on. "Mr. Mahaffey, my name is Monica Rhodes. I'm calling about my mother..." Lowell stopped listening and pecked at his computer keyboard. R-H-O-D-E-S.

A Clinic file popped up right away. Ella Rhodes. She had been extracted from her body two years ago. Next of kin: Monica Rhodes. Whose voice he was now hearing on the phone, insisting that her mother had vanished last night when the lights went out.

Lowell's stomach sank. Even with an utter mist-shrouded void in his brain where a normal person's deductive skills would be, he was detecting what felt a lot like a pattern.

But how much of a pattern? He slowly peeled the electrical tape the rest of the way off his phone, exposing a little LCD status display. And his stomach sank even further when he saw what was on it.

Eighteen more messages.

"I'm calling about my father's father's father's dad. What does that make him? Great, great... whatever. I can't find him. He went to your Clinic a few months ago..."

"My brother became a ghost last April and now he's gone..."

"My husband is gone. He never disappears like this. You should have his name in a file there. He had an appointment two or three years ago..."

All of them. The same thing. All extracted from their bodies by the Clinic where he now worked. All of them annihilated at the exact same moment last night.

Lowell saved all the messages and tore the top blank sheet off his notepad, exposing an even blanker one. He tried to make a list of all the names he had just heard, but his pen still wouldn't leave a mark. He scratched at the pad with it, furiously willing ink to come out.

"Mr. Quinn," he said, "If you have a working pen on you, I'll trade you a burrito for it."

9

By Tuesday afternoon, the Clinic waiting room was full. Every seat taken.

It had been filling up since before lunch, because Margie had taken on several last-minute appointment requests—more ghosts wanting things done in a hurry before the great uncertainty of Friday night's big "Blackout 2" rolled around. There were a lot of them, and Margie was turning none away. She had effectively doubled the Clinic's typical workload for the afternoon, and Ryan was not happy about it.

He didn't want to be working there. All he wanted was to drive to Colorado to make one last grab at Hubert Cereal. Irvin Curry still hadn't made contact. So Ryan felt like his only shot at the cereal now was driving thousands of miles and physically demanding it, in person. But with all these ghosts and their living relatives here with their urgent "problems" and "fears", that wasn't going to happen. He resented them bitterly.

Margie was ready for the next appointment, so he slunk into reception with his back nearly pressed against the wall, trying to blend into the wallpaper like a chameleon. He slid along that way until he was behind the reception desk, where Trudy sat silently surveying the waiting room. Or silently surveying the ceiling. Or silently singing an opera. Who could tell?

"Uh... Trudy?" He kept his voice low. And, out of habit, tried to avoid looking at her neck stump.

If she heard him, she didn't acknowledge it. Her hands remained folded, her shoulders aimed forward.

Ryan cleared his throat. "Trudy... who's next? I'm supposed to prep the next client."

Trudy's hands unfolded. She slowly raised her right arm and pointed at the next client. Then slowly lowered it again, and re-folded her hands in front of her. She shifted ever so slightly in her seat, and her job was done. This was typically the extent of Ryan's interaction with Trudy, and he considered it a pretty healthy working relationship.

The next client was an elderly ghost man, diminutive, with a dense clump of white hair like a dry sponge. His tweedy suit and twisted mustache suggested 19th century. Both his arms were completely blackened from his fingers up past the elbows, and forks of ghostly electricity danced around them, leaving little doubt about how he had died. Ryan still wondered about it given how hard it must have been to find a way to electrocute yourself in the 1800s. The electrified ghost was accompanied by a living man who appeared to be about the same age and resembled him in most ways, apart from the electricity and the death. Clearly a descendant. As Ryan timidly approached, both of them looked up at him with eyes that immediately, wordlessly accused him of having wasted a lot of their precious day. So did the eyes of all the other ghosts waiting around them.

"Uh... you can follow me, please," Ryan said. He said it nicely, but tried to use his eyes to throw some of that accusation right back at them.

The old ghost sprang out of the chair at surprising speed and charged at Ryan aggressively, raving in some northern European language. Ryan took a step back and just let the old man rant for half a minute or so, because what else could he do? Finally the ghost cut off, and turned to his relative for a translation.

"He's angry at you," the relative said.

Ryan swallowed forty-seven potential sarcastic replies, instead motioning helpfully with one hand. "Can you ask him to follow me?"

But before the relative could tell his ancestor what Ryan had said, Lowell whirled into reception like an F4 tornado in a raincoat. Ryan didn't even see where he came from; he was just suddenly *there*.

"Ryan!" Lowell called from across the room. He jogged towards Ryan but only made it halfway before he had to slow down to avoid coronary consequences. "Ryan, good. Where's Margie?"

The electrified ghost hurled another tsunami of Baltic rage and waved his hand through Ryan's head, possibly intending it to be a slap. Ryan got a tingle of electric charge and displeasure with every sweep of the old ghost's hand. "He wants to know why you're talking to that man," the relative said, "and he wants to hurt you."

"I'll be right with you," Ryan said with spectacularly failed politeness. Lowell had already dashed away from him and towards the admin hall, forcing Ryan to chase after him.

"Is she in her office?" Lowell said without turning back.

"Why? What's happening?"

The ghost came after them, sparks leaping up and down his arms. He ranted the whole way. "He's following you," the relative said, shuffling after them, "and he expresses his dissatisfaction using profanity."

Other ghosts in reception began to take notice of the commotion and lean forward in their seats to watch. Ryan ignored the extremely hard-to-ignore ghost and doubled his pace to catch Lowell at the threshold of the hallway. Something about Lowell's sober attitude worried him and he needed to know why. "Lowell? What's happening?"

Lowell stopped and turned to scan all the ghosts in the waiting room. Most of them were paying attention now, sitting forward or standing and no doubt as curious as Ryan to find out what the hubbub might be. They went quiet. Even the old electric ghost sensed the urgency and took a step back.

"I'm not sure," Lowell said, far too loudly, "but I think the Clinic might be killing people. Like, not just dead, but *gone*. Totally gone. *Fwoosh*. Destroyed. So..." He seemed to sense the horrified faces of all the ghosts in reception watching him. He raised his hand to them, and his voice. "Not totally sure, though, folks! I'm wrong a lot. So, you'll all probably be fine." He threw them a crossed-fingers gesture and a "let's hope!" look.

He strode away down the corridor, utterly uncaring about the gasps of horror and shouts of anger from the ghosts in the waiting room. With Lowell gone, they surged at Ryan and engulfed him like a blast of outraged smoke.

◇

It took a few minutes for Ryan to extricate himself from the outraged ghost mob by passing them off to Trudy. By the time he got to Margie's office, Lowell had already apparently delivered whatever dire news he had come to deliver. Ryan found himself playing catch-up immediately.

"Twenty-four?" Margie said. She sat perfectly upright in her desk chair, but her arms were not folded in her lap as they usually were. Instead, she was gripping the armrests hard, her fingers digging into the vinyl. She appeared shell-shocked, struggling to keep her composure. Her voice was level but her eyes were as wide as Ryan had ever seen them.

"Twenty-four what?" Ryan asked. His stomach was knotted already and he hadn't even found out yet what it needed to be knotted about.

"That I know of," Lowell said, talking around Ryan at Margie. "Lester Massey, Derrick Quinn's mom, plus twenty voice mails. And two more called while I was writing down those first twenty. Side note: we need bigger notepads, and more pens."

"So it could be *more* than twenty-four," Margie said. Her fingers plunged deeper into the leather. "There could be more messages by now, and maybe some that haven't been noticed yet, or didn't call you. Has anyone seen Roger since the Blink?"

Ryan looked at Lowell, and Lowell looked at Ryan. Both shook their heads.

"So, possibly twenty-five," Margie said. "Or more."

"Right," Lowell said, "so there's a connection. And I spotted it because it's my job to spot connections, so I did that."

As a brief respite from not knowing what problem they were talking about, Ryan focused on the other problem that he *did* know about: all the irate ghosts in reception. He opened Margie's office door a crack and looked out, checking on the commotion. The ghosts, while obviously concerned, were not yet convinced that Lowell was an expert on anything pertaining to them. So they still expected to keep their appointments. But a bunch of them were clustered around Trudy's desk, pressing her for information that she was obviously ill-equipped to provide. Ryan pushed the door closed before any of them could notice him.

He inserted himself between Lowell and Margie. "Whatever you said when you came in here," he said to Lowell, "say it again. Because I don't like what either of you look or sound like right now."

"At least twenty-five ghosts," Lowell said with a sigh. "Disappeared last night in the Blink. *Kablammo*. Just gone. And every one of them was a customer of this place. My gut tells me that's not a coincidence. So does my head. And they almost never agree. That's gotta mean something." He leaned to look around Ryan at Margie. "Right?"

Ryan looked at her too. He didn't like the look on her face. For her to be so obviously horrified was rare, and all Ryan wanted was to make her feel better. He flailed around for a way to do that. "We don't know that it has anything to do with us," he tried. "Maybe lots of ghosts disappeared. Even ones who weren't clients. Like Abe Lincoln, right? He was never a client. He's gone too."

Much like a restaurant, they had a wall near reception reserved for portraits of famous people who were clients of the Clinic. So far the only portrait on it was of a man who claimed to have been one of the munchkins in *The Wizard of Oz,* despite the fact that he was six foot one. Abraham Lincoln certainly wasn't on that wall, nor were any other presidents. Never mind that it was well known Lincoln had been removed from his body in 1865 without any help from the Clinic at all.

Lowell shook his head. "Have you seen anything else on the news about disappearing ghosts? I haven't. And I called my police friend that I owe a camera to, and he said besides Lincoln there haven't been any unusual reports. But I've got twenty-five ghosts who all had extractions done right here. All completely gone. As of last night."

Margie said nothing else for a long time. Her eyes drifted downwards. Normally Ryan would expect to see them analyzing a steady, shifting stream of ideas in her head. But now, instead, they appeared to be forced downward under the mass of a single idea, horrible and weighty. After a minute or more, Ryan thought he could see a tear in the corner of her eye. But she dabbed it quickly away.

"So..." Ryan dared to push on. "What do we do?"

Margie stood up and smoothed out the sleeves of her lab coat. "Lowell, I need you to go to the Orpheum Theatre. Right away."

"Our deal with the six cases is off, right? I'm not fired?"

"You're not fired. Go to the Orpheum. Lincoln is the only destroyed ghost that wasn't our Client. That means something. There's an investigation going on at the theater right now, so go there and find out what they know. Can you do that?"

"I'm on it!" Lowell said, and saluted like she'd just ordered him to parachute behind enemy lines and destroy a bridge. "But I'm not fired, right? I just wanna make sure we're clear on that."

She didn't answer him. Without another word she strode from the office. She didn't close the door, so Ryan could see her turn and head towards the waiting room.

Ryan and Lowell locked eyes for a moment, silently asking each other "What's she doing?" Neither had an answer to offer the other, so Ryan chased Margie into the hall to find out for himself. He had very little idea what she was thinking or feeling right now—or, indeed, ever—but it was clear that she was worked up. Clients of the Clinic were being obliterated. Clients she had performed procedures on. What if she was blaming herself? What would she do?

He followed her all the way back along the corridor. She marched in brisk, short steps fast enough that he had trouble keeping up. She stared straight ahead the whole way, but didn't seem to be seeing anything. "Margie?" he said a couple of times, getting no reply. He wanted to ask "Are you okay?" but he didn't because the answer seemed obvious. He thought he had never seen her as not okay as she was right now. So what he tried was: "It's not your fault."

That stopped her. She wheeled on him. "How? How is it not my fault?" Ryan's heart flash-froze. She *was* blaming herself. "I invented the equipment. I performed the procedure on all those people with a device that I invented. And apparently it somehow left them vulnerable to total obliteration. So how is it not my fault?" And then she was pleading. Genuinely pleading. "How is it not my fault, Ryan? I need to know. Please."

"I... I..." Ryan stammered unintelligibly. "You didn't know," was all he could think to offer.

Margie dabbed the corner of her eye again. "Exactly the problem," she said. And she strode the rest of the way down the hall.

The majority of the waiting room ghosts had joined the mass around Trudy's desk. Some had just arrived and were pressing forward into the crowd to see what was happening. Others meandered aimlessly, asking each other if they knew what was going on, how long the wait was, what they thought was going to happen on Friday. When they saw Margie and Ryan emerge from the corridor the last stragglers swarmed over to them and immediately started demanding answers, each insisting that their problem was more important than these other peoples'. In seconds there was a mob around Margie.

She didn't look any of the ghosts in the eye, just gazed blankly straight ahead. He waited for her to say something, wondered if he should say something for her. The mob around her grew, and got increasingly restless.

When she spoke, she didn't use her power voice that, given the chance, could subdue a soccer riot. She spoke softly, as though trying not to wake someone in the next room. "I'm afraid we won't be taking any more appointments," she said. "I'm sorry. We're closed."

And then she turned and left.

Only the ghosts closest to her were able to hear it. Some of them looked stunned, others furious. The ones behind them pushed forward, demanding to know what she had said. Gradually the message spread, and the crowd became a mob, and then something like a riot. They surged forward in a clamor of furious, frustrated demands.

Ryan didn't want them to reach Margie so he stepped into their path and made himself the target of their outrage. "We're very sorry!" He tried to make himself heard above the riot, but had no idea how far his voice was carrying. "Just some technical difficulties, that's all! We'll reschedule your appointments! Please move towards the exit! Or just go through the walls if you want, whatever works for you! We're extremely sorry! I'm sure we'll be open again soon!"

If any of the ghosts actually accepted what he was saying and decided to leave, he didn't see them. All he saw was a dense, enraged fog of yelling faces closing in tighter around him, their voices an unintelligible cacophony of outrage.

He looked back and, through a gap in the mob, saw Margie far off down the hall. She was looking at her feet as she rounded the corner into her office and closed the door behind her.

An unwanted thought squirmed into Ryan's mind. A tiny part of him—perhaps a bigger part of him than he wanted to admit—was relieved that the Clinic was closing. Excited, even. Because it meant he was now free. Free to do what he wanted. Free to pursue the buttery gold of Hubert Cereal across most of the country.

And then he felt bad for thinking it. But not *too* bad.

10

This was the kind of investigation that Lowell liked. The kind where other people were doing the investigating, and all he had to do was find out what they already knew. It required much less in the way of deduction than most investigations, and much more in the way of standing around looking like furniture. He was good at that. So he attacked the job with aplomb and made his way to the Orpheum Theatre just minutes after his talk with Margie, stopping only for a donut on the way.

Being the site where a former U.S. president had been annihilated only the night before, the Orpheum Theatre was taped off like a crime scene. It was impossible even to approach the front door, since the police had parked five squad cars around the alley in which the entrance lay, effectively choking both the alley itself and nearby Tremont Street. By now most of the gawkers had figured out they weren't going to see anything interesting from all the way at the mouth of the alley, so only a few living people and a few dozen ghosts lingered outside the barricades. The alley itself was full of curious ghosts because there was no way for the police to block them. But they were keeping a respectful distance from the front door and whispering among themselves. Everyone else passed around the spot without paying much notice, just accepting the police presence as part of the scenery now.

Lowell hovered on the sidewalk across the street from the alley, considering his options. He decided that if he wanted to get into the theater, he had two choices. One was that he could go back to his office and try to fall asleep in his dentist chair. He'd leave his body and then be able to get past the barricades unimpeded, or just go through the walls of an adjoining building. But given the copious quantities of coffee he'd had with his donut, he worried that sleep would be impossible.

So he went with plan B, and called Detective Blair.

Twenty minutes later, Blair pulled into a fortunately vacant spot alongside the Park Street Church across from the alley. Lowell jogged over to meet him, camera in hand. Or rather, camera in *both* hands because it was broken in two pieces.

"Blair! Good! I need you to do something for me."

Blair looked even more weary than usual. And he always looked pretty weary. Or at least, he always looked weary around Lowell. There was no way Lowell could know if that was a specific reaction to him, or just Blair's normal mode of existing. "Is that my camera?" Blair said, as wearily as he looked. He obviously knew the answer.

"Yep!" Lowell said, as brightly as he could manage. "Thanks for the loaner! Really appreciate it." He handed over the camera. And then the rest of the camera. And then something that he had found lying near the camera that he couldn't say for sure was a part of it, but had picked up just in case. And then he stated the obvious. "It broke."

Blair appeared to have expected this all along. "Don't worry about it," he said. He opened his car door and threw the remains of the camera into the back seat. "It didn't work anyway. Mirror was shot. You think I'd give you one of our good cameras?"

Lowell was genuinely stunned. "You loaned me a camera that didn't work?" It offended him a little. But at the same time, his respect for Blair climbed up several points. *Well played, sir.*

"What do you want, Lowell? I'm busy. You *know* I'm busy."

Lowell pointed at one of the uniformed officers guarding the barricade. "I just need you to walk up to that officer with me and say three words. That's it."

"Three words. What three words?"

"'He's with me'. And I need you to say them really casual and show your badge. Then walk into the theater with me, hang around for a few minutes, and then leave. And could you wear sunglasses while you're doing it?"

"Why?"

"Geez, Blair, are you even a real cop? Don't they teach the sunglasses thing at the Academy?"

"No, I mean why do you want in there?" Blair looked tiredly across the street at the blocked alley. "What's this even got to do with you? You know something about the Lincoln case? If you know something you have to tell me."

"I know literally nothing." As much as that answer would frustrate Blair, it was true. Not only did Lowell know nothing about the Lincoln case, he knew very little about Lincoln at all. Beyond the hat and the beard and the appliance stores and the being president, he was mostly at a loss.

Blair sighed. He slipped his hand inside his jacket and withdrew a pair of mirrored sunglasses. "How many times have I said to you 'this is the last favor'?"

Lowell patted his arm. "Sixteen. Thanks."

Blair slipped the sunglasses on and shook his head. "He counts them," he said, apparently to himself. And then he trudged across the street with Lowell half a step behind.

◇

The auditorium seats were mostly empty. A few ghosts, perhaps twenty, occupied spots scattered throughout. But Lowell assumed they were probably stuck haunting the theater and couldn't leave even if they wanted to. They were possibly glad to have something different to watch, because the stage was a hive of police activity. The spot where Lincoln had been standing when he disappeared was entirely roped off with police tape strung around traffic cones. All around it uniformed officers, plainclothes detectives, and various forensic technicians were trying their best to look like there was something they could do about this and they were now doing it. But being a master himself at the art of pretending to look competent, Lowell could recognize that these guys had no clue what to do. A ghost had disappeared; it's not like they could dust for anything or hunt for revealingly-shaped blood splatters. They were good at looking busy, though. He respected that.

He moved through the seats, keeping his distance from the stage and doing his own, well-practiced imitation of somebody who was supposed to be there. And all the while he studied the activity on the stage, watching what all the major players were doing. He tried to focus on whatever conversations he could hear, hunting for useful information. If these guys knew what had happened to Lincoln, he wanted to know. If they even had a theory, he wanted to know that. But he couldn't single out individual threads of conversation in the hubbub. He needed to get closer.

He moved into the aisle and advanced down it towards the stage, pretending to be checking the bottom of every aisle seat as he passed them. There was nothing that he could logically be checking them for; gum was likely irrelevant to the investigation. But he felt like it helped him appear to be an investigator doing some serious investigating.

As he drew nearer to the stage he became aware that there was a whole set of people up there that he couldn't identify. Uniformed cops were obvious, and detectives could be singled out by their sheer detective-ness. Forensic techs all had sterile coveralls on and carried kits of equipment that was no use at all to them on this case. But there were other people too, maybe five or six of them. They were in civilian clothes but didn't appear to be detectives. In fact, they appeared to be interviewing the detectives. *Feds?* he wondered. *FBI maybe?* He decided that he was loving this. The case had taken a turn into coolness.

Just behind the roped-off area and a little to the left on the stage was a small cluster of people, a mix of detectives and uniformed cops, all gathered around one man. From his vantage point he couldn't see through the crowd to tell who the guy was. But whoever it was, he seemed to be in charge. Perhaps the cops were briefing him? Telling him everything they knew? Which was also everything Lowell wanted to know.

He crept closer, passing a few seats without bothering to check under them. If he could get close enough he was sure he could hear what was being said without actually daring to climb onto the stage. He circled to the left, straining to hear.

A moving spot of light caught his eye. It was in the back corner of the stage, far from him and far from the mysterious group he was trying to approach. Far from everyone, in fact. Far enough from everyone that he thought it had to be intentionally avoiding attention. It was a pink blob of light that swung and bobbed and for a moment he thought he was seeing some new kind of pink, fluttering ghost. And then he spotted that someone was holding the light, dangling it from a handle. And when the figure half-turned towards him he was able to see its face and—

Oh no.

Lowell threw all caution aside, clambered gracelessly onto the stage, and strode straight past all the cops and feds and mystery-investigators without stopping. And nobody took notice of him because he was striding with such purpose. They didn't know that his purpose was to get unreasonably indignant with someone, and to forcibly remove her from the building.

He arrived at the light-swinging figure and unleashed his first barrage of bile. "Gwen, what are you doing here?" he hissed.

She let out a startled yelp and spun to face him. As she whirled, the toy-size lantern dangling from her hand with its pink-hued bulb almost clobbered him from the side.

Lowell was surprised to find that, even though he hadn't seen or even thought about Gwen Gilbert in six, seven, maybe even eight years, his feelings for her had not mellowed at all. He still hated her with the kind of intense, bilious contempt that most people normally reserved for genocidal political figures, or villains in movies who murdered the hero's kid. The idea that anybody could regard her with anything but utter loathing never entered his mind. She was horrible in every way that a person could be horrible. And he also hated the little knit sweater she was wearing, although the color did suit her.

She seemed immediately tense upon recognizing him. She glanced over at the investigators across the stage. "Lowell?" she whispered. She clearly didn't want to be noticed any more than he did. "What are you doing here?"

He hated how her voice sounded like a cartoon pony. And he hated very much that she had gotten here before him, because it probably meant that she knew more than he did. "What is this thing?" he demanded, jabbing at her lantern.

She jerked it away from him, almost smacking herself in the face with it. "Don't touch it! And get away from me. I'm working." Again she glanced at the cluster of investigators across the stage, checking if any of them were taking notice of this conversation.

Lowell checked for himself, and could see that some of the mysterious investigators were indeed looking their way. One of them was pointing. If Lowell was going to get anything out of Gwen, he'd have to get it now. "Working how? What do you know?"

She swung the lantern at him, trying to shoo him back. "Get out of here. This one is mine. I thought of it first."

Lowell disliked everything about this conversation so far. For one thing, it had a decided lack of information in it. Plus he was talking to Gwen Gilbert, and that automatically gave him a sour taste in his mouth. He hated the way she was looking at him. He hated that she was looking at him at all. He hated that she was close enough to him that looking at him was even an option. He sort of liked what she had done with her hair since the last time he saw her, but he hated that he liked it.

And then he actually thought about what she had said, and part of it seemed more interesting than it had initially. "Wait, what? Thought of what?"

She narrowed her eyes, baffled by his response. But after a moment, he saw some kind of realization come over her. He didn't know what she had realized, but it was clear that it thrilled her. "You haven't figured it out yet, have you?" she asked, with a note of obvious glee.

"Figured *what* out?"

"I mean, I should have guessed. You never figure anything out. But I really thought—"

A ghost was suddenly between them.

He was neatly crew-cutted and square-jawed like a recruiting poster for the Marine Corps. But he was dressed incongruously in a bathrobe, t-shirt, boxer shorts and socks. It was a testament to the ghost's sheer force of presence that his outfit didn't undermine his air of authority at all. Even though he was a ghost, and dressed like a man rushing to get the trash to the curb on time, Lowell was intimidated.

"Identify yourself," the ghost barked, straight at Lowell. He seemed for the moment to be ignoring Gwen. It irritated Lowell.

A hundred lies ripped through Lowell's mind. Including some truly impressive ones that might work just by their sheer absurdity. But such was this ghost's authority that Lowell felt he had no choice but to do the unthinkable: tell the truth.

"Lowell Mahaffey," he said. He held up his business card. "Detective. Post-Mortal Services." He left off the word "Clinic" because he feared it would undermine all the cool factor he had earned with the word "detective".

The ghost leaned in to examine the card. "Post-Mortal Services Clinic? What is that?"

"We're experts in ghost..." Lowell struggled to remember the name of the particular branch of science that dealt with ghosts. Then he started to think that maybe there wasn't one. "...science. Sciences. All the sciences about ghosts. I thought maybe I could lend a hand with your investigation here." Lowell had impressed himself. Everything he had said sounded halfway convincing to him.

The ghost's granite eyes stayed locked on Lowell's. Lowell couldn't hold the gaze for long. And it didn't help that he could see Gwen creeping away behind the ghost, evidently trying to escape any interrogation herself.

"It's a clinic?" the ghost said. He shifted his feet apart and interlocked his hands behind his back. "Like a medical clinic?"

"We just call it that," Lowell said. "It also has detectives. Well, *a* detective. Me."

"What 'services' exactly are these 'post-mortal services', Mr. Mahaffey?"

Lowell tried to recall some of the words Margie used all the time. He had seen them on the brochure as well. "Besides detective services? Extractions, unhauntings, haunting adjustments, manifestation enhancements..."

Gwen had put ten feet between her and Lowell now, and she was tiptoeing towards the edge of the stage. She was going to get away.

"And this clinic is fully licensed to perform these services?" the ghost said.

Lowell gulped. He had literally no idea. And he had a creeping feeling that this conversation was getting into an area where he'd say things that he'd later wish he hadn't. "Of course it's licensed," he said, convincing neither himself nor the increasingly skeptical-looking government ghost.

"This clinic has regular inspections by the relevant agencies?" the ghost agent asked, clearly thinking he knew the answer already.

Lowell had never seen any kind of inspection hap-pening at the Clinic. But he went for it. "Oh, at least. Weekly, even. Sometimes more than once a week. Inspections, inspections, inspections, we have all the inspections."

"Uh huh," the ghost said, clearly not convinced.

Gwen had reached the edge of the stage and was looking for a quiet way down. Lowell decided that she couldn't get away. It was now or never. He pointed at her. "She's with me!"

The ghost turned and spotted her. Gwen froze in place, one foot half-descended over the edge of the stage.

"You!" the ghost bellowed. "Stop right there!" He turned back to Lowell and jabbed a finger at him. "And you too. Don't move."

Gwen shot Lowell a snarl and he smirked in reply.

The ghost turned away from Lowell and took a few steps towards the other side of the stage, where the small cluster of ghosts was still engaged in their brief-ing. "Director Prewitt?" the ghost called.

Lowell didn't know what Director Prewitt was the director of, and he felt like he didn't want to know. He started to back away. "Look, you've been very helpful. But I think I've got everything I—"

"Stay right there, please," the ghost said. "Director Prewitt?" he called again towards the investigators, louder this time. When there was still no response he turned instead to the closest uniformed cop on the stage. "Get Director Prewitt for me, please."

The ghost's frustration at getting his boss's attention was all the distraction Lowell needed. He took his chance. He bolted straight at Gwen, grabbed her by the arm and pulled them both off the stage. She didn't protest, probably not wanting to be caught any more than he did.

"Stop!" Lowell heard the bathrobed ghost call after them.

He didn't look back, but hurried Gwen down the aisle towards the exit. "Thank you!" he yelled back at the stage. "You've been a big help! We've got everything we need!"

He pushed Gwen ahead of him and tried to estimate the number of steps it would take to get them out of here. But before he could come up with a round number, Gwen shook his hand off her arm and bolted to the left. She was halfway to the emergency exit before he even figured out what had happened. And she was all the way to it before he had decided what to do, which was to stand there stupidly.

The moment she rammed into the door, the fire alarm exploded to life with a deafening wail. Every face on every cop and every federal agent and every forensic technician in the place turned all at once. They looked at the open door, which was already swinging closed. And then they looked at Lowell.

Lowell cursed the name Gwen Gilbert for perhaps the hundredth time in his life. And then he ran.

11

Ryan didn't see Margie for hours after she closed the Clinic. She disappeared into the basement and kept the door to the exam room closed. The most he could get out of her when he tried to open it was a demand that he should close it. Which he did. And he tried not to bother her again. He couldn't imagine what she was going through, blaming herself for the total obliteration of who-knows-how-many ghosts.

But the Clinic being closed didn't mean Ryan had nothing to do. He had to stay here in case Margie needed him. And that meant he had to face the wrath of all the clients who were still coming in.

There was no way to stop them. Locking the door achieved nothing. A locked door is no impediment to a ghost. More of them kept regularly streaming through the walls, and he kept having to tell them their appointments had been cancelled. Most of them got angry, and joined the mob of other angry clients already there. He tried putting up a "Closed" sign, which had no effect at all. So he tried putting up a bigger one. He made it himself out of the plastic floor guard from beneath Margie's desk chair. That sign just seemed to make the ghosts even angrier, so he took it down and put up four smaller signs instead. The ghosts kept coming, and kept angrying. All the chairs in reception were filled, some of them with multiple ghosts. More ghosts were sitting on the floor, apparently intent on staying there until their appointments were kept, no matter how late. A smaller mob still thronged around Trudy's desk.

Through it all, Trudy sat behind her desk and stared at them impassively. Or irritably. Or not at all. As usual, who could tell? The affronted ghosts could get nothing out of her beyond faint movements of her torso, so they always went after Ryan instead. At least he had a face they could be angry at. It started to annoy Ryan because dealing with people in the lobby was specifically Trudy's job, and she wasn't doing it. Decapitated or not, a receptionist should be receptioning. He wasn't sure if he outranked her in the Clinic hierarchy, but he decided to act like he did, and demand better of her.

"Trudy, do you think you could deal with everyone coming in? Please?" It wasn't a great attempt at being boss-like, but it was his first.

She didn't move. Her hands remained folded on the desk.

It annoyed him more, so he pushed harder. "Seriously, Trudy. It's chaos in here. You're the receptionist. Act like one."

That time it came out quite a bit harsher than he had intended. And it provoked a reaction. Not much of one, but a reaction nonetheless. He detected a slight sag in her shoulders, a slight hunching of her posture. He worried that he had wounded her and maybe she was gently crying. But there were no tears to be seen; just the usual spurts of ghostly fluid from the arteries in her neck stump.

He felt like he should apologize, but he didn't know how to calibrate to her reaction because he was unclear on what her reaction was. So he just said: "Please." And he hoped that would be enough.

He was just about to sneak back to the break room for a nap when he noticed someone standing just inside the entrance. Not a ghost. A living man. He stood out immediately because he didn't appear to be heated or impatient. Rather, he stood holding his belt on both hips and surveying the lobby as though it was an ancient Mayan ruin he had just uncovered while digging a pool.

Curious, Ryan approached him around the perimeter of the lobby, trying not to attract the attention of any of the testier ghosts. He wound up unintentionally sneaking up behind the man. And when he said "Can I help you with something?" he mostly anticipated a startled reaction.

Instead, the man turned around as though that was the way he'd expected someone to approach all along. "Hello," he said. "I thought there was no one here. It's so quiet! Slow day?"

Ryan inclined his head towards the rest of the lobby, overflowing with ghosts. "We're actually pretty busy."

"Oh, well, good for you!" The man said it like he meant it. Like he meant it a little too much, as if he was talking to a toddler who had just successfully finger painted without getting any on the table. He fished a leather badge wallet out of his jacket pocket and flipped it open, displaying some kind of I.D. with a government-looking logo that Ryan didn't recognize. Ryan had always thought that there was no un-cool way to flip open one of those things and display a federal agency badge. That was automatic badass in his book. Yet this man had found a way to do it like he was displaying a folder full of tiny surplus carpet samples. "Sidney Prewitt. I'm the Director of the Federal Bureau of Ghost Affairs, East Division."

The Director of the Federal Bureau of Ghost Affairs (East Division), Sidney Prewitt, was the kind of man easier to describe by what he wasn't than what he was. He wasn't tall or short. He wasn't overweight or under. He wasn't striking or bland. His short-cropped, businesslike hair wasn't blond or brown or black, but rather some mix of the three. It even had a few strands of grey because of how young he wasn't in addition to being not very old. He wore a white shirt and tie and a dark windbreaker that wasn't quite casual or professional. He had a beard that wasn't fully grown in. And he spoke in a voice that was clipped and abrupt and could almost pass for a slight German accent. But it wasn't.

"Oh," Ryan said, more stupidly than he intended to. He had never heard of the Bureau of Ghost Affairs. Not any division of it, East or otherwise. And he said so.

"We are a relatively new offshoot of the Immigration Department. Or the Health Department. Some department; I can't remember." Prewitt folded up his badge wallet and urged it back into his jacket pocket like it was a napkin he had just blown his nose into. "Of course, any department dealing with issues related to the spectral population is going to be relatively new, right? That probably went without saying. But yes, the point is, we exist. And we're here. This is my deputy, Agent Shipp." He motioned with his hand towards an empty space off to his right side.

Ryan mentally tested various theories of what that meant. "Imaginary friend" came out on top, yet still seemed like a stretch.

Fortunately, a tall, broad, crew-cutted ghost stepped forward on Prewitt's other side to clear it up. "Here, sir," he said in a voice so flat you could play shuffleboard on it. He assumed an at-attention pose next to

Prewitt with his feet apart and his hands behind his back. His officious, clearly military demeanor was undermined somewhat by the fact that he was dressed in boxer shorts, a white T-shirt, and a tattered bathrobe. Ryan reflected that this guy probably regretted every day that he was wearing that at the time he died. "It's *Special* Agent Shipp, actually," the ghost said. "On special assignment from the Federal—"

"I'm sorry to show up unannounced like this," Prewitt interrupted as though Shipp hadn't been talking at all. Shipp just winced, stepped back to flank Prewitt's shoulder, and let it go. Prewitt went on: "I tried calling on the way over but nobody was answering."

"Well," Ryan said, "like I said, we're busy. So..."

Prewitt shrugged.. "No matter. Do you think I could talk to whoever runs this place? The one in charge, as it were?"

Ryan's brain scrambled to find an excuse not to introduce them to Margie. But it need not have bothered, because she arrived at that moment as if she had sensed something was going on. "What is it? What's going on?" she said, approaching from the corridor. It was the first time Ryan had seen her since she went downstairs, and she looked as though she had been busy disassembling a city bus and then putting it back together again. Her lab coat and face were smeared with dark grease, and strands of her normally tightly drawn hair had burst loose and didn't seem to know what to do with their newfound freedom. In other circumstances, Ryan would have said she looked like a mad scientist. Which, he now realized, she kind of was.

"Uh, Dr. Sandlin, good," Ryan said, deciding that it was best to be formal and keep their relationship secret for now. "There's someone here to see you." He tried to fill his voice with the suggestion that this was important and not at all his fault.

Prewitt strode across the Clinic lobby, making no effort at all to avoid the ghosts in his path. He charged through four of them without blinking or showing any awareness of their presence. The ghosts complained loudly and tried to swat at him as he passed through them. Ryan trotted after Prewitt, having trouble keeping up because he had to zigzag to be conscious of personal ghost space.

Prewitt arrived at Margie and stretched out a hand to her for shaking. "Sidney Prewitt," he said. "Director of the Federal Bureau of Ghost Affairs, East Division."

Shipp followed right on Prewitt's heels and once again assumed a military pose off Prewitt's shoulder, as though at any moment he might be inspected by somebody wearing stars. "I'm Special Agent—"

"I hope I'm not interrupting," Prewitt cut in, interrupting. Shipp winced and resumed his Secret Service pose. Prewitt went on: "I have to be honest, I had no idea this place existed." He tilted his head back and studied the ceiling as though expecting to find a lost Michelangelo there. "If one of your employees had not come by the theater today, I *still* would have no idea."

Ryan was certain Margie was thinking the same thing he was: *what did Lowell say, and what did Lowell do?*

"What can we do for you?" Margie said, with a flat tone that suggested she didn't want to do anything at all for him. "As you can see, we're a little busy." She indicated the crowd of ghosts in the lobby with one hand.

Prewitt glanced behind him. "So I've been told. Busy with what, exactly?"

Margie waved at the crowd of ghosts again. "Um... appointments. Customers. Clients. We have a full schedule." Ryan noticed that she was trying to avoid revealing that they had closed, and made a mental note to do the same himself.

Prewitt looked behind him again and lowered his voice. "Oh, there are ghosts? Here? Now? Where?" He stretched out a hand and waved it through the air behind him as though hunting for a draft. "Here?"

Margie looked at Ryan, clearly as befuddled as he was. Ryan decided that the best way to help was just to ask the question. "You can't see them?"

"That's right," Shipp said wearily from behind Prewitt's shoulder. "He can't—"

"Correct," Prewitt cut in. "I don't see ghosts. I'm like that child in that movie 'The Sixth Sense'." He grinned, clearly having made this comparison numerous times to numerous people, and had it reliably generate hilarity. He paused to let them laugh.

Ryan tried to work out the logic of Prewitt's comparison. He still wasn't sure. "But that kid *could* see ghosts. That was his whole thing."

Margie tried to help. "'I see dead people.' It was in the trailer."

Agent Shipp closed his eyes and massaged his ghostly forehead, losing a little of his perfect posture. "I've tried to explain this—"

Prewitt waved off their protests and interrupted. "I really don't think that's what he said. But I haven't seen it for a while. The point is, I have a genetic anomaly. And it's actually more common than you think. According to a recent study, fully one in three-hundred-and-twenty-five million Americans still can't see ghosts." He gave them an impressed look, as though he was learning this fact for the first time from himself right now, and finding it intriguing.

"Isn't that just about the actual population of the whole country?" Margie asked. "Three hundred and twenty five million?"

"Approximately, yes. Give or take."

"So, in other words," Ryan said, "you're pretty much the only one."

"That is another way of looking at it."

"Wait," Margie said. "You're the Director of the Bureau of Ghost Affairs..."

"East Division."

"Okay. And you can't see ghosts? How does that make any sense at all?"

Prewitt folded his arms like a university professor giving a lecture he had given many times, and enjoyed every single one. "I find it allows me a degree of objectivity that I wouldn't otherwise have. For example, if you were going to appoint someone to be in charge of, say, the environment, would you be better off appointing someone who has studied the environment their whole life and therefore carries strong preconceived notions about it? Or would it be better to appoint someone who has never shown any interest in the environment at all, and could therefore come at it with a fresh mind open to new information. Things like, perhaps: 'what is the environment?' And 'why is it important?' I think we can all agree that the latter would be the better choice."

"No," Margie said. "We can't." Ryan sensed that she was approaching a level of indignation that might actually break through and be obvious.

Prewitt waved the whole discussion off. "We seem to have strayed from the subject. Do you think we could start the tour now?"

Margie blinked at him and shook her head a little, as though trying to wiggle Prewitt's request through a fine mesh in her mind. "I'm sorry? The tour?"

"Yes. I must admit, I was taken aback to find that this place existed. It's my job to know about this kind of thing. Makes me think you've been hiding from me." He waggled a finger at Margie, and included Ryan briefly in the waggle as well. "Naughty naughty. I'm afraid I must demand... oh, I'm sorry. That's such a harsh word. It makes it sound like I'm just throwing my authority around willy nilly." He elbowed Ryan in an approximation of jocularity. "We can be nicer than that, can't we?" He turned his attention back to Margie. "No, let's say 'request'. I *request* a tour of the facility and a demonstration of all relevant equipment, that being any piece of technology designed to impact the existence of any ghost, or the still-internalized ghost of any living person. And while I am not demanding the tour, I am requesting it in a way that is strongly suggestive of the fact that you legally *have* to do it. Kay?"

Margie's face remained, as it typically did, entirely impassive. And Ryan was forced once again to decipher what exactly she was feeling. On this occasion, he did so by measuring how long she spent saying nothing. A brief pause would indicate annoyance. Slightly longer could be anger. Longest was very likely worry. And this pause went on well past the worry threshold. It made Ryan immediately anxious because if Margie was worried, then there was something here that really needed worrying about.

But she let virtually none of it through. Instead she forced a polite smile. "Of course," she said. "But as you can... or rather can't... see, we are very busy. I recommend that we schedule something, say next week?"

"I'm afraid not. It's today or..." He chuckled. "I was going to say 'today or never', but it's not going to be never. It's just today. This afternoon." His smile, while obviously designed to appear chummy, completely failed to obscure the note of menace in his voice. "Now," he said.

12

Margie started Director Prewitt's tour with two big empty rooms. They had once been used as funeral chapels and were now used for wasting air conditioning in the summer and heat in the winter. And they were obviously intended to bore Prewitt and buy her some time.

Ryan followed along, nervous but uncertain why. What's the worst this guy could do? Close them down? They'd already done that themselves. It didn't help his sense of unease the way Prewitt's ghostly, stone-faced deputy, Shipp, lurked along behind them. He stayed far enough away to look like he wasn't really following at all but close enough for it to be obvious that he was. If he was trying to intimidate Ryan, it was working.

Margie next showed Prewitt the utility closet and its collection of highly uncontroversial mops. Prewitt was not impressed. And he appeared to be losing patience. "This is all very nice. But please, let's see where you do your work."

"Did you notice the mops?" Ryan tried as a further distraction. "There are two." He didn't mention that there were supposed to be three but one had broken. Best not to give this guy any ammunition.

It worked about as well as he had expected it would, which was not at all. "Please," Prewitt said, motioning them out of the closet. "I found this pamphlet on the reception desk. It says that one of your services is 'Extraction'. It says that it 'Ensures a comfortable post-mortal existence for all eternity.' That sounds lovely. Where do you do that?"

Those pamphlets had been designed and written by Roger Foster during his management of the Clinic, and Ryan knew that Margie hated their flowery, salesman-like language. But he had to hand it to Roger. They worked. They had worked on him, personally. They made the Clinic seem like a Willy Wonka factory of ghostly delights, and people responded to them.

Margie looked to Ryan for help, but he had none to offer. All he could do was shrug. "I'll, um..." Margie sighed. "I'll show you." She reluctantly led them away from the closet and into the stairwell.

"I have a question for you," Prewitt said as they descended the stairs into the basement. "How many ghosts a day would you estimate that the Clinic services?"

Margie brightened a little as some of her professional pride leaked in. "We average ten procedures per day, not including consultations. That is divided among various services, some of which—"

"So ten is the answer."

She tensed at the interruption. "Yes."

They reached the bottom of the stairs and started down the long subterranean nightmare of ducts and pipes that served as the main artery beneath the Clinic. Ryan expected Prewitt to look disgusted or make negative notes about the state of the basement, but instead he showed no reaction to the corridor at all and looked with keen interest into the nearest door, which was Margie's exam room.

"What is this? Ooh, this is fascinating." Before either Margie or Ryan could intervene, Prewitt had traipsed through into the room and started browsing it like it was a museum exhibit of stuffed cavemen. They hurried after, both of them afraid that he would break something.

Ryan had expected Prewitt to focus on the Box. It was, after all, their key piece of equipment, and really the only substantial piece of equipment they had. What he had not expected was the state they found the Box in. Ryan finally understood what Margie had been up to since closing the Clinic.

The case that enclosed all the Box's components had been unscrewed and peeled back like the wrapping on a brick of butter. And all of its insides had been removed and laid out on the floor in an orderly grid the likes of which only Margie could possibly have managed. Its various attachments were detached and similarly disassembled, their even smaller components arranged around them so that it was easy to tell which parts were supposed to be inside which other parts. It was a collection of baffling bits that Ryan assumed were called things like "capacitor" and "circuit board" and "diode", and he understood the function of absolutely none of them. Yet Margie had arranged them so carefully, in her Margie way, that he almost felt like he'd be able to put the thing back together if he had to. Almost.

If Ryan's assumption was right—and the smears of grease all over her suggested that he was—Margie had spent hours dismantling the Box to figure out if something was wrong with it. She wanted to know why it had made ghosts disappear during the Blink. Because of course she would.

Prewitt stepped slowly around the whole arrangement, on what little floor was left for stepping around on.

"We call it The Box," Margie said, her voice ever-so-slightly pinched with tension. She backed against the wall by the door.

"The Box," Prewitt said with hushed awe. "Why do you call it that?"

"Because it's box-shaped," Margie replied flatly. "When it's assembled. It's down for routine maintenance at the moment, as you can see." She stayed near the door, very clearly ready to escort Prewitt out of the exam room as soon as the opportunity presented itself.

"Don't technology things usually have names made out of capital letters that spell things? And have numbers like '9000' on the end? Like 'FLARC-9000' or something?"

"Well this one doesn't," Margie said, obviously not appreciating Prewitt's critique. "It's just the Box."

"How do you spell it?"

"B-O-X. As in 'box'."

Prewitt concentrated hard as he wrote it on his notepad. "B... O..." He looked up at Margie. "X?"

"Correct."

"X. Excellent." He underlined it with two emphatic strokes of his pen. "What does it do?"

Margie was tense. Ryan could tell because her arms were folded more tightly than usual, and her jawline looked like she was trying to chew a hard candy with a diamond in the middle. "It does... everything."

"Everything?"

"Yes. Virtually every service offered by the Clinic is executed using the Box."

"Like what? Like these..." He consulted his pamphlet. "...unhauntings?"

"Correct."

"It says that's where you help a ghost become un-attached to whatever object or place it's been haunting."

"That's right."

"And you do a lot of those?"

"It's our primary service."

"But you're not doing any right now, because the..." He checked his notes. "...the 'Box' is down for maintenance."

"That's correct."

"But you said you had a full schedule."

"We do. But only appointments that don't use the Box."

"But you said *everything* uses the Box."

Margie's already tightly folded arms folded tighter. Ryan started to worry that she might cut off her own circulation.

He stepped forward to intervene. "Maybe you'd like to see the utility closet again. Did you see both of the mops?" He attempted to usher Prewitt towards the door.

But Prewitt looked from Margie to Ryan with a slightly wounded expression. "I'm sensing some discomfort," he said. "Is there a problem?"

Margie still said nothing. Ryan was forced to attempt a response, as diplomatically as he could muster. "Sorry. It's just... this is kind of new for us. Government inspection. We're not used to it."

Prewitt tried to fan their concerns away with a sweeping hand motion, like their apprehension was a hint of stink and nothing more. "Inspection? This is not an inspection. I never said it was. Shipp, did you say this was an inspection?"

Shipp stepped forward from where he'd been lurking near the sink. "No sir, I—"

Prewitt cut him off. "Shipp must still be upstairs. Always wandering off. Anyway, no no no, this is not an inspection. This is a tour. A tour of what is clearly a very important, very unique facility. I'm fascinated by what you do here."

Margie loosened her arms, surprise on her face. "Really?"

Prewitt stood from his stool. "There are a lot of ghosts in the world—I am told—and they have a lot of needs that are woefully under-served. Especially now, with a potentially cataclysmic new Blackout looming just a few days away. The Bureau of Ghost Affairs exists to help them. As does this facility, apparently. I hope I can support you. I hope *you* can support *me*."

Margie was so taken aback that she stammered. Ryan couldn't remember ever seeing her stammer before. "Well, that's... I... I... well, that's..."

Prewitt bowed slightly, an absurdly formal gesture, and motioned towards the door. "Please. Let's have a look at the rest of the Clinic. Lead on. I want to see everything."

◊

They passed in and out of murky pools of light on their way down the basement hall. Margie led the way with Prewitt half a step behind her, and Ryan another couple of steps behind that. He knew that Shipp was marching with them somewhere even further behind him, but he didn't look back for fear of making eye contact.

"Have you been in charge as long as this place has been open?" Prewitt asked her.

"No, actually, I took over about a year ago. The original manager... well, he left."

It was a lie of omission, obviously, but a justifiable one. Getting into the whole "evil underground body-switching conspiracy" thing was a pretty substantial can of worms.

It occurred to Ryan that in a few moments they'd be entering the storage room, full of the still-living bodies of people whose ghosts had been extracted. Any way you sliced it, that was discomfiting and potentially controversial. He worried that Prewitt might see it as good reason to not only shut them down, but also put them in jail.

"Uh, Margie... Dr. Sandlin," Ryan said, quickening his pace to catch up to them.

If Margie heard him she didn't react. And if she was worried about showing off the storage facility, she didn't show any sign. She marched around the corner and straight in, with Prewitt still right behind her. He stopped as soon as the harsh, cold light hit him, and stared at the wall of cabinets as though he'd just stumbled across an overlook with a scenic view of a dolphin cove.

"Fascinating," he whispered.

Ryan caught up to them. "Uh, Dr. Sandlin, maybe we should..."

Prewitt hurried forward and knocked on one of the cabinet doors. He listened, as though hunting for a secret compartment. "Could you open one, please?"

Ryan emphatically wanted to not do that. But he tried to de-emphasize how strongly he was set against it. "We're not supposed to—"

Prewitt cut him off by yanking the handle and swinging open the cabinet door himself. Before Ryan could protest, Prewitt had already pulled out the sliding drawer. Inside was the body of a middle-aged man, his eyes open and his face locked in an expression of muted disappointment, as though he'd expected his ghost extraction to be like Space Mountain but it had turned out to be more of a Country Bear Jamboree. Various intravenous tubes for keeping his body alive were connected to both of his arms. But aside from that he looked pretty dead.

Prewitt stood alongside the motionless man and studied his face. "He looks good. For a dead man."

"He's not dead," Margie said.

"He certainly looks dead."

"But he's not."

"Look," Prewitt said. He poked the man, sinking his finger alarmingly deep into the man's cheek. "I'm poking him and he's not doing anything. That's exactly how I'd expect a dead person to respond."

Margie snorted derisively, and then quickly tried to pretend it had been a cough. "We tend to use slightly more scientific distinctions. This man is alive. His *body* is alive. We ensure that it remains so. His ghost is just... somewhere else. Like a long-term, or even permanent out-of-body experience."

Ryan's unease was intensifying. They were getting awfully close to having to reveal the problem with the Blink and the annihilated ghosts. This man's ghost could in fact be *gone*. He had been through an extraction here in the Clinic and was therefore possibly one of the missing ghosts on Lowell's list. And if they had to admit that to Prewitt, he didn't know what would happen.

Prewitt seemed for a moment to be giving the idea of a ghostless human body genuine consideration. But the moment passed quickly. He held his hand up to indicate the rows of cabinets. "All of these... these are bodies without ghosts?"

"Yes."

"Those are dead people."

Margie struggled not to snort again. "No. They're actually not."

But Prewitt wasn't listening. He wrote on his notepad and dictated to himself. "Room... full... of... dead... people."

Ryan was very nearly certain that this wasn't going well.

When Prewitt looked up from his notepad he was all smiles again. "Excellent. Shall we move on?"

"That's everything," Margie said.

"That's it?" Prewitt said, with a note of disappointment.

"Yes," Margie said. She had to squeeze the words through her teeth like thick paste. "You've seen it all. There's really not much to it."

Prewitt slid his notepad back into his coat. "Are you sure? An operation this size, there really must be more."

"No, I don't think..." Margie shifted her gaze to Ryan. "Ryan, did we forget anything?"

Ryan shook his head and managed to squeak: "Nope." He felt certain that's what she wanted him to say.

Prewitt stared at both of them for a moment. It was unsettling how he managed to somehow have one eye squarely on Margie and the other squarely on Ryan. Ryan felt compelled to step closer to Margie just to help relieve the obvious strain on Prewitt's eye muscles.

Prewitt drew the corners of his mouth even further out to the sides of his face and nodded. "Great! Then I guess we're done. The exit is back this way?" He took long, echoing steps towards the hall.

It wasn't what Ryan had expected him to say. And from the look on Margie's face he could tell it wasn't what she had expected either. She gave Ryan a "that was a close one" look of half-relief, so Ryan allowed himself a hint of relief as well. Though he had no idea what he was relieved about. What exactly had they avoided?

Ten feet back down the hall, all that relief turned out to have been for nothing. Because Prewitt stopped outside a door. "What's in here?"

In their haste to get to the storage facility they had walked right past that door on the way in. But now here it was, and Prewitt seemed interested. As with virtually everything else that had happened on this tour, Ryan had no idea why.

He jumped in. "That's just storage. Old stuff. Junk. Junk storage."

Prewitt pointed at the label on the door. "It says 'Unhaunted Closet'. What does that mean?"

Ryan had invented that name and put the sign up himself. He liked the name because it sounded like something out of Harry Potter. It wasn't accurate because it was more of a storage room than a closet, but "Unhaunted Storage Room" didn't have the same zing. He had taken down the original sign that said "Soiled Laundry", and now he wished he hadn't. While somewhat less whimsical, that sign wouldn't have drawn nearly as much attention. Probably none, in fact. Nobody wants to inspect soiled laundry.

But what was actually now inside the Unhaunted Closet was almost as uninteresting. The Clinic's most common service was unhaunting ghosts from objects to which they'd been bound. The Box was used to remove —on a molecular level—the ghost's emotional connection to the object, and then the ghost would be able to escape it. A side effect of breaking such emotional bonds was that, once the procedure was done, the client would often find themselves violently disinterested in ever seeing that object again. The Unhaunted Closet was where Ryan or some other member of the Clinic staff would then put the object for safe keeping, in case a relative of the Client ever showed up to claim it. Few ever had. So after hundreds of such procedures, the

Closet was a treasure trove of innocuous curios, each more mundane than the last.

Ryan was about to explain all of that to Prewitt when Margie cut him off. "It's just junk," she said. "Garbage. We take it out to the dumpster once a week."

The "junk" and "garbage" parts of her explanation were true. But the dumpster part wasn't. They hadn't cleaned out the Unhaunted Closet even once as long as Ryan had been working there. And it made Ryan tense. Why was she lying? Margie didn't lie, and certainly not without good reason.

Prewitt tried the handle. The door was, mercifully, locked. "Can I see it?" He then rolled his eyes, apparently mocking his own silly phrasing. "Of course I didn't mean to say it like that. I meant to say: 'show it to me now', because you have to. I mean, you don't *have* to, but yes you do. So, thanks."

There was visible tension in Margie's wrists as Ryan watched her unlock and open the door. Prewitt pushed past her into the darkness.

"Thank you," he said. And he clicked on a pen flashlight that they hadn't known he brought with him. They watched from the door as he moved up and down the aisles, sweeping his light over the shelves. Ryan saw it play across broken bits of furniture, electronics, articles of clothing, a Christmas tree, a doghouse, a jigsaw puzzle of puppies that he had meant to steal and bring home. They watched as Prewitt walked without pausing past a television, a plush purple pillow, a wildly inaccurate globe, stacks of books, a ColecoVision game console, a branch from a tree.

"In 1864," Prewitt said, "nine months before he was assassinated by John Wilkes Booth, President Abraham Lincoln was the subject of another assassination attempt. He was fired upon by an unknown assailant as he rode through Washington."

Margie looked sharply at Ryan. Her face had gone tense. He could see her jaw muscles straining. Why was Prewitt talking about Lincoln? Did he know something they didn't? Ryan pretended to be leaning casually against a shelf, when in fact he was gripping it hard.

Prewitt's light flashed over a metal sculpture of a bird, a whole row of dolls and children's toys, a bowl of plastic fruit. "The musket ball narrowly missed hitting the president's head. His horse was spooked, and galloped off. The President was unharmed, and mostly shrugged off the incident. Some soldiers went back to the spot the next day."

Prewitt stopped. His light had locked onto something, but whatever it was, it was hidden from Ryan's view by a stack of magazines. Prewitt stepped towards it. He reached behind the magazines. His hand disappeared into the dark.

"The soldiers went back to retrieve something the President had lost in the assassination attempt. Something he was very fond of."

His hand came out again holding something. He swung his light up to aim at it.

It was a tall, black stovepipe top hat.

As he held it up for them to see, he shone his flashlight directly into the open bottom. It came out in a thin beam through a small, ragged round hole about a third of the way up from the brim.

Ryan's hand became so sweaty that it slipped right off the shelf he was gripping. He risked a look at Margie. He was afraid of what he'd see, but he looked, and saw it. All the usual superhuman control of her emotional responses had broken. There was flat-out astonishment on her face.

Any government agent or detective who knew anything about drama would have held that moment and let the implication hang in the air. Prewitt didn't. He spoke again at exactly the wrong moment, fully deflating any dramatic effect he might have been going for. "I need to ask a favor," he said. He shook the hat and blew some dust off the brim. "And I hope this doesn't make me into a wet blanket. But I need you to sort of... shut down. I mean, not entirely. You can stay open. Just stop doing things and using your equipment."

"Which equipment?" Margie could barely manage to force out a whisper.

"All of it. Especially the Box."

Ryan's immediate reaction was that it wasn't as bad as Margie's face made it seem. They had already shut down the Clinic anyway, so Prewitt's order from on-high was redundant at best. Margie didn't seem to see it that way, though. She could still scarcely manage to get words out. "For how long?"

"Just until I can come up with some regulations that will then apply to you. Then, of course, I can inspect it to find violations of those regulations and shut things down on a more permanent basis. K?" He tried the hat on. It fell over his head and sat on the bridge of his nose, so he pulled it off again.

"You can do that?" Margie choked out. "You have the authority?"

"Oh yes. I pretty much have carte blank when it comes to inventing regulations. They told me that on my very first day."

Margie pressed both hands against the sides of her face, as though trying to squeeze back a rising rage. "No no no, you can't do this," she said incredulously. "Did you see the lobby? All those ghosts need help now. After Friday there may be no way to help them."

Prewitt shrugged. "I didn't see anyone."

That summoned Margie's rage even closer to the surface. Not quite there, but hovering just below. "I don't understand. What did we do? Why are you doing this? All we do is help people. Why are you even here?"

"Simple." Prewitt held up the hat. "A president disappeared yesterday."

Margie stared at Prewitt with her mouth hanging open. He decided that she wasn't going to get any more words out in that state, so he put some out for her. "We had nothing to do with that. That was the sun."

Prewitt's eyes shifted to Ryan. "If I push you in a river and you drown, did the river kill you? Or did I?" He twirled the hat between his index fingers.

Ryan really wanted Margie to handle this part of the conversation. She always knew what to say and he never did. But she was still paralyzed, and he thought he knew why. But he wanted to know for sure. "So... you think we killed Abraham Lincoln? I mean... again?"

Prewitt fluttered a smile and shrugged. "I don't yet know what to think. But the evidence..." He held up the hat. "...suggests that President Lincoln's ghost was a customer of this place. And now he's been... whatever you want to call it. 'Destroyed.' It certainly bears looking into, don't you think?"

He put his finger through the bullet hole in the hat and pointed it at Ryan like a gun.

13

As the windows drained of day and gradually filled with evening, the reception area fell quiet. Prewitt had left with a genial yet threatening wave shortly after his implied accusation, taking Lincoln's hat with him and leaving Agent Shipp in its place. Shipp's job, apparently, was to make sure that the Clinic did not see any clients or operate any of its equipment, and he took that job as seriously as his cast-iron demeanor suggested. He made a point of telling all the ghosts in the reception area that the Clinic would not be doing any of the things they wanted it to. The ghosts had already been told that several times by Ryan, but Shipp's air of authority, even in a bathrobe and boxers, was apparently much greater than Ryan's because the ghost clients listened to him and fled to wait outside. Some of them came back later to see if he was gone and he scared them away again with a look. After that he divided his time between walking a patrol route through every room in the Clinic and going back to reception to drive off any new ghosts who had come in. He was relentlessly good at both.

What he emphatically did not do was try to be friendly with Ryan, and that suited Ryan just fine. He had enough things to be anxious about without throwing social anxiety into the mix. For one thing, he was worried that either he or Margie would soon be accused of the first-ever second assassination of an already-assassinated president. He didn't know what the punishment for that might be, but it promised to be bad.

On top of that, NASA experts were back on the news, saying that another 'foreshock' was on its way, so they could expect another Blink event. They predicted it would strike around 2:15 AM, and he was worried about what it might do to him. Even if it was nothing more than what had happened the first time, he still wasn't looking forward to it. He wanted Margie nearby in case anything scary happened.

But as night fell she was still in the basement. He walked past the door of her exam room three times in the course of the evening, careful to make sure he didn't cross one of Shipp's patrol routes. The first time past, he heard hammering; the second, beeping; and the third, louder beeping and faster hammering.

Then it got to be 10:00 and apprehension was chewing its way through his organs like an implanted alien. So he ventured another trip past her door. This time he heard nothing. He decided it was worth the risk of annoying her to open it and check in.

To his surprise, she seemed downright thrilled to see him.

"Ryan! Good! Come in, quick!"

He did as she asked, and stepped inside. The Box, in contrast to the last time he had seen it, seemed entirely intact. In the last few hours she had apparently reassembled it and left no trace of it ever having been taken apart. Not a spare part was left on the floor and the Box looked perhaps even more polished than it had before.

Margie hustled him into the room and checked the corridor. "Shipp is due for another patrol soon," she said. "We have to talk fast." She closed the door behind Ryan.

"You put it back together?" Ryan asked, stupidly. He knocked on the Box for extra stupidity.

She waved the question off as though he had just pointed out that she was breathing. "I've been doing a lot. And thinking a lot. I had to be sure that whatever's making these ghosts—" She hesitated, searching for a word. "—making them *be gone*, it couldn't possibly be a defect in the Box. I took it apart and I checked everything backwards and forwards. There's nothing wrong with it. It works perfectly well for unhauntings and we could start doing them again. I'm completely sure of that."

"But the Bureau, that guy Prewitt, closed us down..."

She waved it off. "We can't worry about that. There are a lot of ghosts who need help before Friday. We're going to help them."

"But what if you missed something?"

"I didn't miss anything. I don't miss things. There's nothing wrong with the hardware." From anyone else a statement like that would seem like a boast. From Margie it was just true. She held up a finger in a "eureka" gesture. "But..." She knocked on the Box, and Ryan didn't feel so dumb anymore for having done so. "What if the *software* was changed without my knowing? What if it was something Roger did? He was always experimenting, even when I warned him not to. I undid every change he made but what if he made some I didn't know about?"

"Is that possible?"

She went to the door and checked the hall again. Shipp had apparently not reached this part of his rounds yet. "Shipp will be here soon," she said. "We should whisper."

"Is that possible? Roger changing the software?" Ryan implored again, attempting to get to the ultimate point of this talk.

"Shhh!" She closed the door again and went on in a whisper. "Yes. There's millions of lines of code built into the Box, having to do with SES matching and so forth. Roger's not good at code, but he could have changed it. But why would he? That's why I started thinking about Abraham Lincoln. I didn't unhaunt Lincoln from his hat. But the hat was here. So if it happened, then Roger did it. Secretly."

Ryan was getting edgy. By the clock on the wall it was almost 10:15 and the second Blink was ticking closer by the minute. "I can tell you're excited about figuring something out, so can we maybe jump to that, or—"

Margie ignored him and pressed on. "I looked into it. Abraham Lincoln's last visit to Boston was about two years ago. He threw out the first pitch at a Red Sox game."

"I remember that," Ryan said. Being unable to pick up a baseball, Lincoln hadn't actually thrown anything. Rather, he had stood on the pitcher's mound and mimed the motion of throwing while David Price did the actual throwing from behind him, right through the dead president's chest. As Ryan recalled, Fenway had set an attendance record that day, packing nearly forty million people into 37,000 seats. Countless ghosts had turned the infield into an impenetrable fog and rendered the historic non-pitch nearly impossible to see.

"So," Margie continued, "I thought that would be a likely time for Roger to have performed a procedure on Lincoln's ghost. I pulled up the Clinic records and there was nothing on his schedule around that date. But!" She stopped after the "but" to check the corridor one more time.

Ryan prompted her fretfully. "But you figured out what happened?"

"No, I figured out *part* of what happened. Because I checked on the current status of every ghost we've ever extracted from a body." She leaned closer to him. "There are more than twenty-five that disappeared in the Blink. There are thirty-nine. And all of them had their extractions done *after* that day. Any ghost that we extracted before Lincoln's last time in Boston, they're still here. They weren't affected by the Blink. But all the ghosts we extracted after that date, they're gone. Do you see what that means?"

He did not, but said "Uh huh" like he sort of almost did.

She didn't believe him, quite justifiably. "It means that when Roger secretly unhaunted Lincoln from his hat, he changed something in the Box's software. I don't know why. Some experiment of Roger's that he probably charged a fortune for. And it's something I can't find that never got undone. So every ghost that got extracted after that was affected by it, just like Lincoln. It somehow made them vulnerable to the Blink, in a way that other ghosts are not. That's why the Blink apparently destroyed them."

"But it didn't destroy me because I still have my body. So I'll be okay tonight? They say there's another Blink coming."

"That's what I need to talk to you about. Because I have a theory, and I need your help."

He wanted to say "no" right away, because he was the one who needed help tonight and the last thing he wanted was to be helping someone else. But this was Margie and he had told himself many times he would do anything for her. Until now it had never been tested, apart from her once asking him to let her have the last few Frosted Flakes at the bottom of the box. Agreeing to it had felt like a monumental sacrifice because, obviously, the bottom of the box is where all the loose sugar collects. And he had been forced to have plain toast for breakfast instead, the most offensive of all breakfast foods. In Ryan's view, toast was a curse, a flavorless blight upon breakfast. But he had done it for her, and then basked in the pride of it for weeks.

But he felt like now he was about to find out if he would really do *anything* for her. "Help with what?"

She stepped a little closer. And he found himself even more apprehensive. He could even see pleading in her eyes, which made it even worse. What she was about to ask was probably going to be somehow even bigger than subjecting himself to toast. He braced himself, as much as he could.

But she didn't say anything. She studied his face for a few seconds, and he wondered if she could read the terror in his eyes. He knew they must be wide because he could feel the chill basement air seeping in around their normally warm sides.

And then she stepped back. "No," she said. "Never mind."

Ryan was enormously relieved. Which is why he couldn't believe he was saying: "Why? What is it?" He didn't want to know what it was. At all. But here he was asking it in a weird, squeaky voice.

"It doesn't matter," she said. And she went back to the Box and pretended to be tightening bolts on it that he could tell were already tight.

Ryan knew it did matter. But he also knew that it was something he wouldn't want to do. Because there was only one thing he wanted to do: the thing that he blurted. "Let's just go."

She kept pretending to tighten the bolts, not really hearing him. "Go where?"

"Colorado."

She stopped tightening and turned to him, and as usual he couldn't interpret her expression. She was just looking at him. So he decided to hope for the best, and went for it.

"We just close the Clinic. I mean, we already closed it, and so did Prewitt. It's double-closed. After Friday there's no ghosts anyway, so how much difference can we really make between now and then? So we just let it be closed and we go. Like a vacation. Put all this behind us. Just forget about all of it and deal with it when we get back. Why not?"

He thought he had made a pretty good case. But she stared at him for longer than he was comfortable with. And when she didn't stop, he started to not like it, and to regret every word he had said.

"No?" he said feebly.

But before he could take it all back, Shipp appeared through the closed door. He strode through it like it wasn't there and immediately assumed an accusing hands-behind-his-back pose like a principal who had just caught them smoking. "What's happening in here?" he said. "Are you using that machine?"

Margie looked away from Ryan, and it was the only relief provided by Shipp's appearance. "No," Margie replied flatly. "As a matter of fact I'm disabling it to prevent it from accidentally being used before it can be properly inspected by the relevant authorities."

Shipp lifted his chin towards Ryan. "What's he doing here?"

Margie didn't miss a beat. "We were just discussing what would be the most efficient method to fully comply with Director Prewitt's investigation and enable him to promptly carry out his duties as Director of the department." None of it was sincere, but Margie's professional tone expertly made it impossible to challenge.

Shipp appeared taken aback. His posture loosened slightly. "Oh. Well. That's good." He studied Ryan, and Ryan squeezed what smile he could muster past all the sweaty dread. "So you won't mind if I observe." Shipp widened his stance as a way of indicating that he intended to be a semi-permanent fixture in the room.

Ryan did mind, of course. He desperately wanted Shipp to leave. Immediately. Because there were things Ryan wanted to discuss with Margie more than anything, and he couldn't discuss them with Shipp standing there.

"Of course we don't mind," Margie said. "Anything to assist the execution of your duties in any way we can." It was magnificent how she managed to make it not sound like bitter sarcasm, even though it clearly was.

"Margie," Ryan tried feebly, "should I, um, stay or—"

She sighed. "Just go home for now." She looked at him in a way he didn't like, as though she was seeing him differently now than she ever had before.

On his way out the door he felt like he had physically shrunk.

14

Ryan woke to Benny the Poltergeist poking him in the eye.

Benny had haunted Ryan and Margie's apartment since long before they lived there, and he had spent all that time working out how to be one of those ghosts that played tricks on people. After decades of relative incompetence—and a single well-timed door-opening that had helped save Ryan's life—he was now finally starting to master the art of touching things in the physical world. Where once he had struggled to write "DIE" in the fog on a bathroom mirror, he could now write "YOU WILL DIE" pretty legibly, and was working on expanding it to "YOU ARE GOING TO DIE A TERRIBLE DEATH". In the past it had taken him an entire week to get all the kitchen cupboards open, but now he averaged two an hour. One downside to his growing talent was that he had also figured out how to make noises in the middle of the night by squeaking the floor and slamming doors, and he did both almost every night. Usually he'd call out to them at the same time, like "Ooh, what's that squeaking?" or "Did anybody hear that?" just to make sure they didn't miss how scary he was being. Ryan and Margie had gotten used to it, though, and found that if one of them got up and pretended to be investigating the "mysterious" noise, that made Benny happy and he'd leave them alone the rest of the night. But the other downside to his skills was that he could now directly contact them when he wanted to.

And he was doing that now by poking Ryan in the eye.

"Yo! Ryan!" He jabbed again.

It didn't feel so much like a poke as like a fly landing on his eyelid. But it was enough to rouse Ryan and make him irritably try to swat Benny away.

"Ryan! I hear a noise."

Great, Ryan thought through the sludge of unconsciousness. *He probably figured out a new way to make the faucet drip.* It was still very much dark out, and it was Margie's turn to go "investigate" whatever Benny had done, so he rolled over and left her to it. Seconds later he was already diving back into the murky depths of sleep when—

Ping!

"There it is again!" Benny sounded genuinely frightened.

Ryan sighed. Having died in the 80s, Benny was unfamiliar with cell phones. And ghosts, as a fact of their static, limbo-like existence, were mostly unable to absorb new understanding. So no matter how many times Benny saw Ryan and Margie use their cell phones, he was constantly surprised when their phones did things. Like make noises.

Ping!

"What *is* that? I think it's coming from the lamp!"

Ryan mumbled: "It's a message, Benny, go away."

Wait. A message? The thought woke him up like a slap.

He rolled over fast. So fast that he rolled right off the couch and landed on top of his empty cereal bowl on the floor.

A rush of questions flooded his mind. *Why was I on the couch? What time is it? What day is it? Am I late for something? Who's messaging me?*

He crawled to the side table and grabbed his phone. Immediately all the answers came to him. He had sat on the couch after coming home alone from the Clinic. He had watched an awful reality show called "Digging Up" where ghosts were reunited with their exhumed remains and apparent hilarity ensued. He had fallen asleep because it was terrible. It was now 1:57 AM, early Wednesday morning. And Margie was messaging him.

Eight messages and three calls.

"Are you here?" "Where are you?" "Running out of time." "Answer your phone!" "I need you here now." "Did you fall asleep?" "Wake up!" "Get here ASAP".

Ryan cursed loudly and toppled the side table as he pulled himself to his feet. The lamp tumbled, but he was all the way to the door before it hit the floor and shattered.

As he took the stairs down three at a time he heard Benny shouting: "I didn't do that!"

◊

It was 2:12 by the time Ryan made it to the Clinic. Three minutes until the new Blink. He fumbled with his key, ripped open the Clinic door, and plunged inside. As he charged across the lobby the muted thumps of his feet on the carpet echoed heavily. The place had never felt so abandoned. So dead. Even in his rush to get to Margie he was dimly relieved to see that Shipp wasn't in the reception area. Only Trudy sat resolutely at her desk, acknowledging Ryan only by folding her hands in front of her as if waiting professionally for him to request an appointment. He decided that Shipp must be out on one of his patrols, which was either lucky or unlucky.

The lights in the stairwell were shut off except for one stark pot light directly overhead. The fixture was loose and wobbled as he passed. As he descended, his deep shadow spread wider around him like a puddle of dark he was leaking into. Halfway down the stairs the metal pipes in the basement corridor caught the echoes of his footsteps, throwing hollowed-out versions of them back at him seconds later.

He paused at the bottom of the stairs to let the echoes subside. The basement was utterly silent but for the soft thrumming in the pipes of whatever thrummed in them. The corridor stretched endlessly through illuminated pools into the distance. Only the sharp-edged rectangle of light spilling out of Margie's exam room broke the pattern of the overhead lights.

There was no sound of Margie. No sound of anything.

Hesitant for some reason to step into the darkness, Ryan called out from the bottom of the stairs. "Margie?"

When there was no reply he turned cold. Something was wrong. Something was definitely wrong, and his heart was trying to tell him so by frantically drumming in his ears like it was testing them to see if it could escape that way and flee back up the stairs.

He dashed the last few steps to the door of Margie's exam room, hurled it open the rest of the way and dove through.

The first thing he saw was Agent Shipp. Standing with his back to Ryan just inside the door. When he heard Ryan enter, he turned to look at him. And he smirked. Like he had known Ryan would be here, and here Ryan was doing exactly what he'd expected.

Ryan didn't bother to go around him. He went right through him, felt a chill as he passed and shook off whatever other emotions of Shipp's he picked up on the way. He didn't want to know.

He stopped just on the other side of Shipp. Because when he saw what was past him, his heart stopped completely.

Margie was there. But she wasn't working on the Box anymore.

She was attached to it.

Her body lay on the exam table, clutching something to her sternum. The back of her head hung over the end of the table a few inches, which was how she always positioned her patients, with the giant metal "spider" gripping the back of her head. Wires snaked across the several feet from the spider to the Box. And the Box, Ryan could see from here, was powered on. But rather than being plugged into the wall, it was wired to several car batteries piled up beneath its cart. There were a couple of numeric readouts that hadn't been there before, but he saw immediately that its charge was at zero, which meant either that it hadn't been fully charged yet, or that it had been recently discharged. One more look at Margie told him which. Because he could see thin threads of white smoke flowing around the sides of her head and tracing undulant lines in the air above her.

Questions rioted through Ryan's head. *Did Shipp do this? Why would he do this? He's a ghost, so* how *could he do this? Why wasn't I here? How do I fix this?*

He was so dazed by all the questions that he barely noticed Margie herself standing next to the table, looking down at her body.

The same moment he noticed her, she turned her translucent head to look at him. "Ryan?" was all she said. The word was unformed, not quite her voice. And it pitched up at the end like a question. Like she wanted him to tell her what was happening, and what he was going to do about it.

All the questions stampeded through his head again. "What do I do?" was all he could blurt out. It was the only one that mattered now. He had to get her back into her body. The rest could wait.

She looked up at the wall behind him.

He turned to follow her gaze. She was looking at the clock.

2:16. The Blink was late. Or the clock was wrong. Or the prediction of the Blink's timing was wrong.

But he knew immediately what would happen when it came. Margie had been extracted from her body like all the others, and that meant she was vulnerable like all the others. And she would be obliterated like they had been.

He had no time.

He dashed across the room and slammed the reset button on the Box, then set the charge to 100%. The hum began rising as the capacitor charged. Then he hunted for the paddles. "We're putting you back in! Get above your body!" He had never seen a ghost put back into its body, because it almost never happened. But he knew it could be done because it had been done to him. How hard could it be?

He couldn't find the paddles. They were supposed to be hanging on the cart with the Box, but they weren't. He grabbed the wires running from the Box and fol- lowed them. Found one of the paddles clutched in Margie's hands on her chest, like she had been trying to force it off of her. Trying to save herself. *Save herself from who? Who did this to her?!*

He snatched the paddle away from her and held it over her body like he'd seen her do many times before. Her ghost looked at him with a kind of desperation in her eyes. She struggled, trying to form more words, but couldn't get the air to make them. She wasn't used to being a ghost, didn't know how to make her particles do things. He didn't want her to have time to learn.

The Box rose through the middle octaves.

"Get above your body!" he barked again. "I can do this!"

"Ryan," she said. Her voice was taking form gradually, sounding more like her. She was shaking her head. "Ryan," she said again, "Listen. Listen. Listen."

And then all the lights went abruptly, utterly dark.

Ryan froze. The Blink had arrived.

The only light left in the exam room came from Margie's ghost and from Shipp in the doorway, a faint diffuse blue that reflected off the walls and counter tops.

The Box kept rising through the octaves, its glowing display a piercing point of light in the dark.

Margie's ghost hadn't moved. She was watching him with wide eyes and the faintest hint of apology in the way the corners of her mouth curled up. Like she was sorry for having put him through this.

"No!" Ryan cried. He threw the paddles down and dashed towards her, reaching out like he could grab her and hurl her physically back into her body.

He was a foot away when he saw her molecules fly apart like an air cannon had been fired at her from behind. It blasted all her particles straight at Ryan and he felt the electric surge of them tearing through him, felt a flood of her fear and regret and worry. And then she was gone.

Ryan stood in the black. He was cold. He listened to his own ragged breathing, not knowing what he could possibly do.

And then whatever had hit Margie hit him too.

The world pitched up on its side like a ship running aground. The floor punched him hard in the temple, and then the dark got darker and dragged him into a deep hole.

15

"You haven't figured it out yet, have you?"

The words echoed in Lowell's mind long after he escaped from the Orpheum. And because the echo was in Gwen Gilbert's voice, every word was like a stab in the brain with a fork. And what added poison to the brain-forking was that he had no idea what the words meant.

Lowell always thought best when he was a ghost. So after fleeing the Orpheum he sneaked back into the Clinic, careful to avoid Margie who would be expecting him to provide information he didn't yet have, locked his office door, and lay down in his dentist chair. It took more than an hour but he eventually drifted off, and then drifted up, and then drifted out.

Well into the night he wandered, ghostly, around the dark paths of Boston Common, trying to figure out what Gwen knew that he didn't. He often came to the Common at night. His body could get some well-earned rest in the dentist chair while he meandered the pathways, watching the British infantry gear up and march out for the Battles of Lexington and Concord. There were about twenty of the soldiers haunting the park who for some reason re-enacted the deployment again and again, probably confused as to why they never actually made it to the battle. It had become something of a tourist attraction, like one of those stunt shows at Universal Studios. And he found it fascinating. Or at least much moreso than all the other thousands of ghosts in the Common, most of whom were confused farmers and hippies who didn't have muskets or cool uniforms.

But tonight Lowell was distracted by his ruminations, so he only watched the soldiers' deployment twice. He spent the rest of the night just meandering and thinking, blending in with the rest of the ghosts.

"You haven't figured it out yet, have you?"

Lowell dug deep, trying to recall what else Gwen had said. Surely there would be a clue to what she was talking about. Something that he could deduce to ensure that she didn't get to screw him over, which she was most certainly attempting to do. Because that's what Gwen Gilbert did. She existed on this Earth for the sole purpose of screwing over Lowell Mahaffey.

◇

He first encountered Gwen during the brief period in his life when things were actually going pretty well. For a while before the Blackout and after discovering that he could leave his body by creative use of a dentist chair and red wine, Lowell was a spectacularly successful detective. It was easy when he could communicate with ghosts that nobody else could see. He just walked up to the ghosts of murder victims and asked them who did it, and the case was closed. For a time he was the BPD's go-to paranormal consultant whenever they hit a dead end in a case, and they paid well for it. He had a great detective agency office with a desk and a filing cabinet and a big stack of business cards with his picture on them. They were mostly matte, but had a glossy finish where his smiling teeth were so if you held a card just right, his confident detective's grin would sparkle in a way that said "I am ridiculously cool".

The case he was working when he met Gwen was a difficult one. Not difficult in the sense that it was particularly hard, but difficult in the sense that it required effort to cheat at. A man named Jan Boelens had been murdered in some kind of business disagreement. His business was manufacturing decorative screw-on knobs for the ends of curtain rods, which didn't seem to Lowell like it should be all that cutthroat. Organized crime wasn't exactly falling over itself to get in on the decorative curtain rod knob racket. Nevertheless, Mr. Boelens had been murdered. Disappointingly, not with a decorative knob, but rather by the more conventional method of bullets through the chest. And his three business partners were the prime suspects. Detective Blair had worked the case for months and found no hard evidence that could pin the crime on any one of the three. So he turned, naturally, to Lowell.

It should have been an open-and-shut case for someone of Lowell's abilities. But the problem was that upon the death of his body, Mr. Boelens's ghost had gone hurtling across the Atlantic to the Netherlands where he was from and where, apparently, decorative curtain rod knobs were all the rage. And Lowell didn't much feel like making the trip to Leeuwarden to talk to him. It was a chore. It was too far to go as a ghost—his body would wake up and pull him back before he got there. And he couldn't haul his dentist chair halfway across the world without incurring major shipping charges.

So he stalled. He told Blair he was working on it, and did no such thing. He assumed that the motivation would come to him eventually, but it never did. And the Boelens case went stale. Until one day Lowell went into the station to visit Blair and find out what easier cases he had, and found him at his desk talking to a psychic medium.

Lowell didn't know her, but she immediately annoyed him because she was sitting in the chair where he should be, and talking to the guy he should be talking to. She was diminutive; Lowell guessed no more than an even five feet. She had a round face and narrow-set eyes, and a curl to her lip like a perpetual smirk. Her frizzy dark brown hair stuck out to both sides like a set of motorcycle handlebars. He would have expected a psychic medium to be dressed in some kind of draped robe with lots of beads and scarves, but instead she wore a wool cardigan undoubtedly knit by somebody's grandmother.

Lowell felt the urge to interrupt whatever was happening here, and fast. "Blair," he said, "I'm here."

He thought that should be enough to capture Blair's full attention. But Blair just held up a finger to shush him, and never took his eyes off the psychic. "Boelens," Blair said. "With a B."

The psychic glanced at Lowell, then away. "Who's this guy? I'm getting such bad energy." Her voice was in a register so high that Lowell thought it might be imperceptible to many humans.

"That's Lowell," Blair said. "He's one like you with the talking to dead people stuff."

Lowell had no desire to be associated with this woman. "What's this, Blair? What are you doing?"

"Shut up, Lowell," Blair said. "Go ahead, Madame Gwendolyn."

The psychic, evidently Madame Gwendolyn, closed her eyes, drilled her thumbs into her temples, and seemed to be concentrating. It all seemed wildly exaggerated, and Lowell felt his dislike for her growing by the minute. "Yes, it's him," she said. "Bollins."

"Boelens," Blair said again.

"Really? I'll tell him." The psychic closed her eyes tighter and twisted her thumbs in deeper. "Stop saying your name wrong!" she yelled as if trying to be heard down a long tunnel. "It's Boelens!"

"What's he saying?" Blair asked, evidently fascinated. "Anything about the murder?"

At that, Lowell went from annoyance to full-on alarm. Not only was this person sitting in his chair, but she was also muscling in on one of his cases. One that he had been tirelessly ignoring for weeks now. He refused to let that all that non-effort be wasted. "Are you really buying this?" he said to Blair. "This stuff isn't real. She's a fake. Nobody can talk to ghosts like that."

"You do," Blair said.

"Yeah but, like, to their faces. This is just dumb." He jiggled the back of the chair, trying to shake her off of it.

Her eyes sprang open, but not because he was shaking her chair. She had apparently had some kind of revelatory communication. "P!" she shrieked.

Every detective in the office wheeled their chairs out and stood up to see what was going on. Blair held up a hand to let them all know everything was okay. "P?" he said.

"The man who killed him. His name starts with P!"

Blair checked his file. "B?"

"Yes! D!"

Blair checked his file again. "B?"

"Yes! B!"

Blair checked his file one more time. "You're sure?"

"Positive. He's telling me B."

Lowell shook the chair harder. "Okay, that's it. Get out. Just get out. I'm serious."

Blair tried to wave Lowell away. "Lowell, stop it. That's rude. She's trying to help us out here."

"She's a wacko and she's taking you for a ride. Just because the guy's dead he starts spelling stuff? That's B-U-L-L-S-H..."

Madame Gwendolyn leaped out of her chair and tore her thumbs away from her head. "Bruce Floyd!" she yelped. "He was murdered by Bruce Floyd, his business partner. Shot him twice in the chest with an illegal FN-Browning handgun. You'll find it in the bottom drawer of the filing cabinet in his office. Also, he's a Gemini."

Lowell stopped shaking the now-empty chair. He was sure that his stunned expression matched Blair's exactly, and he didn't like that because Blair's looked stupid.

Blair looked at his file one more time. Then flipped it closed. Madame Gwendolyn threw Lowell a spiteful, triumphant look.

Lowell sneered. "No. Way."

As it turned out, she was right. Bruce Floyd was arrested three hours later after a handgun matching Jan Boelens's wounds was found in the bottom of his filing cabinet. The only comfort Lowell could take was that Bruce Floyd turned out to be a Leo. At least she had been wrong about that. But she was dead-on correct about everything else, and he had no idea how.

That was the first case Madame Gwendolyn—nee Gwen Gilbert—stole from him. After she stole three he started to feel like she was specifically targeting him. And after six he decided that he truly, genuinely despised her.

Then the Blackout happened, and the ghosts appeared, and everybody in the world could talk to murder victims whenever they wanted. So all that remained of Lowell's police consulting business went rapidly in the dumper. The only consolation was that he heard Gwen's business had also gone into that very same dumper.

That his life started to go badly after that wasn't Gwen's fault, but he still chose to blame it partly on her merely because she existed.

◇

A shift in the general tone of the conversations around him wiggled into Lowell's awareness. He started paying attention, and it took a few moments for him to grasp what was going on.

The lights had gone out.

The lamps along the Common paths were black, and the buildings he could see past the Frog Pond were nothing more than black silhouettes against a sky that had turned an odd, ghostly green. He realized that a second Blink had hit, and he hadn't even noticed. It took him another moment, maybe even pushing into two solid moments, to figure out *why* he hadn't noticed.

It was because he could still see the ghosts. The lights had gone out but the ghosts were still there. During the first Blink they had all vanished, but this time they had not. They mostly stopped their wandering, though, and paused to look up at the shimmering green sky. Even the British soldiers seemed to decide that the aurora overhead justified delaying their march on Lexington just this one time.

Lowell drifted through the ghosts, watching their reactions. There was a lot of pointing and ooh-ing and aah-ing, but no fear. Because nothing, really, had happened, apart from the park getting slightly darker.

But something *had* happened. It took him more than just a few moments to figure it out. It took a full-on *while*. But he did, eventually, notice it. Not among the ghosts, but among the living people. Being so late at night there weren't many of them in the park, and it wasn't until after he had passed several little groups of them that he started to notice that their reaction was different from that of the ghosts. The living people weren't looking up. They were looking around them-selves, at the park. They were pointing into empty space, at trees and lamps, and whispering curiously. He couldn't figure out what had them so freaked out. So he approached a pair of them, a middle-aged couple in sweaters and tennis shoes who apparently and wrongly thought it was cute to dress exactly the same as each other.

"Hey folks," he said, as non-threateningly as he could. He held up his hands to indicate that he had no plans to rob them or, more plausibly, possess them.

They didn't respond. One of them seemed to be look-ing at him for a moment but almost immediately looked away again.

He tried again, amplifying his non-threatening tone to the level of outright chumminess. "Pretty weird, eh? How are you guys—"

He hadn't finished his sentence when one of them, the apparent husband of the pair, interrupted him. "I forgot how dark it could get," he said.

"I know, right?" Lowell said, joining them in looking around the park. "But it's weird, I—"

"I know," the wife said. "It feels so empty."

Lowell clued in that they weren't talking to him. They were talking to each other. They weren't even looking at him, and hadn't been since he approached them.

The realization fell into place like a sliced bagel into a toaster. They couldn't see him. They couldn't see any of the ghosts. The ghosts *had* disappeared. He just couldn't tell because this time he was one of them.

He tested it by moving in front of the couple, inches from their faces. And when he got no reaction he tested it further by waving his arms above his head and screaming at the top of his ghostly, non-material lungs.

It drew stares from many of the ghosts around, but no reaction at all from the couple.

Until the lights snapped suddenly on again. The Blink was over. The city lit up in flickers and the couple both reeled backwards from Lowell, screaming.

Lowell tried to apologize as they staggered back from him, but he decided that it would be best for all three of them if he just turned and ran away into the Frog Pond. So that's what he did, not looking back to see if either of them had suffered a heart attack. He made a mental note to come back later and find out if he had killed one or both of them, and to apologize for it.

He got to the middle of the pond, his feet completely failing to make splashes or ripples in the water. And then an enormous revelation dropped on him so hard it almost sank him into the earth. He finally understood what Gwen had meant. *You haven't figured it out yet, have you?* And the shock of the realization transmitted all the way back to his body and snapped it awake.

He felt himself ripped across the city, hurtling through buildings and trees and cars and suddenly into the dentist chair in his office at the Clinic. He slammed into his body so hard that it toppled off the chair. And he knew he was back in his body because it hurt when he hit the floor.

Without getting up he went over the realization in his mind, and he could see no holes in it. It was thrilling, and optimistic, and perfect.

After the big Blackout this Friday, the world would be back to the way it had been. Nobody would be able to see the ghosts anymore.

Nobody except him.

And that meant he would be back in business. Not just back in business the way he had been before. No, it would be better than that. Because now everybody *knew* the ghosts were there. It wasn't just some crackpot theory exploited by scam artists. It was a known thing. And people would want a way to talk to the ghosts they knew were there but couldn't see for themselves.

After Friday, Lowell wouldn't need the Clinic anymore. After Friday, people like Lowell would be in demand. And Gwen Gilbert was, he hated to admit, a person like him. They would be at war again.

She was already trying to get ahead of him somehow, and he needed to know how before it was too late.

16

Ryan woke this time to a drain under his face smelling strongly of formaldehyde and weakly of lemonade. When he managed to roll onto his back and forcibly wrench his eyes open the overhead light drilled into them immediately. He tried to raise a hand to shade them and found that his shoulder ached. He tried to grip his shoulder to squeeze out the ache, and found that his fingers were tingling. So he tried to flex them and got a sharp pain in his wrist. He decided that maybe if he stopped looking for injuries there wouldn't be any more, so he just lay there and let everything hurt.

And then a single thought yanked him off the floor: *Margie.*

He sprang upright, hoping desperately that he'd been wrong about what happened. He clutched the exam table and pulled himself to his feet.

She wasn't there.

The Box was there, parked next to the table with its paddles and attachments strewn on the floor amidst a spaghetti dinner of wires. The power toggle was on, but the display was dark, suggesting that the car batteries had been depleted. The spider was there too, resting on the table with its spindly legs rigidly sticking upwards, as though it had died of convulsions in the night. But Margie's body was definitely not there.

Feeble hope dared to poke its head up in his mind and wave a little flag. Maybe he *had* been wrong. Maybe Margie had climbed back into her body after a brief ghostly trial. But then why was he on the floor? Why was the Box so disorderly, in a way that Margie would never, ever leave it?

He dashed for the door, staggered, and missed it by a solid foot. The shoulder that didn't hurt slammed hard into the frame and started hurting.

He stumbled up the stairs and into the admin hall. He was stunned to find that it was daylight. How long had he been unconscious on the exam room floor? The Blink had happened just after 2:15 AM, so five or six hours at least? Maybe more.

He kicked Margie's office door open, which didn't work at all so he had to grab the knob and open it the normal way. She wasn't there.

Call her. He whipped out his cell and speed-dialed. It rang three times, finally clicked through. "Margie?"

"This is Margie Sandlin recording a voice mail greeting. Please keep your message brief. Thank you." *Beep.* Ryan hung up. He caught a glimpse of the time on his phone. It was 9:12 A.M. So, seven hours then. The time had passed in an instant.

Where else could she be? Would she have gone home? If so, why leave him on the floor? And the whole idea ignored the fact that he had seen her ghost outside of her body and blown apart by the Blink. But still, hope continued winking at him and waving that little flag.

He heard heavy footfalls in the corridor and for a moment thought it could be her. But she never stomped like that. It could only be the orderlies, Ethan and/or Ewan. Ryan ripped the door open and almost collided with one of them on his way through it. "Ethan! Ewan!" He didn't have time to check if they were both there, and it didn't matter anyway because he had no idea which one was which. Throwing out both names covered all the bases.

The huge man had been on his way to the stairs but he stopped at the sound of his name, and the other name. His ghostly brother was in front of him, leading the way, and also stopped. They looked at Ryan like he was a smudgy fingerprint on a window they'd have to come back and Windex later. One or both of them grunted in reply.

"Have you seen Margie—Dr. Sandlin—this morning? Is she here?"

The ghostly brother jabbed a thumb towards the stairs. "She's downstairs," he growled.

"You saw her? She's here?" Ryan was already trying to squeeze past them to get to the stairs. They left precious little space in the hall. He wondered how they ever rode buses, but presumed that nobody rode a bus who had the capacity to carry one.

The living brother frowned. "Yeah, we saw her. She's downstairs."

Ryan got past them with minimal contact and plunged down the stairs. Dangerously fast, apparently, because he stumbled at the bottom and cracked both his kneecaps on the floor. But he was up again immediately, ignoring the pain. He checked her exam room, knowing she wasn't there. And she wasn't.

Downstairs? Downstairs where?

The understanding dropped like a heavy rock that crushed his feeble, misguided hope back into its hole.

He continued down the hall, slow now because he didn't want to get where he was going. If the corridor went on forever and he never got to the storage facility, he'd be fine with that. He'd just keep walking and never see what he was about to see. And he could live with that.

He found himself under the flickering green lights, typing Margie's name into the computer to search the directory of storage cabinets. He hoped faintly that it wouldn't show up.

But that hope, like the others, was soon mashed into the ground. Her name was there among the others, with a number telling him which cabinet to open and various measurements of her vital signs.

It was vaguely comforting to see that her heart was beating, her temperature was good, and she was still breathing. But he knew it meant nothing, really. She wasn't going to leap out of the drawer when he opened it. Because she wasn't in it. Her body was, but she wasn't. And she never would be, because everything that made her Margie had been utterly annihilated the night before, right in front of him.

He didn't allow himself any hope at all as he opened it. Hope tried to emerge yet again and say that maybe she wouldn't be in there, maybe it would be mistaken identity and not her body at all. But he kicked that hope until it retreated back into the dark. And he pulled the cabinet open.

There her body was. She looked for all the world like she was asleep. Her right arm was connected to the various tubes and sensors that would keep her body alive— Ethan and Ewan were good at their jobs and apparently hadn't questioned at all why the latest body was their boss and not a client. Aside from those attachments she might just have been taking a nap in there. He shook her arm, gently so as not to disturb the serenity of her pose. She didn't respond at all. Her eyes didn't flicker. No part of her moved.

It had all happened exactly as he remembered. She was gone. She had been taken out of her body and totally obliterated, and he hadn't been able to stop it. Ryan stood holding her arm under the pallid lights until his feet hurt as much as the rest of him. She never moved, and it was a long time before he gave up hope that she would.

◇

He didn't start to think again until he was walking back up the hall towards the stairs. But as he trudged past all of Margie's handiwork, this Clinic that she had worked so hard to build, he realized something terrifying that he didn't have the mental capacity to process.

He was in charge of this place now.

He didn't want that. He wanted to close it for good, or to let Prewitt go ahead and shut it down. Then he could spend his time doing what he really felt like doing: eating poorly, staring, and being generally sad. And after Blackout 2 on Friday there wouldn't be any need for the Clinic anyway, so he would only be shutting it down a couple of days early. Would that really be so bad?

He desperately tried to justify the idea. For one thing, Prewitt had already told them to shut down, on suspicion that they had been responsible for Lincoln's re-assassination. If Ryan kept the place open he'd be violating orders from a government agency, and could wind up fined or in jail.

Then he took that line of thinking even further. He rationalized that his keeping the Clinic open would almost certainly put him in mortal danger. There was only one person whom he could realistically suspect of having murdered Margie. It had to be Director Prewitt. His goon, Agent Shipp, had been there in the room, probably somehow doing his boss's bidding. Behind all his Mr. Rogers-esque geniality, Prewitt clearly had an agenda. Ryan just couldn't figure out what that agenda was, or why it required Margie to be taken out of the picture. He already held supreme power over the Clinic, so what purpose did it serve getting rid of her? It made no sense. But if it was somehow true that Prewitt had murdered Margie merely for being in charge of the Clinic, and then Ryan took over the Clinic in her place, then Prewitt would almost certainly try to murder him too. And for obvious reasons, Ryan didn't want that.

All of those were good reasons to just walk away. He could lock the door, say goodbye to Trudy, leave a note for Lowell, and head to Colorado to find Irvin Curry and his box of Hubert Cereal. He would never, ever come back to this place. All of that would be easy. He could do it right now.

But Margie wouldn't want that. He knew she wouldn't. This place was her life's work, and if there was any way she could keep it going and keep helping ghosts all the way up to Blackout 2 on Friday, then she would. And she would want him to do it too.

But on the other hand, all that other stuff.

No. I can't do it. I'm sorry, Margie, I can't.

He made up his mind. He was going to leave, and lock the door. Margie would forgive him. He had a plan and he was sticking to it.

His plan failed thirty seconds later when he found the waiting room packed with clients.

17

Lowell sat in his car in the tiny parking lot of a paint store in a depressingly cramped part of Malden. He didn't know how long stakeouts were supposed to last, but he had been sitting there for about an hour and it seemed excessive. The first half of that hour he had spent deep in thought, carefully going over events in his head, analyzing and trying to spot any connections he might have missed. The second half of the hour he had spent wishing he had some onion rings. Now he was just bored.

He wasn't interested in the paint store he was parked at. It was closed, because paint stores seemed to have universally agreed to adopt maximally inconvenient hours. But it had a three-space parking lot which he was taking up two spots of, because it afforded him a view of the building next door. This was a squat, drab little commercial building whose designer must have dropped out of architecture school after the first day, when they learned to draw rectangles. It was barely bigger than an average-sized family home, with another dismally tiny three-spot parking lot in front where all but the smallest cars would have their rear bumpers protruding into traffic. The bottom floor of the building was a dealership that sold scooters out of a small garage attached to the side. The scooter dealership was not the reason he was there, although after staring at it all day he found himself wondering if maybe a scooter might be right for his lifestyle. The reason he was actually there was the second floor. There were three identical windows across the top of the building, each with a blind covering it on the inside. The third window was taken up mostly by an air conditioner that looked like it might soon fall and bring someone's scooter shopping to an abrupt and scooterless end. But the first two had words painted in them in large purple letters. The middle window said "Psychic Medium", and had a phone number which was useless because two of its digits were scratched off. And the first window said "Madame Gwendolyn".

Lowell disliked having to search for people. He had only ever gotten into the business of tracking people down because he had found various ways of cheating at it. When he had to legitimately hunt for them, it frustrated him. It was hard. Real detectives did that kind of thing, not him.

Besides which, on the list of all the people he didn't want to be searching for, Gwen Gilbert was near the top. Tracking her down meant seeing her, and potentially even talking to her again. Both possibilities gave him chills. But he had done it, using all the specialized detective resources at his disposal. Mostly Google. And now here he was, looking at Gwen Gilbert's office window and waiting for her to come out. He was pretty sure she was in there because he had seen a shadow moving around in the crack above the air conditioner. If she had clients in for palm readings or aura adjustments or whatever nonsense she did, their appointments wouldn't likely have lasted this long. He'd have seen them leave by now. So it had to be her in there, just Gwenning around being all Gwennish.

His plan was this: he would wait for her to come out, and then follow her. After that it got a bit hazy. But whatever Lowell-screwing plan she was up to, he wanted to know about it. And then he wanted to steal it from her. The prospect made him dizzy with delight, and would hopefully make all this sitting-around-at-paint-stores worth the effort.

He saw a shadow move behind the air conditioner again, and he wished that in addition to the onion rings, he had some binoculars. And maybe a scooter. He had just decided what color of scooter he would prefer—black—when Gwen Gilbert emerged from the front door of the building.

Lowell sat up. And then thought better of it and hunched down so he could barely see over the dashboard.

Gwen moved in a rapid shuffle around the side of the building. She seemed to be in a hurry, maybe even flustered. Something was up. Lowell congratulated himself on his detective work. He had been right to stake out her office and now it was going to pay off somehow if he could just stay with her.

She disappeared behind the building and Lowell took the opportunity to start up his engine. Starting his car was often a lengthy process so he thought he better get a jump on it. He was on his fourth attempt when he saw Gwen drive out from behind the building in a dented green Mini that had seen better days, the majority of them in the 90s. While she waited at the edge of the parking lot for traffic to clear, Lowell fought with his own car until it finally, complainingly came to life. Gwen turned left onto the street and passed right in front of him, and he was eventually able to escape the little parking lot and pull in behind her.

Pretty good so far, he thought. Maybe he was better at this detective stuff than he thought he was. Then she stopped at a light and he couldn't stop fast enough and bumped into the back of her.

Lowell froze, wondering if that had just happened. And if it did, then why couldn't it have happened to somebody else? He ducked beneath his steering wheel, because her thinking she'd been hit by a driverless car might be slightly better than her seeing him.

Miraculously, despite the jolt and the *thump,* Gwen didn't seem to notice. Maybe her Mini had better collision absorption than his car did. Because she just waited for the light to turn green and then accelerated away. Lowell sat up and followed, thanking whatever power in the universe had saved him.

A few turns later, Gwen swerved down a side street next to a bakery cafe and slowed down, evidently hunting for a parking spot. Lowell slowed and pondered his options. If he turned down the same street she'd definitely see him creeping along behind her. There wasn't another side street, nor were there any free spots on the main road.

So he stopped. Right there in the middle of the road. What else could he do but stop there, watch, and hope that nobody came up behind him? Which somebody immediately did, with honking.

Lowell cursed and clicked on his hazard lights, hoping the driver behind him would assume he was broken down. Who honks at someone broken down in the middle of the street? This guy, apparently.

A ghost who appeared to have been angry since the 16th century decided to take up the other driver's case and stood in front of Lowell's hood, yelling curse words at him that nobody had used since 1770. Lowell made a mental note to look up what a "bobolyne" was.

Despite all that, he was able to watch Gwen leave her car and go through the side entrance of the bakery, then emerge right away onto the patio. No stopping to buy anything. The patio was mostly empty but for two small ghost gatherings in the corners and one living person: a slight, bookish man, sitting alone. Gwen sat at the table with the man and leaned across the table towards him. The man looked surprised to see her. He glanced around the patio, maybe checking if anyone was listening in, while Gwen seemed to be talking quietly to him. It did not appear to Lowell like a social call. It looked like a meeting.

Neither of them seemed to notice the honking in the street nearby. Which was surprising, given that the driver behind Lowell had decided to put his full body weight onto his horn. *Shut up shut up shut up.* Lowell flipped him the telepathic bird.

Gwen finished talking to the man on the patio and patted him on the forearm. Then she stood, went through the bakery again, and headed back to her car.

Lowell was again torn about what to do. Stick with Gwen and lose Patio Guy forever, or interrogate Patio Guy and find out what this meeting was about. In a flash he decided that, impossible though it seemed, he was going to attempt both.

He threw open his door, leaving behind his car, the honking driver, and the bobolyne ghost, and dashed across to the bakery. He vaulted the cast-iron rail around the patio, stumbled badly into some chairs, and plowed through a cluster of ghosts having an intense conversation around a table. Around the corner of the bakery he saw Gwen's Mini, still parked. She hadn't left yet. He still had time. But not much time, because the honks from the driver in the street had been joined by another.

He collapsed into the chair across from Patio Guy, out of breath. Patio Guy gave him the exact same surprised look he had given to Gwen just moments earlier.

Lowell fought his desperately gasping lungs to get words out. He didn't have time to be subtle, or polite, or threatening. So he just demanded and hoped for the best. "I don't know who you are," he gasped. "But tell me what Gwen Gilbert just said to you."

Patio Guy's surprise changed shape from one kind of surprise to another. Lowell wasn't sure which kind either of them was. "Are you... Lowell?" he said carefully.

Now it was Lowell's turn to be surprised. "How did you know that?" he wheezed.

"That lady," Patio Guy said. He thumbed towards the bakery, where Gwen had recently departed. "The lady who was just here."

This wasn't going anything like Lowell had expected. He stuck with his interrogator voice. "Yeah. How do you know her?"

"I don't. I've never seen her before. She just came up and said that somebody named Lowell would ask me about her. She said to say you can stop following her. And that if you want to talk, she's in the coffee shop across the street."

Lowell reluctantly shifted around in his chair to look across the street, past where a line of four cars was now stuck behind his and a crowd of ghosts was yelling in front of it.

Gwen Gilbert sat at a table in the front window of a little coffee shop, looking across at him with what he assumed was a triumphant smirk. She waved cheerily, waggling her fingers in the air, and raised her coffee cup in a toast.

◇

Lowell never expected to be having coffee with Gwen Gilbert. Yet here he was, sitting across from her in a coffee shop. And he hated that she had out-clevered him somehow, and could now justifiably look smug. He tried not to look at her, fearing it would cause him actual physical pain. Instead he focused on the cheerful ghost barista behind the counter, who was gamely trying to serve everyone despite being unable to physically move cups, plates, or any controls on any of the coffee machines. The ghost customers didn't seem to mind because they couldn't drink coffee anyway. And a sign on the counter read "Living customers please serve yourself", which explained how the shop stayed in business at all.

"What do you want, Gwen?"

"What do *you* want? *You* were following *me*."

Lowell hunted for an excuse, but failed to find one. So he said: "No I wasn't." Which already made him feel like this wasn't going well. But he was prepared to lean into it if pressed.

Gwen sipped smugly. "I think you're following me because you know I can find him, and you're hoping you can slide in there and find him first. But I've got news for you, Lowell. It's not going to work that way. I'm all over this, and you've got *nothing*."

He had to admit, she was right. He had nothing. He had less than nothing, because he didn't even know what she was talking about. He deliberated between trying to subtly eke out of her what she meant, or just getting it over with and asking her. He settled on the latter. "What are you talking about, Gwen? Find who?"

She stopped sipping in mid sip and blinked at him. She slowly lowered her cup. "Are you really that dense? Lincoln!"

Lowell dared to look at her. Was she serious? Did she know something *else* that he didn't? "Wait... so you're saying Abraham Lincoln is... alive?"

"No, Lowell. That's stupid. He hasn't been alive since 1865. All I'm saying is he's not as dead as people think he is."

"So where is he?"

She put her coffee cup on the table and leaned towards him. He leaned back because he didn't want to be touched by air that Gwen Gilbert had breathed. "I have a theory. You know how back before the ghosts were everywhere, we always said they were on 'the other side'? Well now, because of the Blackout, 'the other side' is on the same side as us. There's no 'other side' anymore. There's just a side."

"Uh huh," Lowell said. He was looking at her hair and wondering how she got it to stay sticking out at the sides like that.

"Only... what if there's *another* side? An 'other other side'? And just like how when people died, they used to go to the 'other side', when a ghost dies, it goes to the 'other other side'." She grinned like it was genius.

But it wasn't genius. It was stupid and she was nuts. Or she was playing at something, probably with the end goal of humiliating him somehow. But it was more comfortable for him to assume it was stupid. "That's stupid," he said.

"Is it, though?"

"You made it up."

"It's a scientific theory."

"A scientific theory that you made up."

"So?"

"It doesn't get to be a scientific theory just because you call it that. Only scientists can make up theories." He didn't know if that was true. But he was pretty sure she didn't either, so he felt like he got away with it.

"Well it doesn't matter. It's true. I know, because I talked to him."

This was getting worse by the second. Lowell prepared to get up and leave. He didn't do it yet, but he prepared. "You talked to Lincoln's ghost. On the other other side."

"That's right. And I think I can find him. With this." She held up the little pink lantern she had been using at the theater. It was turned off now, and looked even dumber when it was dark. It was plastic, and he wondered if it had been made for a doll. "Think about it, Lowell. After Friday, it could be a golden age for people like you and me. But there will only be room for so many of us. If you want to come out on top, you have to make a splash. Something that gets you on talk shows. I'm going to be the psychic that found Abraham Lincoln. Who are you going to be?"

So there it was. She did have a plan to screw him over. Only it didn't seem as bad as he had expected, because of how totally nuts it was. Or so he wanted to believe. Yet still, some small part of his mind nagged at him. *What if she's right?*

He shook it off, pushed away from the table and stood up. "I'm outta here."

"I heard you talking to that ghost agent at the theater," she said quickly, recognizing that she was losing him. "Are you really working at the Post-Mortal Services Clinic now?"

"Until I get fired for wasting my time talking to you." He turned to leave.

Gwen took his arm to hold him back, and he hated that any part of her was touching any part of him. He was genuinely amazed that his skin didn't smoke and blister beneath her fingers.

"Has Lincoln ever been there? To have, you know, Clinic stuff done to him?"

"No. Why?"

Gwen talked fast, maybe sensing that she'd lose him if she didn't get through it. "Because until about two years ago, Lincoln never went anywhere without his hat. He made assistants carry it to his speaking engagements, because he could never be apart from it. But then, after he was in Boston for that Red Sox game, all of a sudden... no more hat. I think he got unhaunted from it. There's nowhere else he could do that but your Clinic. Is is possible he went there and you didn't know it?"

Lowell knew that it was. Lots of things happened at the Clinic that he didn't know about, because he usually tried to avoid its business. He didn't want to admit that it was possible, but he did. "Maybe."

Gwen gripped his arm tighter. "Then I think we just became best friends."

18

The waiting room was even more densely packed with ghosts and their living escorts than it had been the day before. Shipp was no longer there to scare them off so they had come back in force. Ryan guessed that the second Blink through the night had frightened them. More of them were figuring out that they would be invisible again after Friday, and they needed the Clinic's services before it was too late. So here they were.

But despite their great numbers, they were not a mob this time. They were organized and orderly. None of them swarmed him when he appeared from the admin hall. They definitely noticed him, and they seemed neither happy nor patient. But they didn't rush at him and demand service. Instead the ones that had chairs stayed in them, and the ones that didn't have chairs stayed in a single-file line that snaked around from Trudy's desk through all the available space in reception and out the door. And they waited like good clients to be dealt with.

With so many concerns already gladiator-wrestling in Ryan's mind, he couldn't begin to guess the reason for the shift in tone. But as he tried to shrink away from

the waiting room and get back to more pressing matters, he noticed another surprising detail: Trudy was
not at her desk. Trudy was literally *always* at her desk.
But right now she wasn't.

And then he spotted her. She was out in the waiting
area with the crowd, deftly moving between all the waiting clients and steering fast towards him. She had a
hand in the air towards him and she waggled it, trying
to get his attention as she approached.

He had no attention to give, so he put up his own
hands defensively and waved them in the universal gesture of "not right now". But if she saw it she gave no
indication. She reached him and tried to usher him over
to her desk with a sweeping motion of both arms.

"I... I can't," Ryan stammered. "I really can't."

At the front of the long line was a ghostly old woman
in a hospital gown, accompanied by what Ryan
assumed was her still-living husband. The husband,
despite his advanced age, was lugging a 20-pound gym
weight. If his wife's ghost was haunting it for some reason, he probably carried it everywhere. And that was
likely the reason for his pronounced and painful-look-
ing hunch. No wonder they had come in to the Clinic.
He had probably been carrying that literal weight for
years, and now sensed his last chance to get rid of it.

But just as Trudy was gesturing at Ryan to come help
them, another freshly-arrived ghost shoved through the
line to her desk. He had the appearance, demeanor, and
expensive fashion sense of a high-powered banker or
corporate executive. Specifically, one who had jumped
or fallen out of a very high window, judging by his bent
limbs and cracked skull. Probably a victim of a tech
bubble bursting, Ryan judged.

"I've been here an hour already," he snarled at Trudy.
He pointed a finger at Ryan. His finger was so star-
tlingly snapped that he had to aim the rest of his hand

downwards just to get the fingertip to point generally in Ryan's direction. "Is he the one? Is he the doctor?"

Ryan was ready to bolt. He couldn't deal with this on the best of days. And today was seriously far from the best of days. But he needn't have worried, because Trudy inserted herself between the executive and Ryan. She assumed a commanding posture, and pointed firmly out the door where the end of the line presumably was.

The executive smirked and shook his head. "No freaking way. Do you know who I was?"

And then Trudy did something Ryan had never seen her do before, but had always feared that she *could* do. She seemed to grow larger, and darker, like a storm cloud gathering energy and shaping itself into a tornado. And she downright loomed. Her neck stump towered over the executive, spurting, and her shoulders broadened into veritable mountains that he would have to overcome if he wanted to get past her. She stretched out one hand and pointed at the door, and tapped her foot rhythmically. So much power had she summoned that Ryan was almost sure he could hear her foot actually making contact with the floor like a clock timing how long it took the guy to react.

The executive cowered. He turned and fled out the door, sweeping other ghosts aside like swarms of gnats as he passed.

And then Trudy was suddenly back to her usual self as if nothing had happened. She turned back to Ryan and motioned him over to her desk.

Ryan realized now the reason for the organized waiting room. "You did this?" He motioned towards the orderly crowd. "Seriously?" Apparently his boss-like order-giving the day before had had an impact. More of one than he could have anticipated.

Trudy moved to the elderly couple at the front of the line and put an arm gently behind the old woman's back. With her other arm she gestured towards Ryan.

As impressed as Ryan was with Trudy's sudden transformation, he wanted no part of this right now. He wanted to leave, before Prewitt had the chance to murder anyone else. "Sorry, no," he said to the old couple. "We're closed. By order of the government. Maybe Trudy didn't make that clear."

The couple paused and looked to Trudy for confirmation. Ryan could see that he had made all the hope in their faces drop away, replaced by despair. The husband gave Trudy a wet-eyed look. "Please," was all he said. But his eyes and his pleading hands were saying it too, so really he said it three times.

Trudy stepped closer to Ryan, and he backed reflexively away. She folded her arms and did the same stern foot-tapping thing she had done with the executive. And he feared that at any moment she might do that looming thing again, this time directed at him.

Ryan looked at the couple, who were now watching him with those wide, pleading eyes. Even though Margie had said there was no risk in using the Box for unhauntings, there were countless reasons why he couldn't—and shouldn't—do so: he was inexpert at best with the Box; given Prewitt's order, it was probably illegal to use it; he might get caught if Shipp happened to come back; Margie had told him never to touch it without her present; and, maybe the strongest reason of all, he really, really didn't want to.

But he also didn't think he could tell them no, because Trudy might hurt him.

He stepped up as close to Trudy as his revulsion would allow and whispered into where he thought her ear might be. "Just them," he said. "Everybody else gets cancelled."

He selected a smile from his artificial smile reserve, put it on, and motioned for the couple to follow him. "Hello," he said, as brightly as he could. "I'm Dr. Matney, apparently. But just so you know, I'm not really a doctor. What can we do for you today?"

"Thank you," both husband and wife said. "Thank you so much."

As they followed Ryan into the hall, he looked back to make sure Trudy was clearing all the other clients from reception. But she wasn't. She was waving the next client forward and moving them into place, like they were in line to ride a roller coaster. He tried to tell her with his eyes to stop doing that. But if she saw him, he couldn't tell.

◇

The old couple were called the Waldrops, and their procedure went surprisingly well considering it was the first time Ryan had done one himself. He was nervous on two fronts the whole time. He was nervous that he would mess it up and cause some harm to the ghostly lady, and nervous that either Prewitt or Shipp would come in the door and cause some harm to him for violating their order. But in spite of his nerves he managed to get through it and successfully detach Mrs. Waldrop from the weight which, according to her husband, she had been bench-pressing at the time of her death. Ryan resisted the urge to try to picture that and wished the couple well. He did allow himself to feel very slightly good about how happy they looked when they left.

After that he went back to the reception desk, sneaking so that nobody would see him, and hoped that Trudy might have cleared the place out by now. But of course she hadn't. And she spotted him immediately and sent the next client back, evidently a musician from the 1930s accompanied by some distant relative carrying a trombone. Fearing another look at Trudy's new talent for intimidation, Ryan accepted the clients and helped them too. The trombone vibrated when he jolted it with the Box and for a moment it almost seemed to be playing a tune as happy as its owner looked. And again, he found himself taking a slight thrill from their gratitude on the way out.

Then he was back at reception again, and didn't even try to put up a fight when Trudy brought the next client forward. There was no point. Soon he was working his way efficiently through the line of ghosts and their living relatives, and had all but forgotten about the constant threat of fines, arrest, and annihilation. He kept telling himself that he would leave after the next one, or he would leave after the next five, or he would sneak out the back where Trudy couldn't come after him.

But after a while, he even stopped thinking about leaving. Partly it was the fear of Trudy's wrath. But it was also the knowledge, the absolute certainty, that if Margie was here, this is what she would be doing. She would be helping as many of these people as she could before the great unknown of Friday night.

He was wearing short sleeves, but in his mind he rolled up some long ones. And for hours he kept running the Clinic even though he didn't want to.

And then he saw Prewitt yank open the door and skip through it.

19

Prewitt danced over to Ryan, smiling even with parts of his face that didn't normally participate in such expressions. He looked like a man about to receive an oversize check from a lottery commissioner. Shipp moved with his usual bathrobed stoicism right behind Prewitt and assumed his usual military pose, evidently ready to prevent anything resembling nonsense from happening. And behind both of them, four more agents in caps and government-issue windbreakers took up flanking positions and looked uncertain why they were here.

Ryan had expected to be scared when he saw Prewitt again. Instead, he found himself enraged. He was almost certain that Prewitt and/or Shipp were responsible for what had happened to Margie. And here they were, smiling. Smiling like it didn't matter, like she had been a minor obstacle in their path that they had swept aside like an errant branch. They had taken everything from her, and almost everything from Ryan. He wished he was the kind of man who would stride across a room and, without caring what the consequences might be, punch someone in the face. But Ryan was not that kind of man.

Which is why he was so surprised when he did it.

Prewitt reeled backwards, clutching his nose. Ryan managed to get in a pointless swing through Shipp's head too, and Shipp didn't flinch at all. Then Prewitt's agents surged forward and seized both Ryan's arms. They dragged him backwards away from Prewitt while he struggled feebly against them. He had only managed to get in one punch, but it had felt *good*. He wanted to hurt Prewitt more.

"It's okay," Prewitt said through his hand. He was already smiling again. He prodded at his nose. "Nothing's broken. No harm done. In fact I'm not even sure it hurt. Did it leave a mark?"

He leaned his face towards the agents closest to him and they studied his nose. There was a chorus of no's and unh-uh's and seems-fine's. One even claimed that Prewitt's face looked better than it had before.

It was Ryan's first-ever attempt at punching someone, and it hadn't gone well. But the humiliation barely made a dent in his rage. "Why?" he hurled at Prewitt. Then added for clarity: "Why?"

Prewitt's cheerful expression didn't break, but his eyebrows descended ever-so-slightly. "I'm sorry? Why what?"

Ryan re-directed his rage at Shipp instead. "Why?" It was the only syllable he could form and it didn't work any better aimed that way. He suspected that this wasn't coming across as the rock-solid accusation he wanted it to. But he leaned into it anyway. "I don't understand!"

Shipp was unmoved, but Prewitt nodded sympathetically. "That's very clear," he said. "But it's good to ask questions. Or rather, question, since that was only one." He clapped his hands together and rubbed them as though warming them over the heat of Ryan's fury. "But don't worry. As long as you cooperate, stay where I can find you, provide everything I ask for, and don't do—" He waved at his recently punched nose. "—whatever that was again, we won't have a problem. Kay?"

Ryan wished he'd spent more time coming up with a plan and less time doing non-plan-related things. He decided to delay at least a bit by playing dumb himself. "What do you want? What's happening?"

Prewitt gave him a knowing smile, like they were sharing a private joke. "I think you know," he said. He slapped Ryan jovially on the shoulder. "Nothing to worry about. We're just taking over today. All standard procedure. Not that we have any standard procedures per se. We are pretty much making this up as we go."

"You can't do that without a warrant or something," Ryan said with attempted indignation.

"Oh yes!" Prewitt said as though it had slipped his mind. He turned to an agent lingering behind Shipp. "Do you have that?" The agent produced some papers from inside his jacket and fanned them out for Prewitt to see. Prewitt browsed them like he was choosing a card for a magic trick. "Not that. Not that; that's the criminal negligence thing for later. Not that one either, though I like the font there where it says 'prosecution'. No, it's this one. With the stamp that judge put on it. I liked that judge. Very stern." He withdrew it from the agent's deck of court papers and held it up proudly like a painting he had just finished. "All good?"

Ryan was still furiously trying to come up with a plan. By now he was forced to admit that he didn't even have the beginnings of an inkling of a hint of a plan.

But it didn't matter. Prewitt didn't wait for him. He slid back to the door, pushed it open, and called outside: "We're all good in here!"

Ryan had always thought that when government agents raided a place for any reason, they blitzkrieged in like SWAT cops. He thought they'd beat down the door with one of those battering ram things and then swarm through in cover formation, aiming guns in all directions yelling things like "Clear left! Clear right! Everybody down! This is a raid!" Even though they were coming to destroy everything Margie cared about, he was at least looking forward to the entrance, because it promised to look cool.

But it didn't happen that way at all. Instead, a few bored-looking agents strolled in. They looked like tax accountants in blue jackets, and universally seemed to have the attitude that today would have been a good day to call in sick. In addition to all the other things Prewitt lacked, he also profoundly lacked a sense of awesome.

"Excellent!" Prewitt enthused, responding to nothing specific. He rubbed his hands together. "Now then, where is Dr. Sandlin?"

Ryan's heart was squeezed just hearing her last name spoken out loud. He tried to keep the feeling off his face. "You know where she is," he growled.

"No, I don't," Prewitt said. He did a full turn, scanning the waiting room around him. "Is she not here?"

Ryan considered the two possibilities. Either Prewitt had been involved in Margie's destruction the night before, and he was now playing dumb with a truly awards-caliber performance. Or he was, somehow, not. Ryan looked at Shipp for some kind of hint. But the ghost remained utterly impassive. His spectral eyes were so dark and empty, Ryan couldn't even tell which way they were looking.

He knew that if Margie were here she'd be throwing up barricades, locking doors, maybe even flooding the corridor with knock-out gas. She'd force Prewitt out the door with the sheer force of her glare. She'd do whatever it took to save the Clinic and keep helping all its clients. He wasn't sure he could do any of those things. But he did want to find a chance to hit Prewitt again and maybe leave a mark this time.

Prewitt looked past Ryan into the admin hall, still apparently hunting for Margie. "Well, whether she's here or not, we really must get started. Isn't this exciting? I've never done anything like this before!" He checked Ryan's face and seemed mildly disappointed that Ryan didn't share his enthusiasm. "Oh, its fine. We're all friends here. Everybody likes everybody. We all want the right thing to be done. Together. Nobody is forcing anybody to do anything, or accusing anybody of anything. So cheer up!" He patted Ryan's arm. "But just be aware that I have cordoned off the parking lot and the neighboring streets as a precaution, so nobody can go in or out without my explicit permission. Good? Okay!" He clapped his hands together again as though about to dig in to a Thanksgiving dinner. "Let's begin."

◇

Ryan watched, helpless, as Prewitt's agents "stormed" the Clinic. But "stormed" was the wrong word, because they appeared more like a tour group exploring a house where a famous Tudor poet had been born. They opened doors delicately, talked in whispers, pointed things out with muted interest, and generally acted like this wasn't as interesting as they'd hoped and they were ready to move on to the gift shop. Still, Ryan couldn't help feeling utterly violated. Maybe he was feeling it on Margie's behalf, or maybe he was more attached to the Clinic than he realized, but every time one of Prewitt's agents touched one of the Clinic computers or opened one of their filing cabinets, he wanted to try that punch thing again.

Worst of all was having to deal with the clients at reception. Their orderly line-up completely broke down once Prewitt started his genteel rampage, and Ryan once again had to face an onslaught of frustration from innumerable ghosts. He had no answers for them, and this time he couldn't blame them for being upset. He tried to direct all their anger at Prewitt, but that didn't work because Prewitt couldn't see them, which made them angrier and brought them right back to Ryan.

Prewitt genially demanded that Ryan follow along with him—under escort from Shipp and some of his disinterested goons—to unlock doors and explain what things were. Ryan at first refused, but then decided it was his best chance of getting in the way. But the most rebellion he managed was fumbling for keys and just being generally unfriendly, neither of which slowed them down much. He was mostly forced to linger behind and do nothing while Prewitt gave his agents orders (or as Prewitt called them, "suggestions") to confiscate and dismantle, invade and violate. It quickly became almost too emotionally taxing for Ryan to take. And then the raid moved towards the basement, and he was seriously thinking about fleeing. Until he remembered something.

Margie's body was in the basement. Where Prewitt was heading right now.

He didn't know what Prewitt's plan was for the bodies in the storage lockers. But whatever it was, he couldn't stand the thought of Margie's being subjected to it. Not yet. Not by these people.

As he descended the stairs with Prewitt and his agents, Ryan started to realize that he had inadvertently created an opportunity. He had been so quiet and cooperative through most of the raid that Prewitt seemed to have largely forgotten he was there. And now that Prewitt was outright giddy about getting to the exam room and the Box, it occupied his full attention.

"Hurry up, now!" he enthused to his agents as he led them into the exam room. "You're going to love this!"

Ryan was at the back of the pack, still in the stairs with Shipp and his escorting agents. But even they were spurred on by Prewitt's enthusiasm and rushed to follow. They left Ryan by himself at the bottom of the stairs, with a gap between him and them.

A gap that he used to quietly slip away.

He slid to the side and hurried down the tunnel towards the storage facility. He knew he didn't have long—they would surely notice his absence in mere seconds. And he had no idea what he was going to do. But he was away, and he would think of something.

He accelerated as he neared the storage facility, and his amazement at not being discovered grew by the second. Especially with his footsteps echoing off the pipes, he thought they would surely detect him at any second. So he sped up, running at a full sprint by the time he got near the turn into the storage area.

And then the door to the Unhaunted Closet opened into the hall right in front of him, and he slammed face-first into it with a deafening *clong*.

Ryan bounced backwards off the door, dizzy and reeling. He stumbled, his legs went out from under him, and he fell hard onto his back on the damp concrete floor.

Lowell emerged from the behind the door and looked down at him. "Oh. Ryan!" he said, like they had just run into each other shopping for produce at the grocery store. "Good, I need your help. Have you seen a hat?"

◇

Ryan pulled Lowell into the Unhaunted Closet, and hauled the door shut. He expected to hear the footfalls of agents coming for them any second, but so far they were lucky.

"Lowell, what are you doing down here?"

"I just said. I'm looking for a hat. What's going on? There's cars, like, everywhere outside. They blocked off the road."

"I know! How did you even get in here?"

"I snuck. I'm pretty good at that." Lowell started browsing the shelves full of unhaunted objects. He shoved things aside and dug into piles, clearly hunting for something.

Ryan let it go. None of this mattered. There was only one thing he wanted right now. "Lowell, I need your help. I need to get Margie out of here."

"Why can't she get out herself?" Lowell shoved over a pile of People Magazines to look behind them. Finding nothing, he moved on.

"She's not in her body. She's..." He shivered. He didn't want to say it. "She's gone, Lowell. She's gone. In the second Blink last night."

Lowell stopped hunting and looked at Ryan sharply. "Gone? Like *gone* gone? When the lights went out?"

"Yeah."

"You mean like Abraham Lincoln?"

Ryan's frantic mind couldn't deal with figuring out Lowell's line of thinking. "Yeah?"

Lowell paused and thought about that. Ryan had rarely seen Lowell think about anything, so he could tell the moment was significant.

Lowell looked back at Ryan. "Well then I got news for you. She might not be as gone as you think she is."

20

Ryan opened the Unhaunted Closet door a crack and tried to look through it down the hall. He could hear voices vibrating down the pipes, but they were still distant. He gently pulled the door closed again. They had time, but not much.

He rarely put much stock in anything Lowell said. But as nonsensical as he was sure this would turn out to be, it had brought a small flicker of hope back. "What are you talking about?" He was certain he'd regret asking.

Lowell sat on a little plastic shoe shelf that buckled beneath him. "Okay, here it is. I have this friend who's not my friend that I hate." Ryan regretted asking, in possibly record time. Lowell went on, ensuring that Ryan would regret it further: "But here's the thing: she says Abraham Lincoln is still around."

"She says? How does she know?"

"It's a long story. It's probably better if she tells it. But the point is, she's been right about stuff like this before. I don't know how, because she's a total nutcase and a liar and a fraud and I hate her. But she has."

"So you believe her?"

"I dunno. Maybe. Kind of."

Ryan squeezed his eyes. "Why are we talking about this? Why am I here? What's happening right now?" He silently berated himself for having let Lowell suggest any kind of hope.

Lowell stood off the shoe shelf, which had miraculously not broken. "So if Lincoln really is somewhere, and he got where he is because the lights went out, maybe Margie's in the same place he is. Right?"

"Because your friend says so?"

"She's not my friend. I told you, I hate her. Let's try to get that right, okay?" Lowell seemed genuinely offended.

Ryan had to accept that there was a certain logic to what Lowell's non-friend was saying, if he accepted that she existed and had some kind of special knowledge. Which was a lot to ask.

"And here's the thing," Lowell continued, "she also says she can find him. Which means we can maybe bring him back and get on TV. And I guess maybe also find Margie."

Ryan didn't know what the TV part meant, but he ignored it. "How? How is that possible?"

Lowell waved off the question like it didn't matter. "She's got like this pink doll lantern thing." Ryan regretted asking even more. "She says it can follow these trails between ghosts and things or people they like, even if they're not attached to them anymore. She was going to dig up Lincoln's body and follow the trail from that. But I don't know if you've seen Lincoln's tomb—it's like a Fort Knox for corpses. So she said she can try to use his hat instead. And she thinks his hat will be right here. So, yeah. That's it."

It was absurd. All of it. But whoever Lowell's hated non-friend was, she was right about the location of the hat. Or at least, she had been. "The hat's not here," he said. "The government confiscated it."

Lowell cursed and punched a fifty-year-old stuffed giraffe, which burst in an explosion of feathers. Then he took a moment to calm himself and steady his breathing.

"Okay," he said. "Forget everything I just said. I'll see you later." He moved for the door.

Ryan could not make himself believe any of what Lowell had said. Lowell didn't seem to fully believe it himself. But at the same time, Ryan wanted desperately to get Margie's body out of the storage facility before Prewitt got to it. And Lowell could potentially help him with that. Plus, faint insane hope was faintly, insanely better than no hope at all. On his list of plans for what to do now, Lowell's was right at the bottom.

But the rest of the list was empty.

So before Lowell could get out the door, Ryan made his decision. "You said if she had Lincoln's body she could find him?"

Lowell paused with his hand on the door handle. "Yeah?"

"Okay. So... if she had somebody else's body, could she find them?"

◇

Lowell went down the hall towards the stairs with a promise to "cause a diversion". Ryan was afraid to ask how he planned to do that, and decided to just hope Lowell would handle it. He also hoped that it wouldn't involve fire, which it probably would. So while Lowell went that way, Ryan went to the left, into the storage facility.

He crept in, keeping to what few shadows there were. He didn't think any of Prewitt's people had made it this far yet, but it was possible he had missed them. He was relieved to find the storage facility as silent, sickly, and creepy as ever. Hoping that Lowell was working on that diversion, he dashed into the room and went straight for where he knew Margie's body was stored.

He felt a jab at his heart when he pulled the cabinet open and saw Margie's face again. He wished she would sit up and tell him he was being stupid and careless. He already knew he was being stupid and careless, but he really wanted to hear it from her.

He brushed her hair back from her forehead, then looked to the tubes and contacts attached to her arm. It looked like he could just pull them all out, but would that do her harm? What if it made her bleed? He had no idea. He leaned in and tugged at them, testing how firmly they were attached.

He was so focused on them that he didn't notice the footsteps approaching until they were right behind him.

A shadow fell across Margie's face, and Ryan whirled around.

An enormous form was coming at him, clearly bent on aggression. Ryan stumbled backwards until his back slammed against the wall of cabinets. He slid down them to the floor, shielding himself with both arms against whoever was attacking him.

Right before the figure was upon him, he saw who it was. "Ethan! Or Ewan! Whatever!"

Ehan/Ewan didn't seem to hear him. He grabbed Ryan by both arms and hauled him off the floor, then tossed him easily across the room. "Get out! This is my place!"

Ryan hit the floor hard, shoulders first, and slid several feet until his head struck the wall harder than he would have liked.

Ethan/Ewan's ghostly brother Ewan/Ethan joined the attack, towering over Ryan and swinging at him with gigantic ghostly fists. They passed right through him, but he still couldn't help flinching. "Nobody touches our customers!" the huge ghost bellowed. "Nobody! Get out!"

Ryan admired the giant orderlies' commitment to their customers at the same time as he rolled over and tried to scramble away from them. "Wait! Wait! It's me, it's Ryan!"

The big ghost paused, fist raised, and squinted at Ryan. His material brother stepped up to his side and they both looked down at him, uncertain what to do. "It's that guy," the ghostly one said to his brother. "Do we keep hitting him?"

Ryan panted and nursed his shoulder. "I need your help. Seriously. Help me get Margie into the House Call Wagon. I might be able to get her back."

The brothers looked at each other, exchanging a wordless brotherly communication. They didn't resume hitting him, and Ryan took that to be a positive sign. He pulled himself up the wall until he was standing relatively vertical. "I'm going to need to move her," he said. "Will you help me?"

And then the fire alarm went off, and Ryan silently cursed Lowell.

21

Moments later, sweating and clenched and already imagining his first day in prison—he had decided that his prison nickname would be "Skinny"—Ryan watched Ethan/Ewan position Margie's body in the House Call Wagon's left hammock and strap her in. The fire alarm was still blasting inside the Clinic and almost certainly causing chaos. And maybe it was working as a diversion because nobody had tried to stop them coming up the casket elevator and out into the loading dock.

Ethan/Ewan checked the buckle on the last strap. It held fast. "Done," he mumbled, so low it was like the shifting of tectonic plates.

"Great! Thanks! Seriously, I couldn't have done it without you," Ryan said, trying to sound like he couldn't feel sweat stains spreading from his armpits all the way to his knees. He tested the straps holding Margie in and found them snug and well placed. Ethan/Ewan, for all his clumsy shambling, was actually quite good at this part of the job.

The big man motioned at his ghostly brother with one giant arm. "He did most of the work," he said. The ghost brother nodded.

Ryan found that claim wildly improbable, but he had other concerns right now. "Ethan," he said, "and Ewan." He waved vaguely somewhere between them so they wouldn't be able to guess which name he was assigning to each of them. "You're probably wondering what this is about."

"Nope," one of the brothers said.

"It's important that you understand what you're getting into before you get any deeper in this," Ryan said. He was reluctant about bringing them along at all. But nobody knew how to keep a ghostless body alive and comfortable better than they did. That slightly superseded the fact that they always seemed to want to hurt him, and that they had once stolen all the mini Froot Loops boxes out of his variety pack in the break room. Under present circumstances, he felt he could put such things aside. He needed them to come with him. "What we're doing could be seen as illegal, and—"

"Don't care," Ethan/Ewan said. The big living man shifted himself out the back door and the van groaned in relief and bounced a foot higher on its suspension. His ghostly twin followed, with no response at all from the van's moving parts. And then they were gone, leaving Ryan to rationalize that he was better off without them. Which, clearly, he wasn't.

He moved forward to the driver's seat, resisting the urge to tell Margie everything would be fine. Aside from very shallow breathing, she remained utterly still.

He slid into the driver's seat, his heart thudding around in his ribcage like a bat trying to get out of a box. He was about to prove beyond all doubt that he would do literally anything for Margie. For example, he would evade government agents, defy the justice system, and probably become a wanted fugitive for the rest of his life. It was a start.

He started the engine.

The back door of the Clinic burst open. Terror shot up Ryan's spine and fresh sweat fountained from him like a lawn sprinkler. *They're coming for me already! I haven't even left and I'm already caught.*

But he was relieved to see that it was Lowell. Lowell's raincoat billowed behind him as he ran across the loading dock to the van. It was only ten feet but he was out of breath by the time he got to Ryan's window.

"I'm here!" he said breathlessly. "It's all good. I bought us some time."

"That was your diversion? You pulled the fire alarm?"

"No I didn't. The fire probably set it off." He yanked Ryan's door open. "Shove over. I'll drive."

◇

Lowell backed the van gently out of its spot and crawled it along the edge of the parking lot until they had a clear view of the exit. He shifted into park and they studied their situation. From here they could see that Prewitt's agents had blocked the entrance to the lot with an uneven line of wooden A-frame traffic barricades. These were overseen by a single, entirely non-threatening agent who could easily be mistaken for an office drone taking a break from fixing the photocopier. He leaned against one of the barriers, watching the ghosts passing in the street and paying no attention at all to the Clinic or the lot he was supposed to be guarding.

"Let me do the talking," Ryan said. This was generally good practice with Lowell on the best of days, but even more so when subtlety was required.

Lowell snorted. "What's to talk about? I say we Vin Diesel it. Straight through."

"We don't want to draw attention to ourselves. Just let me talk to him. I'll think of something."

Lowell snorted again, even snortier. "Whatever."

He shifted into gear and adopted the posture of a French resistance fighter about to drive through a Nazi border crossing. He even pulled his raincoat collar up over half his face and put on a pair of sunglasses, which Ryan thought made him look significantly more suspicious.

Still, Ryan almost pulled his own collar up as well. It just seemed like the thing to do.

The guard must have heard the engine behind him. He stood up from against the barricade and looked back at them, then approached Lowell's window. Up close he looked even less how Ryan imagined a government roadblock guard should look. He was heavy set and balding, with a goatee that appeared thinly painted-on like a Lego character's.

Ryan braced for Lego Goatee to tell them to turn back. He had his story prepared: he would claim that Prewitt had asked them to retrieve all the files Ryan and Margie had taken home, along with some laptops that belonged to the Clinic. They were just going to run home and get them, and would be back in ten minutes, tops. He figured that he had earned quite a bit of good will by appearing to be cooperative with Prewitt during the raid, so the guard would be receptive.

But Ryan didn't get to tell his story. "Hold on," Lego Goatee said before Ryan or Lowell got to say anything at all. "I'll get this out of the way. It's heavier than it looks!" And he walked ahead, grabbed hold of the end of the closest barrier, and started to drag it out of the way.

Ryan was astonished. They were about to make an entirely clean getaway, without having to crash through anything or put any kind of pedal to any sort of metal. It could not possibly have gone any better than it was going right now.

"Well that sucks," Lowell said, disappointed.

Ryan admitted to himself that he was slightly disappointed too. "Just go," he said. "Take it slow." He glanced back at Margie's body and was relieved to see that she was just as safely strapped in as she had been the last time he had looked, fifteen seconds earlier.

The barricade got stuck on the curb and Lego Goatee struggled to free it. He waved at them apologetically. Lowell's hands tapped a rhythm on the steering wheel. Ryan couldn't tell if it was out of nervousness or boredom.

Ryan caught some motion out of the corner of his eye and leaned close to his side window so he could see the Clinic back door. He was relieved to see it still closed and nobody in the loading dock. A few ghosts in 19th-Century formal wear were having what appeared to be a festive ball just outside the dock. But Ryan knew that they were regularly there on Wednesdays, so no cause for concern. And the lot was otherwise deserted. There was still, as far as he could tell, nothing to worry about.

And yet he elected semi-voluntarily to worry.

"Come on, come on," Lowell said. His tapping on the steering wheel got faster.

Ryan caught some movement near the loading dock. His subconscious jabbed at the back of his eyes: *You should be looking at this.* And he realized what it was.

Shipp was there. Ryan had missed him when he looked before because Shipp was half mixed-in with the ballroom dancers, perhaps for camouflage. It wasn't very good camouflage, given that the other ghosts were staunchly Victorian formal and he was dressed like someone sneaking down to steal a drumstick from the fridge. But there he was, just outside the back door. And he was looking in their direction.

Ryan pressed himself back into his seat in a way that he hoped obscured him from Shipp's view. But it wouldn't matter. The House Call Wagon was the only Clinic-owned vehicle in the lot, and it was leaving. Shipp would not miss that.

Lego Goatee finally got the barricade unhooked from the curb. He straightened his back and wheezed, evidently suffering from the Herculean effort of moving a few thin pieces of plywood, and then dragged the barrier the rest of the way to the side.

Ryan risked another look back.

Shipp was halfway across the lot towards them. Ballroom dancers whirled around him but he moved through them, unhindered.

Ryan motioned at Lowell. "Go," he said.

Lowell accelerated, but Lego Goatee was crossing in front of them. Lowell had to brake to avoid running him down. They stopped.

"Stop!" The command came from Shipp, across the lot behind them. He was jogging now, coming up fast on Ryan's side.

Lego Goatee saw Shipp coming and appeared uncertain about what to do next. So he stopped directly in front of the van, squinting through the windshield at them as though he had never seen humans before.

Their choices were: stay here and let Shipp catch up, or plow right through the guard. And for a moment, Ryan thought Lowell might take the second option and run Lego Goatee down. But Lowell didn't. He gripped the steering wheel hard, but his foot stayed off the gas.

And then Shipp was in the van with them. He swept in through the side wall right behind Ryan, surged forward and hovered between the seats. For a moment Ryan thought Shipp had shrunk, but it was just that he hadn't bothered to align his feet with the van floor, so they went right through to the asphalt beneath and he appeared eighteen inches shorter than he was. "May I ask where you gentlemen are going?" he asked. His eyes were cold and his voice was hard.

Ryan swallowed hard, and immediately wished he hadn't because it made him look guilty. "Mr. Prewitt asked us to go get all the files I took home, and some laptops—"

"No he didn't," Shipp cut in.

Ryan glanced at Lowell, who was looking out his window and pretending not to be listening to them. Ryan wasn't sure if he was grateful for that, or if he wished Lowell would say something.

"I'll ask you again," Shipp said, emotionless as a house plant. "Where are you going?"

The back door of the Clinic smashed open. Both Ryan and Shipp snapped their heads around to look.

It was Prewitt. He burst out the door onto the loading dock and locked onto them immediately. But rather than running across the lot to them he stopped and cupped his hands around his mouth. "Shipp!" he yelled, "tell them if they leave the premises they'll be guilty of obstructing an official investigation and theft of government property, or whatever! But use the actual names of the laws they're breaking! I don't know them!"

"Yes, sir!" Shipp maintained his rigid attitude and turned back to Ryan. "If you depart the premises during the investigation, you will be guilty of—"

"Shipp?!" Prewitt called from outside. "Are you doing it?"

"I'm doing it!" Shipp yelled back, clearly frustrated. He shook it off and struggled to get his Dirty Harry groove back with Ryan and Lowell. "If you depart the premises—"

"Ryan?" Prewitt yelled again. "Is Shipp in there with you? Is he telling you about the laws you're breaking?"

Ryan rolled his window down halfway to reply. "Yes, he's here! He's doing it!" *Why am I answering him?!*

"Good! Go ahead, Shipp!"

Shipp waited a few seconds, apparently to make sure Prewitt was done. When Prewitt did indeed seem to have fallen silent, Shipp tried again. "If you depart the premises during the investigation—"

"Vin Diesel!" Lowell bellowed suddenly.

He hammered the accelerator and the van lurched forward.

22

Lego Goatee dove completely out of the way, face-first onto the asphalt. The van's front bumper hooked the traffic barrier as Lowell cut the corner hard into the street. Shipp, whose weightless form was still locked to the road rather than the van, disappeared out the back, an expression of menacing annoyance on his face. Ryan could only grip the armrests and fight to keep his stomach in as the van very nearly rolled.

"Woooo!" Lowell whooped. "We're doing it, buddy!"

The van was not built for speed, but Lowell pushed it to its limits. He ran a red light turning left onto Mass Ave and then floored it, weaving in and out of traffic. Ghosts whipped past the windows on both sides or straight through the van from front to back. Ryan got occasional quick glimpses of their faces streaking past him.

Lowell checked the rear view mirror and both sides, clearly expecting to see somebody pursuing them.

"They wouldn't chase us, would they?" Ryan asked. His hands dug gouges into the armrests and he checked the side view mirror. He couldn't see any flashing lights behind them, or any dark government-style cars speeding after them.

The van screamed into Porter Square, drawing a chorus of affronted honks. Lowell weaved through traffic, not caring which lane he was in, and careened through a crowd of colonial settlers making a camp outside CVS.

"Why wouldn't they chase us?" Lowell said, sounding personally insulted. "We're fugitives!" He started scanning the cross streets as they passed, looking for a way off the main road. A loud honk pulled his attention forward again, and he swerved violently to avoid a big U-Haul turning across their path.

Ryan checked his side view mirror again. He still couldn't see anything that looked like a government vehicle chasing them. "I think we're fine! Slow down!"

Lowell unhappily slowed down to barely more than the speed of traffic, and turned sharply at the next cross street. He pulled into the first parking spot he could find, an illegal gap next to a small pharmacy, and left the engine idling.

They both sat still, breathing fast and listening. For engines, or sirens, or any indication of pursuit. For anything, really. But there was nothing.

They had done it.

Ryan rolled his window down and poked his head out. He scanned the street behind them. Nothing but milling ghosts. Nobody paying attention to them. He rolled his window up again.

"I think we're okay," he said. And he couldn't believe it. The full weight of what they had just done had not fallen on him yet. He felt sure that would happen later. But for now, he felt good. He felt jazzed, thrilled, elated. He had escaped with Margie's body, and there was hope of bringing her back.

Then, in a blur, Shipp was between their seats again.

"You're stealing confiscated property and evading—"

Lowell hammered the accelerator and veered into the street. This time Shipp had his feet firmly planted on the van floor and he was adjusting to the crazed shifts in momentum as Lowell swerved and braked.

Having been one himself, Ryan was intimately familiar with how ghosts moved. They could only run and walk at normal human speed, the same as living people. They did have slightly fewer limitations: they didn't get tired, for example, and they could pass through solid objects. But Shipp's movement was impossible. No matter how far they got from the Clinic, he caught up instantly. It was like he was—

The realization clicked so firmly and so emphatically that Ryan thought it might be audible.

"They put something in the van that he's haunting!" he said.

If Shipp was haunting some object, and that object was moving with the van, it would pull him along with it. He wouldn't have a choice, and they wouldn't be able to get rid of him. But what was it? As Lowell continued to speed dangerously along side streets, Ryan feverishly scanned the inside of the van.

"If you turn yourselves in now," Shipp said, "there may be some leniency."

"What are you haunting?" Ryan demanded. "Where is it?"

"I'm not authorized to provide that information."

Ryan looked beneath the empty hammock across from Margie's. Nothing. He ripped open the glove compartment. Van owner's manual and documents. He dropped to the floor and looked under the passenger seat. Gum, candy wrappers, a couple of peanut shells. It seemed unlikely Shipp would be haunting any of those.

"Turning!" Lowell bellowed. He wrenched the wheel to the left and they skidded onto another, wider street. Ryan was flung hard against the wall of the van and onto the floor. A horn blasted at them and tires squealed, and Ryan thought he heard a crunch of metal. But the van didn't slow or stop.

"Why are you driving so fast?!" he yelled to Lowell in the front.

"Because we're escaping!"

"Yeah, but the only guy who's chasing us is already in the van!"

Lowell seemed to be fighting a battle between Ryan's logic and his own nearly irresistible desire to drive fast and crash into things. But the logic eventually won. "I guess that's true," he said.

He slowed down to a safe, non-attention grabbing speed.

Ryan had never noticed before the sheer volume of junk that had accumulated in the House Call Wagon. It was everywhere. Food wrappers, packing peanuts, toys from fast food meals, a couple of inexplicable socks, bits of electronics from Margie's various customizations, Christmas lights, and countless things he hadn't identified yet. Much of it he could personally take blame for, but not all of it. And the object Shipp was haunting could be anywhere. It could even have been affixed to the outside of the van, like a tracking beacon. But he would deal with the stuff inside first. All of it. He dropped to his hands and knees and started plowing it all into a pile.

"It's pointless," Shipp said. "I've got you. Agents are already on their way to this location."

Ryan stopped gathering. Could that be true? Were they going to be caught already, minutes after their escape? As worried as he was, he couldn't help but be skeptical.

Shipp went on: "If you surrender now, it will be better for—"

"How?" Ryan said.

Shipp cocked an eyebrow. "How what?"

"How could agents be on their way to this location? They don't know where we are."

"I notified them."

"How? You can't carry a walkie or a phone or anything. So how did you notify them?"

Shipp fell silent and stared off to Ryan's right, refusing to look at him.

Ryan almost laughed out loud. "You were bluffing."

In the front seat, Lowell laughed too, much more derisively. "Wait, so you guys came up with this system to follow us by haunting the van, but you didn't think of a way for you to tell anyone where we are?"

Shipp's eye twitched. It took him a long time to reply. "It was Director Prewitt's idea. We didn't have time for trial runs. Plus he can't see me or communicate with me."

Lowell laughed again. "That's like, genius and stupid at the same time."

Shipp tried to hold his commanding pose and give nothing away, but from the set of his face Ryan was pretty sure he was trying to pretend he wasn't humiliated.

Ryan stood up and kicked aside the pile of junk he had been gathering. "So I guess you're stuck coming with us. Or you can tell me what you're haunting, and we'll put it outside and drop you off right here."

Shipp stared at nothing, said nothing.

"Fine," Ryan said. He checked on Margie, and found her completely unchanged. But seeing her again squeezed something inside him, hard. He fought to control his voice as he turned back to Shipp. "Why did you do this to her? I don't get it."

"Also how?'" Lowell added.

"Also how?" Ryan amended his question.

Shipp's eyes shifted over to Ryan. He unlocked his jaw. "You think I did this?"

"You were there. I saw you. I went through you."

"I know," Shipp growled. "I felt it. Don't do that again. You have..." A chill seemed to go through him. "...issues."

Any other time, Ryan would have been mildly offended. But he had no time for that now. "So it was Prewitt, right? Prewitt made her a ghost so the Blink would destroy her. Why?"

Shipp's eyes shifted away again. "It wasn't Prewitt," he said. "Director Prewitt is a government-appointed agent with total authority over that Clinic. Why would he need to bring harm to her or to anyone affiliated with it?"

"Then who?"

"You really don't know? You were there."

"Yeah, can we just fast forward to the part where you tell me?"

Shipp's lip curled up on one side. He seemed to relish what he was about to say. And then he said it: "You did."

Panic and dread shot through Ryan, jockeying for the best spots to poke at his clenched heart. It was impossible. He hadn't used the Box. He hadn't done anything but try to save her. Shipp had to be trying to get under his skin, and it was working. All the fight Ryan could muster was: "Did not."

"Did too." Shipp seemed to think the reply was a checkmate.

"Did not! What are you even talking about?!"

Shipp's posture relaxed slightly. He was enjoying having this power to manipulate Ryan's emotions. "She did it herself initially. She used that... that 'Box' to extract her own ghost from her body. I saw her do it. Very impressive."

Ryan paced from one side of the van to the other. It wasn't far enough to be satisfying, but it was better than just standing there in a puddle of anxiety. *Why would she do that?*

Lowell joined in. "So it wasn't Ryan who did it, then. It was her."

"Initially," Shipp said. "But there was a timer."

Ryan paced faster. "A timer?"

"I saw her set a timer. Three hundred seconds. It was counting down. My assumption was that after three hundred seconds, the 'Box' would discharge automatically, and return her to her body. So I was watching to see that happen. And then you entered."

Ryan stopped pacing, frozen in place. The memory of the previous night belted through his mind and he realized what he had done. "I reset it," he rasped.

"Which I'm guessing stopped the timer. Good job." Shipp sneered at him.

So that was it. Ryan knew that Shipp wasn't lying. It all made sense. Somewhere through the day while she was taking the Box apart, Margie had figured out that the missing ghosts weren't obliterated, but rather had gone somewhere. And she had extracted herself right before the Blink to find out where they had gone. The batteries would keep the Box running when the power went out, the Blink would carry her away to wherever the ghosts were, and then the timer would bring her back. It was, like everything Margie did, brilliant. But it was also fraught with risk. To extract herself from her own body had to be difficult, and dangerous. Why would she do that? Why wouldn't she ask him to do it instead?

He went cold. She had been about to.

I have a theory. And I need your help. That's what she had said.

But she had stopped herself because she knew he would say no.

The truth stabbed him in the heart: wherever Margie was, she was stuck there because of him. Because she had done something extreme that he should have been doing for her, and then he had messed it up and ensured that she didn't come back. It was all his fault.

He left Shipp to stare at nothing in the back, and moved back towards the passenger seat. This time, he couldn't bring himself to look at Margie as he passed. He climbed into the seat next to Lowell.

"Forget him," he said. "Let's go find her. Whatever the plan is, let's just do it."

23

It took twenty minutes to get to Malden. Shipp stood resolutely in the back the whole way. He seemed to have chosen the back corner of the van as the spot he could stare to project total disinterest in any further interaction with them.

They parked outside a drab two-story building with a little garage on the side, out of which spilled a collection of scooters. Lowell shut the engine off while Ryan studied the scooters, hoping to find some kind of relevance among them.

"Look up," Lowell said.

Ryan lifted his eyes to the second floor windows. The words "Psychic Medium" were painted across the middle window. Ryan didn't like either of those words, but he said them out loud anyway. "A psychic medium? This is your friend?"

"She's not my friend. But yes."

"What does 'psychic medium' even mean anymore? A psychic medium is someone who can talk to dead people. We're *all* psychic mediums now. What are we even doing here?"

"Come inside. Just trust me," Lowell said, putting his hand awkwardly on Ryan's shoulder. It was apparently meant to convey exactly how serious and trustworthy he was, but instead it just made Ryan uncomfortable.

"I specifically *don't* trust you," Ryan said. "I never have. It's actually a big problem."

Lowell pulled his hand back, which made them both immediately more at ease. "Then just come in and use the bathroom. We're wanted fugitives, so it may be your last chance for a while to pee indoors."

◇

Ryan thought that no building interior had ever so perfectly matched his expectations as this one did. Based on the outside of the building, he had expected to find a peeling wooden door that squeaked at the top of a short, dark staircase that also squeaked. He had definitely expected a curtain of beads just on the other side of the door. He had been pretty sure he'd detect a potpourri of incenses and perfumes and dead rat. And he had certainly counted on there being variously colored lamps combining their dim spheres of mood lighting into a general, muddy atmosphere of mostly discomfort.

He got all of that, plus a slushy machine.

"Ooh," Lowell said, intrigued. "Slushy!"

It raised Ryan's already-high level of annoyance even higher. "Wait, you've never been here before?"

"Not inside, no. And believe me, until today I never wanted to come near this place. But if I'd known she had a slushy machine—"

"So why are we here?"

Lowell cupped his hands around his mouth and called into the office, if indeed that's what this place could be called. "Yo! Gwen!"

They could hear shuffling in the back, but nobody appeared. Ryan idly spun a wire display rack on a cash counter near the entrance. It had little test-tube-shaped bottles on it, each with a printed label bearing the name of a different ailment: "Pink eye", "Pneumonia", "Dry skin". Ryan rolled his eyes and spun the rack faster, trying to make some of the bottles fly off.

It was a second or two before someone—presumably Gwen—pushed through another curtain of beads across the reception area. "Lowell? Where's the hat?"

Lowell grunted. "There was a problem. But I brought something better."

Gwen's eyes shifted over to Ryan. "Him?"

Ryan drew his hand away from the rack, trying to avoid taking responsibility for how fast it was spinning.

"Don't touch those," Gwen said.

"Homeopathic?" he asked, thinking he had her pegged.

"I'm sorry, what?" she said sharply, like he had said something offensive.

"This stuff is homeopathic medicine, right?"

Gwen guffawed. "Yeah, like I want to shill for 'Big Homeo'. Do you know what kind of concentration they produce that stuff at?"

"It's mostly water, isn't it?"

Gwen shuffled behind the counter and stopped the rack spinning. "Exactly! Like one part medicine to a million parts water. I don't know how anyone expects that stuff to do anything. You'll get healthier sucking on a rusty garden hose. My stuff..." She patted the rack like it was a pony she had personally raised from a foal. "... has a medicinal concentration less than one part per *billion*."

Lowell held up one of the tiny bottles and pointed at the printed label on the back. "Says on here the concentration is zero."

"You shouldn't believe everything you read on labels, Lowell. But yes, it's zero. And zero is in fact less than one part per billion. As I said."

"So it's just water?" Ryan thought he was right about that, but at the same time was convinced that he couldn't possibly be.

"Yes. On a purely chemical level. And also on every other level."

"Where do you get the water from?"

"The sink, dummy. Where do you get your water from?"

Ryan considered expending mental resources trying to figure out what she was getting at, but decided against it. "Uh huh," he said, hoping desperately that it would bring the conversation to an end.

It didn't. Gwen seemed to be waiting for him to ask a follow-up. When he didn't, she frowned at him, annoyed. "You're not the curious type, are you? Aren't you going to ask how it works? Everyone always asks that."

Ryan was pretty sure—no, entirely certain—that it *didn't* work. So if he was going to ask a question, "how does it work?" was not likely to be it.

"I'll bite," Lowell said, "I have like this sniffle thing going on. You got anything for that?"

"Sure do!" Gwen spun the rack and grabbed one of the larger bottles off of it. The printed label wrapped around it said, in unabashed Comic Sans, "Cold and Flu". She carried it to the slushy machine, twisted open a sealed lid on top of the mixing tank, and dumped the little bottle into it. The slushy machine whirred and sloshed, and then she jammed a paper cup under it and opened a spigot.

Ryan was agog. And yet he couldn't help being slightly impressed. "Homeopathic slushies?"

"I know," Gwen said. "Great idea, right? I'm trying to get a patent. I also have grape." She handed the cup to Lowell. "There you go. Drink the whole thing or it won't work. But not too fast. Brain freeze."

Lowell gave a "why not?" shrug, and sipped. "Can you put the grape in with the medicine?"

"Yeah, if you wanna get sicker. The grape is pretty expired."

Ryan had seen about all he needed to see of Gwen. If she was his only hope of finding Margie, then he was starting to think that maybe risking life imprisonment by defying a court order and stealing confiscated property to evade interrogation on suspicion of committing a federal crime was a bad idea. If she didn't convince him right now that there was truly hope, he was ready to storm out and slam the curtain of beads behind him. "Lowell says you know Abraham Lincoln's still around. How?"

Gwen ignored him. "Lowell, where's the hat? Tell me you got the hat."

Lowell threw back a gulp of his semi-medicinal slushy. "The hat's gone. No way we can get it."

Gwen threw up her arms in frustration. "So why are you here? Why are we even talking? You're no use to me now!" She snatched what was left of the slushy out of Lowell's hand and threw it on the floor. It splattered colorless crushed ice in a little pool at his feet.

Lowell seemed about to hurl some vitriol back at her, but Ryan had no desire to see them argue. So he interjected. "Tell me about Lincoln. How do you know he's not gone?"

She tore her eyes off Lowell and turned them to Ryan. "I talked to him."

Ryan's skepticism fought hard against his natural curiosity and, for the moment, lost. "You saw him?"

"No. I talked to him."

"He was here?"

"No."

"Where was he?"

"I didn't get to ask him. The connection was a little fuzzy."

"So what did he say?"

"Nothing."

"But you said you talked to him."

"Yeah. I talked to him. He didn't talk back."

Ryan wrestled all the pieces of what she was saying into one big picture. It seemed to still be missing entire giant sections but he made an attempt at summing up in the hopes that the gaps might fill in. "So, you talked to him but couldn't hear him or see him, and he's somewhere but you don't know where?"

"Mm hmm. That's why I needed the hat. So I guess now we're back to square one."

Frustration swelled deep in Ryan's gut and he was momentarily tempted to pick up the rack of "medicine" and dump everything off of it in a fit of anger. He only stopped himself because he knew it was pointless; they were all water and she could just refill them in the bathroom.

Lowell jumped in. "I told you. I brought something better. A body."

Gwen looked skeptical. Which didn't suit her, because Ryan was pretty sure she had never been properly skeptical of anything, ever. "Lincoln's? How did you manage that?"

"I didn't. It's somebody who's in the same place Lincoln is. So you track her down with your magic Barbie lantern, and you'll find him. Genius, right?"

Gwen patted both handlebars of her hair dubiously. "It's not ideal."

Ryan regarded that as a colossal understatement. "I don't believe this," he said. He was fed up. And he did the fed-uppiest thing he could think of to do, which was to leave. And for good measure, he tried to pull down one of the strings of beads at the door on his way out. The string wouldn't come loose, though, so he gave up after one tug and didn't achieve even close to the indignant effect he wanted.

He had to go. He had to get away from crazy people and go sit with Margie and maybe talk to her and pretend she could hear him.

"Ryan, wait!" Lowell called after him before he could reach the stairs.

Against his better judgment, Ryan stopped. He would not do them the courtesy of turning around, though.

"Let her just try talking to Margie. What can it hurt?" He turned to Gwen, who seemed to need persuasion almost as much as Ryan. "Gwen, try it."

Ryan didn't know if he wanted that. The idea of sitting through a demonstration of this woman's supposed talents filled him with the kind of hostility he usually reserved for people who kicked puppies. But he didn't know where he was going. He didn't know how to be sad about Margie when there was even the faintest glimmer of hope that he didn't have to be sad about her at all. *Maybe*, he told himself, *the world is just messed up enough that there's something to this. Maybe she can do what she says. Maybe Margie is still out there and this woman is my only hope of finding her.*

So he turned around and pushed the beads aside. "Okay. Let's try it."

24

"Her name is... something that starts with N or M. No, definitely M." Gwen thought hard, scrunching her face up tight until it fit into half its usual space. "Or N," she added.

She knelt between the hammocks in the back of the van, resting one hand gently on Margie's shoulder. Lowell watched from the driver's seat, evidently fascinated. Even Shipp, while still pretending to steadfastly gaze at the blank spot in the back of the van, kept glancing over to see what was happening.

Only Ryan was unmoved. He had seen this kind of thing before. It was cold reading, and it was common before the Blackout, when psychics couldn't actually talk to ghosts but wanted to convince people that they could. So they'd fish around with random words until they saw a reaction from their audience, however subtle, to let them know they were onto something. From that point they could pretty much wing it. Now that ghosts were as common as the living—or rather, roughly ten times *more* common—there was no reason why anyone would ever have to do a cold reading again, and even less reason why anyone would ever believe someone who was doing it.

And yet here Gwen was, clearly doing a cold reading. And the fact that she had happened to guess the first letter of Margie's name almost right didn't convince Ryan for a second that she was actually in touch with Margie across vast distances. Instead, it just made him want to kick her out the side door and drive away as fast as he could.

But he decided that if this cold reading was going to happen, he wasn't going to be a factor in it. He wasn't going to give her any hints, any help. He locked his facial expression, kept his arms at his sides. *You're not getting anything from me.*

"Which is it?" he asked coldly. "M or N?"

She placed her hand on Margie's forehead as though checking for a fever. Then, weirdly, she pinched both Margie's eyebrows between her fingers and worked them up and down, apparently with great concentration. It gave Margie a look of surprise, then anger, then surprise again, then anger again.

Ryan was about to put a stop to it when Gwen blurted. "Margie!"

Ryan was impressed in spite of himself. In direct violation of his plan to show no reaction at all, he was sure he looked amazed. "How... how did...?"

"Lowell said it inside."

Every part of Ryan that had been impressed stopped being impressed. "Then why did you do the whole 'N or M' thing?!"

"It was M. Was I wrong? Pretty impressive, right?"

"No! It's not!" Ryan flailed hysterically, frustration and anger interacting in a way that created wildly amplified waves of flinging his arms around. But he let himself do it despite how crazy it probably made him look. "You can remember a name you heard five minutes ago—but only after sifting through the alphabet trying to figure out what the first letter was. That is not impressive! It's whatever the opposite of impressive is!"

"Unimpressive?" Lowell offered, looking like he agreed.

"Yes! That!"

Gwen wasn't paying attention to him anymore. She had her eyes closed, and her thumb and index finger pressed to Margie's forehead. "Margie? Margie, can you hear me?" She asked it loudly, as though talking to someone with a bad cell signal.

Ryan waited, certain that he'd regret the misuse of these few seconds.

Gwen concentrated. She put her other thumb and index finger on her own forehead, maybe to channel the signal directly into her brain. Or something. After a second of that, she seemed to be jolted, as though something had just fallen on her head. Her eyes sprang open. "She hears me!"

Ryan was afraid to ask, but asked. "What's she saying?"

Gwen closed her eyes again and leaned in, maybe trying to give the signal a shorter distance to travel. "She's saying..." She paused, silently mouthing words. Then: "She's saying 'Tell Brian I'm okay'!" She opened her eyes and grinned with glee at Ryan. "She's okay, Brian!"

Ryan sighed. "It's Ryan."

"What?"

"Ryan."

To her credit, Gwen managed to not let the correction impact her gleeful response at all. "She's okay, Ryan! That's good, right?"

Ryan needed air. He needed to be a long way away from both of these people for a long time. "I'm sorry, Gwen. I'm sorry, Lowell. I think we're done here. I need to get back to, I don't know, fugitiving." He shifted to the back of the van, shaking his head, and navigated carefully around Shipp to avoid going through him.

"She's in the dark," Gwen said behind him.

Ryan stopped halfway out the door. All of his frustration and annoyance got out of the way for a second. He didn't turn around; that would be granting Gwen too much unearned faith. But he listened.

"Wherever she is, it's dark there," Gwen said. Her tone had shifted completely. She sounded grave, even urgent. "And she's not alone."

Ryan turned fully around. Gwen had her hand resting on Margie's arm, like she was trying to comfort her. And it warmed Ryan to her a little. While she was still clearly a charlatan, as least she was a sympathetic charlatan.

"Where is she?" he demanded.

"I don't know."

"Then how do you know it's dark? Did she tell you?"

"No. Sort of. Not really. Yes. But no." Even she seemed to be frustrated by that answer, and waved him over instead. "Look at this."

Ryan hesitated. Already he had given this woman a chance and she had proven herself, if not insane, then definitely a con artist. Was he really prepared to give her another chance?

He reluctantly turned and shuffled back to her.

She pointed at Margie's eyes, which were still closed and impassive. "Look. See how they're squinting?"

Ryan leaned in close to try to make sense of this. Margie's eyes were most definitely closed. So he said so. "They're not squinting. They're closed."

"Right. But she wants them to be squinting. Look at the muscles here and here." She ran her finger around the corners of Margie's eyes. "Look at the eyebrows. Wherever she is, it's dark. Her mind is trying to make her squint so she can see better in the dark. And the

connection between her mind and her body is not completely broken, so her muscles are responding."

Ryan looked at Margie's eyes again. He couldn't see
what Gwen was pointing out at all. Margie looked as
absent and motionless as ever.

Sensing that he couldn't see it, Gwen pointed again
at the corner of Margie's eye. "Trust me, it's happening."

"How can you possibly...?"

Gwen sighed. "Okay, yes, the way I used to do business, I had to occasionally do cold readings. But only
when I wasn't getting anything from the other side and
I still had to make a good show of it. Which was pretty
frequently. Stop judging me. I can see you judging me.
Stop it."

Ryan tried to stop judging her so she'd get to the
point. He failed. He still thought she was a fraud. But he
was starting to think she could be a useful fraud.

"The point is, I got pretty good at picking up on little
cues. If I said the letter D and somebody there knew
someone named David, I'd have to be able to see that
little flicker in their face, right? I got good at it. I see
things in faces maybe you don't see. And right now, I
see that Margie is in the dark."

Ryan found himself being reluctantly persuaded. He
studied Margie's face as closely as he could and started
to think that maybe, just maybe, there was something
about her eyes that wasn't her usual, neutral look.
Maybe she was trying to see in the dark. But he needed
more. He couldn't get completely on board with it just
yet. "Okay," he said, "how can you tell she's not alone?"

Gwen traced her finger along Margie's jawline and
around the corners of her mouth. "See here? She's talking."

Once again, Ryan couldn't see anything at all. There
was no motion he could detect. The muscles were still.

"It stops and starts," Gwen said. "But she's talking. Her mind is trying to make her jaw move, and her lips. The connection isn't strong enough to actually move them. But it's trying. So unless she talks to herself a lot, somebody's there with her."

"Lincoln?" Lowell asked, eager.

Gwen shrugged. "Can't say. Unless we get lucky and she happens to say his name out loud. But that's probably not happening."

"Okay," Lowell said, "so how do we find her?"

"That's where things get mystical." She picked up the little pink lantern she had carried out to the van with her. It was like an old kerosene lamp that a lighthouse keeper might carry, but half the size, made of pink molded plastic, and with a tiny incandescent bulb inside it like a Christmas light. Ryan's skepticism returned in force as she twisted the little knob on the bottom and the bulb faded up, also pink. "It reveals the unseen spectral pathways of the ether," Gwen said. "And it attracts and kills mosquitoes."

She lowered the lantern towards Margie's face and dangled it there, swooping it in a tight circle. Evidently not finding what she was after, she shifted it up to Margie's forehead and circled it again. Her mouth was moving the whole time like she was uttering silent incantations that Ryan was glad he couldn't hear.

"How long does this take?" he asked, wishing he had a watch to look at for emphasis.

"I'm gonna need lots more batteries," she said. "Are there any double-A's in here?"

It was not the answer Ryan wanted, or indeed an answer at all. He found himself wanting to run her over with the van on his way out of the parking lot. He turned and gave Lowell the hardest look he could.

Lowell turned up his hands in a "what can I do?" shrug. "Hey Gwen," he said, "is there any way we can speed this up?"

"Nope." She twisted the knob and made the little bulb slightly brighter. "Unless you know somebody she loves."

Ryan froze. Lowell's head snapped around to look at him with an expression of fresh hope. He pointed. "Him! Totally!"

Gwen looked Ryan up and down. Then looked at Margie. Then back at Ryan. She frowned skeptically. "Really?"

The urgency let Ryan avoid being offended. "Maybe! Does that help?"

"Sort of. Not really. I mean, love is the essence, the very pulsating lifeblood, of the universe. The pathways formed by love are stronger than any other. So I can see them more clearly, and they'll be easier to follow."

Crackpot. Ryan wanted to leave again. For a moment he imagined the look of shock on Gwen's face as the van rolled over her.

"Oh stop it," she said, as if reading his thoughts. "Is it so ridiculous? What does your Clinic do most of the time? You use your electric zapper machines to break the connection between a ghost and the thing they're emotionally attached to. You know those connections exist. Is it really so ridiculous that I might be able to *see* those connections? Technically I could follow a path all the way from you to her. Wherever she is."

"So do it!" Lowell said. He bounced in the driver's seat, excited about this plan now.

"I can't," Gwen said. "He's not a ghost. Maybe if she was right next to him it'd work. But when there's distance, the body hides it. He has to be a ghost."

Ryan knew the solution to that right away. And it was terrifying, and dangerous, and wildly implausible. But he entertained it anyway. Because he had literally nowhere else to go, no-one else to turn to, and no other hope of ever finding Margie. And if she was out there, and he didn't find her before Friday's new Blackout, she would be rendered invisible and he would never see her again.

Against all his better judgment, and against all his judgment that wasn't better but was still pretty good, he was going to have to give this woman a shot.

"Then let's make me a ghost," he said.

25

Minutes later Ryan was strapped into the empty hammock opposite Margie's, and had the huge and always-threatening metal spider gripped to the back of his head. Lowell fiddled with the wires snaked across the floor of the van, and Gwen swung the little pink lantern above Ryan and poked at him. She studied him much too closely for comfort, as though she was trying to see his ghost through his skin.

It had been more than a year since he had last had his ghost ripped out, and he wasn't looking forward to repeating it. If anything he was even more frightened this time because he knew what to expect. And because this time the procedure was going to be performed by people who were not only inexperienced at it, but also possibly crazy.

"You're sweating," Gwen said, leaning close over his face.

"Sorry."

"It's just an observation. I wasn't going to say that it's gross."

"Okay."

"You *are* sweating, though."

Ryan changed the subject. "What if she's a long way away? Like China?"

"Or the moon?" Lowell suggested. He unhooked the paddles from the Box and struck them against each other, trying to create sparks like he would with jumper cables. It didn't work and he hung them up again, disappointed.

Gwen wrinkled her forehead. "The other other side could be anywhere. It could be in a parallel dimension, or in another universe, or right here mixed in with our own reality but out of phase so we can't see it. I'm guessing when we find where this trail leads, it'll be some kind of spiritual energy portal. You're going to want sunglasses. Did you bring any?"

"That's not the point," Ryan said irritably. "Portal or not, what if it's far away? Will your..." He didn't know what to call it, so he invented a term. "Will your 'pink-light' still work?"

"It'll work no matter where it is. All it gives me is a direction. Everybody's in a direction from other things. It's how directions work."

"So how long will this take?"

"Totally depends on how far away she is."

"No, I mean, to get the direction. You can do it fast, right?"

"I have to keep doing it until we find her. Otherwise it's possible we could go right past her and not know it. If you're navigating a ship you can't just look at your compass every once in a while. You have to have it open all the time. And what if she's moving? Even harder. You're going to need to stay a ghost until we get there. Are you cool with that?"

"No! I'm very *not* cool with that!" Just pulling him out of his body one brief time could destroy him. Margie had cautioned him about it numerous times, reminding him that when his body eventually died and his ghost left it, he would be gone. For real, and for good. So it was a monumental risk just to attempt this plan for a few seconds, much less for an entire trip of indeterminate length. "It has to be fast. I can't stay a ghost. So you'll just have to get your direction quick, and that's it."

Gwen tapped on her teeth with the tip of her finger, pondering. "I guess we could keep doing it. Pull you out for a few seconds, get a reading, then put you back in. And do it all again later."

He didn't like that idea either. Even if he survived the first time, he imagined that every time they did it was going to wear down the stability of his ghost a little bit further. Eventually they'd do it one too many times, and he'd be gone.

But he decided to be optimistic. Maybe Margie wasn't far. Maybe they'd find her after only one reading. It wasn't totally impossible. Just really, really not very possible at all.

"Let's do it," Ryan said.

"Great!" Her enthusiasm was more than he wanted. She was like a kid opening presents. "Lowell, proceed!"

Ryan's dread transformed instantly to outright terror. He sat bolt upright. The cord on the spider, too short for him to sit up all the way, snapped tight and the spider tore off the back of his head. "Wait, Lowell's doing it?"

"Duh. He's the only one who sort of halfway knows how. Plus I need to have all my thirty-one senses attuned to my reading, so I'll be busy."

Lowell studied the controls on the Box and rubbed his hands together like he was about to count poker chips.

Ryan squirmed to the back of the hammock. "He is *not* doing this. I thought you were doing it." Even as he said it, he realized that having her do it might in fact be scarier. She was clearly a fruitcake. Lowell, while incompetent in virtually every way, was somehow the better choice. So why was he protesting?

"I can do it," Lowell said. "I watched Margie do this a bunch of times." He lifted the paddles and turned them over in his hands. "Am I holding these the right way?"

"Yep!" Gwen said cheerily, and threw Lowell a thumbs-up.

Ryan shrank back even further. "No, he's not!"

Lowell flipped them around. "He's right. I wasn't. That wasn't gonna work." He chuckled, bemused.

Ryan wished Margie was doing it. He wouldn't be scared at all if she was doing it. And she'd track her missing self down in no time. Then they'd be back home watching terrible TV about real estate and eating Sugar Crisp to put this all behind them.

Shipp spoke up from the back of the van. Ryan had completely forgotten he was there. "You people have been ordered not to use that equipment until it's been cleared."

"Yeah?" Lowell said, challenging. "How are you gonna stop us? Talk to us when you're less transparent."

"What's that guy even doing here?" Gwen said. "His energy is bringing me right down."

Shipp seemed to want to storm over and drag them all off to jail. But he turned away and went back to staring at his empty spot in the corner of the van. Ryan could almost see the energy Gwen was talking about, and it was dark.

"Anyway," Lowell said, "are we ready? I am totally ready."

Ryan clamped his eyes closed and nodded. And resigned himself to the fact that these would likely be his last few moments spent existing.

"Here we go," Lowell said. And he powered on the Box.

Inside the Clinic, the Box made a noise that was intimidating at best. Despite all Margie's efforts to make her clients comfortable, as soon as she turned on the Box and they heard that high-voltage whine rising all the way to that piercing shriek, the client's heart rate would inevitably spike. Here in the van, the sound was amplified and made genuinely monstrous by the metal walls. So even though he heard that sound several times every day, Ryan felt his heart accelerate and the sweat on his forehead turn to waterfalls cascading down his hairline to the back of his neck.

He felt the cool metal of one of the paddles touch his chest, and the other press against his scalp. He was slightly comforted by the fact that Lowell at least seemed to have the positioning right. Maybe he *did* know how to do this. He didn't know how to do literally anything else, but maybe he knew this.

They waited, Ryan with his eyes firmly closed, while the Box's charge rose, and rose.

"Ready, Gwen?" Lowell said.

Ryan didn't hear any response from Gwen, but thought perhaps she had nodded because Lowell went on.

"Okay," Lowell said. Ryan felt him adjust the positioning of the paddles. A millimetre here, twisting one degree to the left there. Was he making expertly calculated minute adjustments? Or was he just not paying attention and they were drifting around? That seemed more likely.

Then the tone reached its peak and Ryan knew the moment was coming. Lowell waited a second too long. Then: "I just step on this, right?"

Ryan heard the *clunk* of Lowell stepping on the pedal.

He had vivid memories of the first time this procedure had been done to him. The white light ripping through him. The burning inside and out. The world dipping out from under him and careening around him. And the sudden overwhelming rush of sensation, all the particle waves and energy fields of the physical world slamming into him hard like crashing tsunamis from all directions.

This time was just like that, but with the addition of Lowell laughing.

He felt his body get out of his way, and then he was outside it. Visual information flooded into his mind, drowning him. He saw the world through a three-hundred-and-sixty-degree lens, unfiltered, unfocused, a cascade of baffling information. But as soon as the sensations settled down and let him get his bearings, a familiarity set in. He had already been through this several times and the routine came back to him quickly: focus your vision on a narrow cone, exclude everything else, look down at your body, let your form take shape, adjust your height and features, move the air like you still have vocal cords.

There beneath him, no less shocking than the last time he had done this, was his own body. This, he had not gotten used to. This was—and he was sure would always be—a profoundly unsettling experience. Just as it had done the first time, it threatened to snap something in his mind. Some part of his rational being identified that body down there as being him, and couldn't process the fact that he was up here looking at it. On a raw existential level, it felt wrong. Impossible to accept. And on an entirely different level, it felt wrong that his body was drooling out of one corner of its mouth.

Still, he cycled through the things he knew he had to do in order to properly assume his ghost form. What had taken him several minutes to get through a year ago, he whipped through in seconds. He was officially excellent at being a ghost.

He swung his vision around until he sensed a form that had to be Gwen. He processed the visual input, compared it to his memory of her, and adjusted the whole rush of information until he felt like he was just simply seeing Gwen. And there she was, looking dazzled at him.

"I'm ready," he said.

And then it hit him. With all the other things he had to fear, he had almost forgotten that being outside his body wasn't going to be the same this time. It was going to be dangerous.

Moments after he thought it, it punched him hard in the face he no longer had.

Everything he had just fought to bring into focus went out of focus again. He couldn't keep his shape, or his position in space. His extremities turned quickly to shifting tendrils of vapor and he fought to bring them back to a familiar shape. But the particles wouldn't cooperate. He sank to the floor, pooling out at the edges as the energy that made up his form spread apart.

This was a mistake. I can't do it.

Gwen was yelling something at him. His name, maybe? What was his name? He couldn't remember it. It was gone, dissipated along with everything else that made him himself.

But he could remember one thing.

Margie.

With the most powerful concentration of effort that he could muster, he fought his form back together. The world pulled itself briefly back into focus. Somewhere in the chaotic swirling of energy he found his voice again.

"Do it!" He hurled the words at Gwen. The voice didn't sound like him, but the words were clear enough.

Ryan fought his cone of vision down to Gwen. He wanted to see what she was doing.

She twisted the little knob on the base of her lantern, and the bulb glowed softly pink. She held the lantern by the little wire handle on top and swung it around him, as close to him as she could get it without having it contact him. She let it rock gently on its handle as though using it to spread incense smoke.

If it was having any effect on him, he couldn't see it yet. It was just a soft pink light. Yet she gazed at it with unbreakable focus.

Shouldn't it be doing something? I don't have all day. No sooner had he thought that than he felt himself drifting apart again, spreading in all directions like dissolving gelatin.

"Just a few more seconds!" Gwen insisted.

Ryan yanked himself back together. He stopped trying to see what she was doing and concentrated every piece of energy he had on just maintaining his form. It was getting more difficult by the second. He could feel himself slipping away.

"I... I...." His voice was a blob of sound. His words drowned in mush before they could get out.

"Got it!" Gwen said.

Lowell leaped in with far too much enthusiasm, waving the paddles in the air. He slapped one of them onto Ryan's body's chest and jammed the other straight into the substance of Ryan's ghostly torso. "Like this?" he asked.

Ryan didn't know if Lowell was asking him or Gwen, but it didn't matter because Lowell didn't wait for an answer. He thumped his foot onto the pedal and the Box made a screeching electric *snap*.

Ryan's ghost had re-entered his body several times before. But he'd always been unconscious for it, or busy fighting with someone else also trying to get into his

body. This was the first time he'd had enough awareness to pay attention to how it felt. And it was strangely
underwhelming. One second he was floating in the air
wondering if Lowell was doing this right, and the next
he was looking up at the roof of the van. His fingers and
toes were cold, and he could smell burnt hair and
ozone. Smoke drifted in oily clouds through his vision,
and from the heat on the back of his head, he was pretty
sure he knew where the smoke was coming from.

He sat up sharply, and again the cable attached to
the spider pulled taut and ripped the device off his
head. He forced himself to breathe, gulped down air,
gripped Lowell by the shoulder for balance as he waited
for his body to adjust to his presence in it. The Box was
winding down, its voice already dipping into the lower
octaves, the metal parts of it creaking and cracking as
they cooled.

"You okay there?" Lowell asked. "Want me to zap you
again?"

Ryan shook his head as emphatically as he could, and
waved for Lowell to hang up the paddles.

He noticed that Gwen was grinning at him, and he
didn't know why. Through his rapid, gulping breaths he
managed to choke out: "Did... you... get..."

She nodded, and raised a hand to point in a direction
just a little to the right of the front passenger seat.
"She's that way."

"How... far?"

"I told you, we only get direction. We'll have to figure
out distance on the way."

Ryan was only slightly encouraged. Margie could be
ten feet away, or a thousand miles. There was no way to
know. And they had only two days to get her back. The
whole plan was starting to feel futile. And based on how
traumatic this first extraction/re-entry procedure had

been, he strongly suspected he wouldn't be able to go through it many more times.

Gwen was still grinning at him. He wondered if she was more optimistic than him, and what reason she might have for it. "What?" he asked with a tinge of hope.

"You love her," she said, through a giggle.

Ryan felt himself blush.

"No, I mean, you really love her. I've seen a lot of connections before, but this is one of the strongest ever. Like, I mean, can't-live-without-her, Jack-and-Rose-from-Titanic kind of love."

"Really?" Ryan didn't like that he sounded surprised. But he did sound surprised, because he was. He knew that he wanted to be around her all the time, but it astonished him how strong it apparently was. "You can tell?"

"Yep. Big time. There's a stream between you and her about this big." She made a circle with her hands about the size of a volleyball. "I could almost see it without the lamp."

"Wow," Ryan said. He glanced around, half-expecting to see the stream himself.

Gwen touched him on the arm. "Now I really hope we find her. Not just for keeping her alive and making sure she keeps on existing and all that. But also because it's, like, romantic now."

26

The first thing Ryan did was take a compass bearing. If they turned the van it would mess up Gwen's only frame of reference, so he wanted a definite, consistent direction to go. His phone provided a workable compass and they determined that the direction was something like west-southwest. Ryan tried to get Gwen to be more precise about what she had seen, but in trying to describe it she actually got less so, waving her hand vaguely at the front of the van and ending every word with "ish". So he went with the way she had first pointed.

Ryan didn't believe for a second that Margie was in some alternate dimension or "other other side". If she was out there, she was somewhere he could find on a map. So he pulled up a map on his phone and scaled it to show twenty miles or so. He took a screenshot of it and with a basic painting app, drew a line through it west-southwest of their position.

His first idea was to check the map along that line for any places he knew Margie was familiar with. Maybe she had been taken somewhere she had an emotional connection to. Or, failing that, maybe after her initial disappearance she had made her way to one of those places on purpose. He had some feeble hope that the line would pass through their apartment, the Clinic, or the library—anywhere she might have been drawn to. It would certainly make this job much easier. But the line didn't pass even close to the Clinic, any of her favorite restaurants, her parents' house, her friends' houses, or where she grew up. All hope of this quest being easy quickly turned to a certainty that it would be a pain.

Lowell, ever eager to play the part of the man on the run, asked if he could start driving. And then, before Ryan could answer, he started driving.

Lowell promised to go west-southwest as much as possible, but driving in any compass direction through the city for any length of time was impossible. Roads curved, buildings got in the way, or there were no streets going in the right direction at all. The best they could manage was a crude zig-zag that occasionally passed over the path of the map line. Ryan had never wished so much that he owned a helicopter. Or rather, he had never before wished it at all, and now he did.

He took to simply looking out the windshield, hoping to spot her. The day was overcast so ghosts outside were mostly easy to see. Of course there was a chance that he would happen to see her face go by in the crowd. But the futility of that, too, quickly became apparent. The ghosts were so densely packed, and flashed past the van so quickly, that even if she did happen to pass nearby his odds of spotting her in the crowd were virtually zero. Plus he found watching the ghosts hypnotic, and it quickly lulled him into a near-catatonic state.

Gwen suggested that for the first little while at least, they would extract Ryan every hour and take a new reading. If the tracking radically changed direction they would know they had gone too far, but this way they would never have to backtrack more than an hour. Ryan feared having the procedure done to him again at all. But Lowell was, bizarrely, downright giddy about it. He even made the case for doing it every half hour instead, which Ryan quickly shot down.

So after an hour of zig-zagging through the city they pulled into a relatively secluded spot next to a Shell station in West Newton. It had a playground next door and a quiet street without much traffic. They waited for a small, curious mob of 1940s-era ghosts to stop paying attention to them and go back to criticizing customers at the gas pumps about not saving for the war effort. Once the ghosts were gone and they had a modicum of privacy they extracted Ryan again. Ryan was tense the whole time. He had feared that the first extraction might destroy him, but he feared it doubly this time.

The sensation was so fresh in his mind and so familiar by this point that once he was out, he went through the whole acclimation process in seconds. But the feeling that quickly followed, of drifting apart and vanishing, was even more frightening this time. Fortunately Gwen was more efficient with the lamp and Lowell seemed to know much better what he was doing with the Box. The whole process was finished in less than a minute, and Ryan was back in his body, gasping and blinking with his hair only a little on fire. Given what could have happened, he considered that a win.

The reading showed the exact same compass direction: west-southwest. And the stream was, as Gwen described it, "adorable". But it seemed like they were not going to find Margie as close to Boston as Ryan had hoped, so they decided to try going some serious distance and got onto the Mass Pike. It went in approximately the right direction, so maybe they could cover some real miles before extracting Ryan again. Ryan liked that idea. The longer between extractions, the happier he would be.

But soon Gwen lost her confidence in the reading and Lowell got hungry. So after forty-five minutes they stopped at a Park-and-Ride at the Worcester exit and extracted Ryan again in the shade of a parked transport trailer with cookies painted on the side.

Lowell rushed through the extraction because he wanted to go to the Wendy's just up the road. Afterwards, Ryan implored him to take this whole thing more seriously and Lowell insisted, around a mouthful of chili, that this was as seriously as he ever took anything. Which was true. But Ryan still found it annoying that Lowell concentrated harder on getting chili out of the little paper bowl than he had on either of the two times he had ripped Ryan's soul out of his body.

This latest extraction gave them the exact same direction. West-southwest. So they got back on the Mass Pike and drove for another half hour. Though the highway was never completely empty of ghosts, they did thin out significantly the further they got from the city. Ryan regarded that as a good thing. If Margie happened to be out here wandering for some reason, she'd be easy to spot. He started to irrationally feel like maybe this plan had a chance of working.

But then the Turnpike angled too far north and the only other choice, I-84, angled too far south. So all that hope he'd drummed up fell away. He started to feel again like the whole thing was impossible and he'd been a fool to trust these lunatics. By the time they got as far as the little town of Sturbridge, he had given up almost entirely.

He didn't want to give up because he didn't know what else he could do if he wasn't looking for Margie. But going further felt wrong, and going back felt even more so, so stopping seemed like the best thing for now.

They pulled off at the Sturbridge Walmart and parked in a secluded spot behind the garden center to talk about options. And, in Lowell's case, to have a nasally loud nap on the roof of the van.

Gwen tapped her teeth pensively. "The chances she'll be in a city are bigger than the chances she'll be in the middle of nowhere. Just, like, statistically. So what cities are along that line?"

Ryan scanned around the map, sliding it south-southwest. "Poughkeepsie, Scranton, Pittsburgh, Columbus, Cincinnati..." The more he zoomed the map out, the more intimidating it looked. "She could be anywhere," he said. "Literally anywhere. She could be in Siberia. How would we know?" His voice broke as he said it. He wished it was an old-fashioned paper map because he wanted to rip it up and hurl it out the window.

Shipp snorted derisively, but continued looking at the back corner of the van. Ryan ignored him.

"I say we take another reading," Gwen said. "I'm feeling, like, way more in tune now and maybe if I focus I can try again to communicate with her and use the stream as a conduit."

"That would work?" Ryan asked, unable to keep the skepticism from his voice.

"No idea. It'd be cool if it did, though. I'm always figuring out new things I can do."

"You mean you're always making them up." This time he didn't even attempt to keep the skepticism from his voice. Instead, he dunked his voice in thick, gooey skepticism and let it drip off.

"You doubt me?" she growled. "I've solved crimes."

"How many?"

"More than I can count."

"So that'd be what, three?"

"You shouldn't get huffy with me!" Gwen said. Her face was red now, in a wide blotchy pattern that stood out against the pale like a climate map. "I'm the only chance you have of finding her!"

"And that's why there's *no* chance! She could be in Australia! She could be in Botswana!"

Shipp snorted again and didn't look over. It was starting to annoy Ryan. "Why do you keep doing that?"

Shipp twisted his head around just barely enough to look at them. "Because you people are stupid. The Earth is round."

Gwen snorted. "You still believe that? In the twenty-first century?"

Ryan stepped in front of Gwen so Shipp wouldn't have to listen to her. "What do you mean?"

Shipp cinched his robe tie and put his hands behind his back like he was addressing an officer. . "This 'stream' that your friend is seeing is presumably a straight line. The Earth's surface is not. If the target of your search was in Siberia or Australia or Botswana, the stream would point downwards. It doesn't." Shipp looked back at the empty corner, evidently done inter-acting for now. "You people are idiots," he added.

Ryan stared at him, fairly certain that what Shipp was saying made sense. It was the first time anything had made sense in a while and Ryan couldn't remember how to cope with it. "Gwen, the stream you saw wasn't pointing into the ground, right?"

"No." She pointed towards the front of the van. "Straight out."

Ryan felt hope surging back. "So she's close. Or close-ish." He was reluctant to let the hope take over, because in spite of Shipp's logic this all still felt like a fool's errand. But at least he wouldn't have to sit still anymore. "Gwen, get your toy lamp ready." He pounded on the ceiling of the van. "Lowell! We're doing it again!"

◊

This time was worse than the others. It *hurt*. And not just because Lowell got over-enthusiastic with the paddles and jolted Ryan twice, gleefully. This time, Ryan felt like his body was holding onto him. Some kind of body/ghost immune system had had enough and was trying to keep his ghost inside his flesh where it belonged. And the extraction procedure had to fight against it. Violently. In a way that it never had before.

As soon as he was out of his body he tried to run through the now-familiar acclimation again, but this time he had to struggle more than ever before. Nothing worked the way he was used to. He couldn't staunch the flood of sensory information, instead succumbing to it like waves crashing over him, too powerful to fight. He couldn't get his form into a human shape. He couldn't speak, couldn't move, couldn't think. After only a few seconds he lost consciousness entirely, and he fully expected, as the darkness took him, never to wake up again.

But he did wake up. There was a surprise of light and he exhaled explosively. He sat up and kicked so violently that the bottom of the hammock tore off the wall and his feet thudded to the van floor. It took him a full minute to catch his breath and figure out how to speak. "Did you get it?" he managed to gasp out.

"We got it!" Gwen said brightly, thrilled. "And you're not going to believe this."

Ryan tried to roll off the hammock, but didn't have the strength. He lay back instead. "Believe what?"

"She's moving," Lowell said from the driver's seat.

Gwen huffed. "I was going to tell him!"

Ryan disentangled himself from the hammock and stood up. "Moving? Where?"

Lowell pointed out the side of the van. "We got east this time. So either we passed her, or she passed us."

Gwen huffed and swatted the side of Lowell's seat. "I was going to tell him! Stop it!"

"East?" Ryan lost the battle he'd been fighting against hope. Hope stormed through him, victorious, running little hope flags up every flagpole within him. East could be back towards the city. "She's going home," he said. "Let's go! What are we waiting for?!

"Yeah baby!" Lowell said. He threw Ryan a salute, then sprang back into the driver's seat and turned the key.

The engine choked, and died.

27

The debate over what to do next was short and contentious. Clearly they had used the Box too much without charging the van's battery in between. Lowell proposed that he would prowl the parking lot talking nicely to people until he found someone willing to give them a boost. He would then knock that person unconscious and steal the battery out of their car. Ryan objected, saying that the plan had an unnecessary extra step and that if the person was willing to boost them, nobody had to be knocked unconscious and they should just let them. Lowell seemed unhappy with the change, but also willing to allow it. Gwen had an entirely different idea, which was to focus their collective energies through meditation and start the van with the power of their auras. Ryan shot that one down quickly, still insisting that they go with the boost thing. And Shipp's idea was that they should all turn themselves in because they were stupid and this was all going to fail. Nobody else liked that plan, and Shipp went back to silently looking at nothing.

So with their course of action more or less settled, Lowell went off to prowl the parking lot in search of someone who would boost them. He soon disappeared out of sight around the garden center, leaving Ryan to fidget nervously in the passenger seat, constantly looking back to check on Margie. She hadn't moved at all, and he knew she wouldn't, but it comforted him to keep seeing her there.

Once in a while he'd catch a glimpse of Lowell far off across the lot chasing someone to their car, or making small talk next to where the shopping carts were parked. And a worry started to nag at Ryan. Was it safe to have Lowell out there advertising their presence when they were wanted fugitives? What if somebody recognized him?

It seemed ridiculous to Ryan. Having never been a fugitive before, he wondered how famous it could make them, really. Was the apparent destruction of a 200-year-old ghost due to possible accidental negligence really enough to make them into Bonnie and Clyde?

A few minutes of searching on his phone found him the answer, in the form of a clip on a news site. It was Director Prewitt himself, addressing a small cluster of reporters outside the Clinic front entrance. Ryan's blood chilled as he started it playing.

"At this point we have good cause to suspect that these individuals are directly responsible for the death of Abraham Lincoln." Prewitt paused and considered that for a second, then qualified it. "Not the first death; we already know who did that. No, the second one. From this past Monday."

Three portraits appeared on the screen. Margie's, Ryan's, and Lowell's. Along with the dread feeling of seeing himself presented as a wanted fugitive, he also wished they hadn't somehow found a picture of him toasting the camera with a frozen strawberry daiquiri.

"Oh my god," Ryan said. He gripped the sides of his head. *This can not be happening.*

"It is too early to say," Prewitt went on, "whether this was an accidental death as a result of negligence on the part of these suspects, or whether this was done intentionally as an assassination type thing. Both are bad. But it's almost certainly the latter. And I have to say I'm very disappointed in these people. I thought they were my friends."

"Oh my god," Ryan said again. He gripped his head tighter.

"I will now take a few questions," Prewitt said.

A ghostly hand in the front row of reporters went up. At least half the reporters present were ghosts, most of them crowded at the front so they'd be picked first. The ghost reporter's voice was faint, off-microphone, but still audible. "Mr. Prewitt, are these suspects dangerous?"

Prewitt didn't answer. He scanned the field of reporters for a few seconds. "Any questions? Nobody? Okay then." He stepped away from the mic and off camera. And the clip stopped playing.

Ryan hid his phone in his pocket, which at least made him feel like if the clip was somewhere he couldn't see it, all of this would go away.

"This is great!" Gwen said, startling him. He hadn't known she was watching over his shoulder. She danced in a circle between the hammocks. "Finding a missing president is one thing. Clearing the names of falsely accused fugitives... that's PR gold! Can you send them my picture too? I'll pose." She started adjusting her hair, which had the effect only of making it more bizarre.

Before Ryan could reply in the negative he spotted Lowell again, chatting with a white-haired man and three ghosts across the parking lot. As Ryan watched,

Lowell pointed straight across the lot at the van. The man nodded and raised a hand as if to say "no need to thank me, it's no problem at all", and Lowell thanked him profusely. Then the man and his three ghosts got into an SUV, and Lowell jogged straight towards Ryan, looking pleased with himself.

With the news clip still fresh in his mind, Ryan was starting to think Gwen's aura plan might have been the safer idea. He threw open his door and dashed out to meet Lowell.

"I found someone!" Lowell said as he approached, already out of breath.

Ryan couldn't share Lowell's excitement, or keep the worry out of his voice. "Did he say anything about you looking familiar?"

"No. Why?"

"We can't go around showing our faces! Did he show any sign that he recognized you?"

Lowell shrugged. "I dunno."

Then they had to step back as the SUV arrived in front of the van. The white-haired man carefully aligned his hood with the van's, then cut his engine. As the man climbed out, Lowell looked at Ryan questioningly and mimed knocking someone unconscious with a club, as if to ask "Should I?" Ryan shook his head subtly.

White-hair came around to them. He looked to be in his late 50s, with the genial but slightly know-it-all attitude of someone who thought he had seen far more than they ever would and so they should just defer to him on everything. His three ghosts got out of the SUV behind him. And they all looked remarkably like him. Each about the same age, each white-haired, each completely in charge of this situation.

Lowell introduced them. "These are the Stuarts. This is Stuart. That's his father Stuart. That's *his* father Stuart. And that's Stuart's father. Stuart."

"Stuart the first," said the last-introduced one.

"Stuarts," Lowell said, "this is Ryan." Ryan shook his head again and Lowell course-corrected. "I mean, not Ryan. This is..." He had to think far too long to come up with a false name, and came up with the worst one. "... Humphrey."

"Pop your hood," Stuart IV said, evidently not interested in Humphrey's biography, or in shaking his hand.

His father, Stuart III, leaned down to look at the gap between the two cars. "You need to pull forward."

"He's close enough," Stuart II said.

"He's not," Stuart I said. "Battery's on the other side."

Stuart IV, the living one, closed his eyes and sought some elusive kind of zen. "Pop your hood, Humphrey," he said again.

Ryan, wary of the whole situation, searched Stuart IV's face for any sign of recognition. But the man was clearly preoccupied with his ancestors and hardly seemed to be looking at the fugitives at all. So Ryan obliged, climbed into the van, and popped the hood.

Stuart IV, still silently insisting that he knew everything about everything, propped the hood open while his host of fathers gathered around the engine in a circle to supervise.

Lowell attempted to distract them. "So, you guys from around here?"

They ignored him. "Battery's cooked," Stuart II said.

"It's fine," Stuart I said.

"Don't touch the terminals," Stuart III said.

Stuart IV, evidently fed up with this, fished deep into his pocket and dug out an ancient brass pocket watch. Without a word he tossed it over the van and into some bushes in the garden center. All three ghostly Stuarts immediately rushed off to follow it, clearing the space around the van considerably. "Heirloom," Stuart IV muttered to Lowell. "I may have mercy on my son and not pass it down." And then he went to get jumper cables from the back of his SUV.

Ryan's tension gradually deflated the longer Stuart IV spent attaching his cables to both batteries. He didn't seem interested in the humans present at all, only in finishing the job and going to gather up his heirloom watch and three immediate ancestors. So Ryan just backed off and let him do it, hopeful that they'd be back on the road soon.

Lowell climbed into the van driver's seat and waited with his window open. "Should I start it up?"

"Hold on," Stuart IV said, triple-checking the connection.

Then, suddenly, Shipp was standing between Stuart IV and Ryan. He seemed to appear out of nowhere, and Ryan let out a little yelp and jumped back.

"Excuse me, sir," Shipp said.

All Ryan's tension came rushing back. What was Shipp up to?

Stuart IV straightened and looked at Shipp suspiciously.

"Sir, if you have a cell phone, could I trouble you to call the Federal Bureau of Ghost Affairs. Give your location, and request that they send—"

"Starting it up!" Lowell yelled from inside the van. He turned the key, and the van made choked grinding noises but didn't start.

"What's this about?" Stuart IV asked Shipp, even more suspicious now.

"Nothing!" Ryan said. He swished his hand through Shipp, trying to waft him back into the van.

"These men are wanted by the FBGA on suspicion of —"

"Thank you, Stuart!" Ryan said. He jumped right through Shipp to get in front of him. "You've been a big help. Start it, Lowell!"

Lowell tried the engine again. And again, it wheezed and died.

Shipp appeared again right behind Stuart IV. "— actively contributing to the re-assassination of President Abraham Lincoln. Now if you would be so kind, sir..."

Stuart IV looked for the first time straight at Ryan, his eyes wide and alarmed. Then into the van at Lowell. Ryan could tell the situation was fully out of control.

"Start it, Lowell!"

Lowell tried again. The engine coughed, coughed again.

And started.

Ryan ripped the jumper cables off the battery and tossed them back towards the Stuarts' car. They struck each other in the air and spat sparks over him as he yanked the van hood closed. "Thank you, Stuart!"

He ripped the van door open and jumped in just as Lowell jammed it into reverse and backed them clear over a curb and onto the grass.

Shipp took his last few seconds of opportunity. "Tell them we're headed east, sir," he said quickly.

And then as the van tore across a lawn and onto the road behind Walmart, Shipp was seized by whatever object he was haunting, and ripped away from the stunned-looking Stuart IV.

The last thing Ryan saw as they cut into a fast U-turn was the dazed white-haired man reaching into his jacket for his phone.

28

Lowell aimed them straight at the turnpike, eastbound into the city.

"Try not to draw too much attention," Ryan told him from the back.

"Got it!"

Lowell screeched off the on-ramp, squealing their tires, and then wove crazily through traffic, leaning on the horn and flashing the headlights. He rolled down the window and yelled "Get out of the way! Move it!" even at cars they had already passed.

But with the whole family of Stuarts probably calling Prewitt right now, Ryan couldn't complain. Speed— even loud, obnoxious speed—seemed like the way to go.

"Thanks for this," he said bitterly to Shipp, who had resumed his position in the back staring at the corner.

"For doing my job?" Shipp replied without turning around. He saluted sarcastically. "Any time."

Ryan wondered what Prewitt would do when he got the call from Stuart IV. Send the police after them maybe? He wondered if they should get off the turnpike and use back roads. But that would cost them significant time, during which Margie could move again. They had to catch up to her while they could.

Ryan was tempted to have his ghost extracted again right now to make sure Margie hadn't moved again. But that seemed unwise. For one thing, it would mean they had to stop. And for another, it would probably destroy him. Neither would be helpful. He thought the best bet was to assume she was headed back to the Clinic, or to their home. Which was she more likely to be headed for? Which mattered to her more?

"The Clinic," he said without hesitation. "She's heading for the Clinic. Go! Get us there!"

"Are you nuts?!" Lowell said. "We can't go there!"

He was right. Prewitt was probably still at the Clinic, along with all his bored, bookish goons. The idea of going back to the place they had just fled from seemed inadvisable. Still, if that's where Margie was...

"Just get us close. We'll figure something out."

Shipp, in the back, chuckled. Ryan took that to mean that Shipp believed that they would not, in fact, figure something out. He didn't need to hear any more of Shipp's snorts or scoffs or chuckles. And he certainly didn't need Shipp giving them away when they got wherever they were going.

An idea struck. He berated his brain for keeping such an obvious idea to itself for so long.

"Gwen, can you use your pinklight to tell what Shipp's haunting? It's something in the van."

"It's not called that. But yes!" Gwen enthused. She swung the lantern around her finger and cranked the little dimmer on the bottom to full power. It cast a feeble pink tinge, not nearly as impressive as the phrase "full power" might usually imply. But still bright enough, in its soft pink way. Shipp watched her suspiciously as she shuffled past Ryan towards him. She dangled the lantern tauntingly with one hand and steadied herself against the van's insane weaving with the other.

Shipp smirked. And then he jumped straight upwards, arms outstretched above him. Both hands went through the roof of the van and held somehow onto the outside. Then, as though he was doing chin-ups, he hauled himself up through the metal and onto the roof. Where, Ryan assumed, he intended to spend the rest of the ride out of their reach.

Gwen looked crushed. "That's not fair!"

"Forget him," Lowell said from the front. "Everybody hold on!"

They already were. But Lowell hadn't warned them to do so for all the insane driving he had done up to this point. If he felt the need to warn them now, then Ryan thought he had better find a seat belt.

◊

By the time they arrived back in the city, Ryan was nauseous from what amounted to a forty-minute off-the-rails roller coaster ride without the safety. And Gwen looked ready to pass out. Only Lowell was still whooping in the front, leaning side to side in the driver's seat, like he wanted to pretend they were turning even when they weren't.

They had not encountered any resistance on the way back into town. They had heard sirens on their way past Framingham, but the sound had faded quickly and no lights had ever appeared. Ryan wondered if Stuart IV's various father figures had prevented him somehow from making the call. Or perhaps he had made it, but Prewitt just assumed where they were going and was lying in wait for them rather than mounting some form of pursuit.

Finally they were back on Mass Ave and through Porter Square, Lowell had slowed to a more sane speed, and soon the Clinic would be in sight.

Ryan unwound himself from the empty hammock he'd been hanging onto and pulled himself forward into the passenger seat next to Lowell. They both looked ahead, waiting for the Clinic to come into view. Ryan's feet danced on the van floor and he fidgeted with the seat controls. He was tense and scared, certainly, but more than that he felt a thrill. Because Margie was nearby. He'd thought she was gone forever but now she was nearby. And soon, he would bring her back. The thought made him lightheaded, even overpowering the lingering nausea.

"How bad do you think it's going to be?" Lowell asked. "Like, cops? Feds? What? How bad?"

Ryan didn't answer. He was pretty sure the answer was "really pretty very bad", but he worried that saying it might make it true. Maybe if he didn't say anything, the Clinic would be wide open and surrounded only by softly fluttering cartoon butterflies.

Lowell gasped, thinking of something. "They wouldn't touch my chair, would they? I need that chair!"

Ryan didn't answer that either, but not because he didn't know the answer. Only because he didn't care. Margie was close by.

Maybe a hundred yards to go. Ryan leaned forward, straining to see. Where would Margie be? Inside? Downstairs in her exam room? Looking for her body? They'd need to get into the basement and meet her there.

Gwen spoke up from the back. "Are you guys seeing this?"

Whatever it was, they weren't. Ryan wasn't seeing anything but the road ahead. But he worried that she had spotted some mortal danger he was missing. "Seeing what?"

Gwen climbed into the space between the front seats. She dangled her lantern so close to Ryan and swung it around him so wildly that he thought she was trying to hit him with it. "Look at that!" Gwen said, thrilled.

Ryan still didn't see anything, and he wanted her to not be so close. "What? What is it?"

"She must be really close, because the stream coming off you is wicked bright right now!"

"You can see it? Now?"

"Yeah! She must be super close, because your guts can't even block this!"

"We're almost there!" Ryan leaned forward. Once they cleared the trees ahead, the Clinic would be in sight.

"No. No no no, it's not that way!" Gwen said. She slammed the lantern against his chest and studied it. Then she pointed out the side window next to Ryan. "It's going that way!"

Ryan knew immediately what that meant. "Lowell, stop!"

Lowell hammered the brake and they stopped dead in the street. Immediately someone was honking behind them. Lowell and Gwen looked at Ryan, waiting for an explanation.

"She didn't go to the Clinic," Ryan said. "She went home."

◇

They were there in five minutes.

Lowell turned far too sharply and the van bounced up over the curb and bumped the little fence in front of the house, nudging a plank loose. Ryan hurled open his door and crossed the lawn in five loping steps. He kicked a stray cardboard box on the porch out of the way and slammed into the front door with his shoulder, hoping the door would just give so he wouldn't have to unlock it. But it held, and he dropped his keys twice trying to get it open too fast.

And then he was inside and charging up the stairs three at a time. He tripped and his knee slammed into one of the risers but he barely noticed, just sprang up and kept going.

"Margie?!" he kept yelling, as loud as his lungs would allow. "Margie?!"

He arrived at the door of their top floor apartment and tried it. Locked. He started desperately fighting with the keys again. *If she's home, why is it locked?* But of course it would be. He chastised himself silently for being so stupid. *She's a ghost. She can't unlock anything. Just get inside.*

The key finally slid in and he rammed the door open. "Margie?!"

No answer. The apartment was totally silent. Even Benny was apparently not home. Sye and Sye's Wife sat at their table, gazing at each other, not even noticing that Ryan was there. "Sye, is Margie here? Have you seen her?" They didn't answer, because they never did.

He scanned the kitchen. Sprinted to the bedroom door and threw on the lights. Nothing.

Had Gwen been wrong about the stream? Or had Margie been here looking for him and left already? They would have to take another reading with the lamp. Right now. They had to find out where she had gone.

He crashed back out the door and down the stairs, slipped down the last few stairs, fell backwards and landed hard on his hands, shoved himself up and over to the front door, which still hung open from his passage a minute earlier. He charged through it and nearly tripped on the cardboard box on the porch. He kicked it further aside.

Lowell and Gwen were halfway across the front lawn, coming towards him with hopeful looks on their faces. Even Shipp climbed down off the roof of the van to watch, clearly interested in what was going on.

Ryan didn't wait for them to ask. "She's not here," he said, with a sharpness that implied it was their fault even though he didn't think it was. "Do you see the stream, Gwen? If she just left, we can catch up. Check me!"

Gwen ran up to him and circled him, letting the lantern bump against him as she searched for the stream. Ryan danced the whole time. Finally she stopped right behind him. "It goes straight to the house! Right up to the porch! I can see it!"

But Margie wasn't there. Ryan couldn't put the pieces together.

But something nagged at him. He had seen something, somewhere between the top of the stairs and here. Something that his mind had filed away and only arrived at processing this moment.

He had seen his name. Handwritten in pen. He could see it in his mind.

Where?

He turned back, looked up at his apartment windows. Had it been on the counter? On the fridge? A note pinned to the wall or the door? How could Margie have left him a note? She was a ghost. Somebody else must have left it, maybe on her behalf. Maybe she had gotten Benny to do it, although it seemed pretty dexterous for him.

Go look, idiot.

He crossed the lawn to the porch again. Up the steps. Across the porch. Through the door. All a blur.

Stop. There.

The cardboard box on the porch.

He had kicked it aside on his way in, and again on his way out. It was about two feet square, and six inches deep. Wrapped in plain brown paper and tied with a string. "Ryan Matney" was written in large letters with a black sharpie above his address. No return address.

Ryan crouched, trembling. Could it be from her, somehow? Could it *be* her, somehow? Maybe she was haunting something, as he had been forced to do with the broken snow globe a year ago, and had shipped it to him. It would make for a brilliant plan to get home. If that was the case, where was she?

He didn't pick it up. Just tore the paper off right there on the porch. An unmarked cardboard box inside, taped closed with packing tape. No way he'd get through that without a knife. So he tore at the corners of the box, heedless.

Styrofoam packing peanuts spilled out of the opening. He gripped the edges and wrenched the box apart, ripping it completely in half. He brushed the peanuts on top aside.

A face looked up at him, smiling.

A spherical caveman made mostly of hair. Bulbous pink clown nose. Clutching a bowl of cereal in one hand and an oversized spoon in the other. His name in giant cartoon letters shaped into an arch above him: Hubert.

There was a slip of paper among the packing peanuts. Ryan grabbed it, pulled it clear. The sweat from his thumb left an immediate stain. It was a hand-written note: "Ryan: Didn't hear from you, but I could tell you really wanted this. It was just gathering dust in my basement anyway. Irvin Curry."

At any other time, in any other circumstance, Ryan would have been bouncing off the walls and running for any spoon within reach. Hubert, finally. After all these months, he had it. But here and now, there was no joy.

Only confusion. His mind careened while Hubert grinned at him from the box.

He sensed Gwen approaching from across the lawn. Her shadow fell across him as she arrived. "What is it?"

And as he thought about telling her she needed to check the stream again, he knew exactly what it would show. They didn't have to do another reading. Not now. What would be the point?

"All this time," he said, "we haven't been tracking her. We've been tracking this."

Gwen looked down at the box. He saw the shadow of her head tilt to the side and then back again. "A box of cereal?"

"Butter-flavored," he whispered.

She was quiet for a long time. Half a minute, he guessed. Then finally: "So that stream I've been seeing coming off you—the strongest, brightest stream I've ever seen coming off anyone—that was for a box of cereal?" She sounded incredulous, and he couldn't blame her. He felt the same way.

"Butter-flavored," he said again.

Hubert grinned at him, and for the first time ever, that grin that had always seemed so comforting, so inviting, seemed to be mocking him.

Gwen shook her head and turned away. She walked back towards the van and left him on the porch with Hubert. He heard her say as she left: "That's messed up."

And he silently agreed. It was.

29

Ryan found it hard to feel good about himself.

It is not a point of pride to discover for incontrovertible fact that a box of cereal is the most important thing in the world to you. Of course, Ryan had already suspected it. He had spent the better part of six months in the obsessive, rabid pursuit of this exact box and the mysterious, alluring, hopefully still crunchy amalgam of synthetic chemicals within. But still, he couldn't help but be devastated knowing for certain that a box of cereal mattered more to him than literally anything.

Now that the box was in his hands, he didn't want to open it. What had always looked like inviting enthusiasm on Hubert's face now looked like derisive laughter. Ryan hadn't even glanced at the list of ingredients despite months of curiosity about whether there was any actual butter included. He had hoped for all these weeks that there wouldn't be, as artificial butter flavoring was likely to taste more like butter than butter would. And he really wanted it to taste a lot like butter without actually being butter.

Until now. Now he didn't want to know what it tasted like. Now he wanted it to be gone.

He wondered what would have happened if he had eaten it. This stuff had mattered to him so much that, according to Gwen, there had been a thick, glowing stream of elemental particles stretching for countless miles between him and it. A link so strong that she had mistaken it for actual *love*. Even stronger, it seemed, than whatever link he had to Margie.

He wondered what would have happened if everything had gone according to plan and he had just eaten the cereal. Would that stream have just dissolved forever, leaving him adrift in the universe without any permanent, meaningful links to anything? Would it have flailed around in search of something else to attach to, that he could then pursue obsessively? Would it have split into smaller streams, distributing his attachment among many small, equally trivial things? Why could it not attach to something where it could stay, and mean something?

Like what, he wondered. And that was answer enough.

He threw the box onto the lawn and sat in the shade of the front porch for a long time while the ghosts of his neighborhood wandered around and past him, indifferent.

Lowell and Gwen eventually got bored of waiting in the van and asked if they could go inside instead. With their plan having failed, they had nothing else to do but go in, raid Ryan and Margie's fridge, and watch TV while Ryan sat on the porch and watched the sun go down. Shipp sat on the back bumper of the van, staring down the road and watching ghosts fill up the street.

Ryan wondered dimly if bugs were getting into the box of Hubert on the lawn, and whether he cared. And most of all he wondered where Margie was.

Again, the truth of it overwhelmed him. Wherever Margie was, it was his fault. If she had asked him, he would have let her extract him and get torn away in her place. Or would he have? He wished he could say he knew for certain, but he didn't.

As darkness descended, the evening sky rippled with waves of blue and green. He wondered if that meant another Blink might be approaching. He was pretty sure the sky had looked like that just before the last one. If there was going to be another, he would have to prepare to be almost torn out of his body yet again. The thought brought his nausea back, and—

He sat up straight.

Another Blink. It gave him an idea.

He leaped up, scattering the ghosts on the lawn as he ran through them, and snapped up the box of Hubert. Then ran inside to find Gwen.

◊

"You followed that stream all the way from me to this box. Could you do the opposite?"

Gwen, reclined on his couch with a bowl of his Cheetos balanced on her stomach, pursed her lips and did an impressive dance with her eyebrows as she tried to decode that. "Follow the box from you to..." She completely lost it, and gave up. "I don't think I'm getting it."

"Me neither," Lowell said from the counter. He had located a bottle of wine somewhere and was exploring its possibilities.

Ryan shook the box. The cereal rattled inside. "Follow the stream backwards from the box to me."

"But I know where you are," Gwen said. "And so do you. You're right there." She pointed at him for emphasis.

Ryan considered what things were around that he could throw at her. "Gwen, listen to me. I have an idea."

Before he said it, he ran through it again in his mind. And it was crazy. Every aspect of it was crazy. It was rampant with things that could go disastrously wrong, and contained precious little that could go right. And some of the things that could go disastrously wrong weren't just inconvenient or annoying. They were fatal. Fatal in a fully existential way. What he was about to propose had the strong potential to end him forever.

And yet, if everything went miraculously right, Margie was at the end of it.

I'm doing it.

He took a deep breath and closed his eyes. "We're going to extract me one more time. Right before there's another Blink. When the Blink happens, I'm pretty sort of sure I'll be taken to the same place Margie is. Then you're going to follow the stream from this cereal box all the way to where I am. Then we can get Margie—and me—back into our bodies before Blackout 2 hits on Friday night. Got it?"

As he was saying it, Ryan hoped that at least one of either Gwen or Lowell would protest and tell him he was crazy. At least then he would feel like they didn't want to risk losing him, which would signal that he actually mattered to them in some way. Instead, they both said the same thing that demonstrated no such concern at all.

They both said: "Cool!"

"But we gotta go. Like, now."

They were into it now. They ran down the stairs and out to the van, where Shipp looked surprised to see them again so soon, but otherwise ignored them.

Ryan lay down in the empty hammock across from Margie's body. Again. And he slid the giant metal spider onto the back of his head. Again. And it all was uncomfortable and painful and terrifying. Again.

I hate this I hate this I hate this.

To settle his frantically pounding heart he looked over at Margie. She lay as always, her face impassive. The same way she looked when she did complex calculus. He wished her eyes were open so he could see them, but just seeing her face was enough to calm him a little and keep him focused on why he was about to do the most insane thing he had ever done.

Lowell read something off his phone. "NASA site says three minutes, give or take," he said. He looked out the windshield of the van. The sky was shimmering green, and the ghosts in the street were taking notice, pointing and whispering to each other. "Everybody looks nervous."

Ryan put his head back and felt the cold lump of the spider dig into his scalp. "Charge it up," he said.

Lowell started the van engine and flipped the master power switch on the Box. It began its slow electric crescendo.

"I think it's amazing that you're doing this," Gwen said. She dangled the lamp from one hand, letting it spin above the cereal box on the floor between Ryan and Margie. "You might die! Like, the real kind."

"Thank you, I was trying not to think about that."

"You should. You *should* think about that."

"Can we not talk now?"

Gwen leaned in closer to Ryan, right over his face. She tapped his sternum with her index finger. "When we found that cereal box I thought you were terrible. But most of that is gone because of what you're doing now."

Ryan didn't care much, but was curious. "Why only most?"

"The cereal that mattered more to you than anything in the world was butter-flavored. That's gross. I think less of you for that."

"If it matters, I think less of me too. How long, Lowell?"

Lowell checked his phone. "Three minutes."

"You said three minutes last time!" Gwen said.

Lowell drew the phone closer to his face and studied something at the top of it. "Oh," he said.

Panic shot through Ryan's nervous system. Lowell discovering something just a few seconds from the critical moment could not possibly be good. "What?!"

"Forgot to refresh the page," Lowell said. He tapped the screen, watched it for a second. "Oh," he said again. "We better start."

Ryan wrenched his neck around, trying to look at Lowell in the driver's seat. The movement yanked the spider off the back of his head, as happened seemingly every time. "Why? How long do we have?"

Lowell jumped out of his seat. "Like, minus ten seconds-ish. I guess it's late."

Ryan's panic bit into his gut. He felt sweat erupt. "The Blink has already started?!"

"Don't freak out. The lights are still on. There's still time."

Ryan slammed his head back onto the spider, but he was off-center. Pain jolted the back of his neck and he felt some of the spider's legs bend out of shape under the force of his head. "Do it!" he screamed. "Just do it now!" He reached back and yanked at the spider's legs, trying to pull them back around his skull.

Lowell snapped up the paddles and clapped them together like blackboard erasers. "Ready!"

Ryan could hear from the pitch of the Box that it wasn't ready. It was still rising, and the ready light remained dark. He wrenched the spider's legs into an approximation of their proper shape and smashed his head between them. They were tighter than before, and carved gouges in his temples. He felt blood mix with the sweat. "I'm in!" he said.

Lowell positioned the paddles. From the look on his face, he was clearly still getting way too much joy from doing this. Ryan thought he might be giggling.

They waited while the Box cleared the upper octaves. Lowell held the paddles poised above Ryan's head and chest while Gwen dangled the lamp above the cereal box. Hubert's eyes looked strangely fearful now, like he was the one about to be ripped out of his body.

The Box made its "ready" *ping*, and Ryan saw the green light shine off the back of the driver's seat.

"Go!" he yelled.

Lowell pressed the paddles to Ryan and jammed the pedal.

Ryan felt his body clinging to his ghost, refusing to release it. It held him in a vice grip as the Box pulled at him in a supernatural tug-of-war. Then the Box won and he was wrenched once again into gravity-less space, and the van flipped upside down around him and stretched out of shape. Everything went briefly dark, and then flooded back at Ryan from all directions, spinning on every axis.

Immediately he could barely hold himself together. He decided to focus only on vision so he could see what was going on. The van snapped into focus around him and Lowell and Gwen were watching him, the bluish glow of his ghostly form making shiny reflections on their faces.

He hovered above his body, staring down into his own face. The spider had indeed scraped his temples rather badly, and blood was creeping down them and around his ears. Smoke was coming out of his nostrils. His eyes were open and for a moment he felt like he could see himself through them, all at once in himself and above himself.

He waited for something to happen, for the solar winds to tear him away. But it didn't happen. He could hear only Lowell and Gwen breathing. And he focused all the rest of his energy on just staying together and not dissolving into non-existence.

Where's the Blink? Why am I not being taken away?

"Are we too late?" He directed the question at Lowell. His voice sounded faint, like a breeze.

Lowell scooped his phone out of the front seat and checked it. "I dunno," he said. "We're past the time!"

Frustrated, Ryan forced himself through the wall of the van and looked up and down the street.

The lights were still on, and the crowds of ghosts still looked expectant. What if NASA was wrong and it wasn't going to happen at all?

He dove back into the van. "What's happen—" he started to say.

But Gwen interrupted him. "Ryan, there's a problem." It was the most earnest he had ever heard her sound. Up until that moment he couldn't possibly have imagined her nasal squeak ever sounding so distressed. But there it was, and it alarmed him.

Fear was like a shot of spectral adrenaline. It gave him the strength to pull himself into focus, to hold his shape a little longer. "What problem? What's happening?"

Gwen waved the lamp over the cereal box. She picked up the box, flipped it over, waved the lamp over it again. She shook her head. "There's no stream."

"No stream? How can that be? We followed it all the way here."

She tried the lamp again, turning the cereal box to every possible angle beneath it. "Yeah, but it's gone!"

"How?! Why?!"

She flipped the box upright to look at the top. And she cocked an eyebrow. "It's still closed."

"Yeah! So?!"

"You didn't open it? Why didn't you open it?"

"I didn't want any!"

"This was the most important thing in the world to you and you didn't want any?"

Something that Ryan could only describe as a chill started right in the middle of his substance and quickly jumped from molecule to molecule until it permeated him entirely. He had never felt anything like it in his body, but he interpreted it as some form of terror. Because he had realized exactly why the stream between him and the cereal was gone.

He didn't care about the cereal anymore.

From the moment he had found it on his front porch, it had seemed insignificant. Wasteful. Frivolous. In those moments, now that he looked back on them, he had practically felt the invisible stream that connected him to the cereal snapping like a ghostly umbilical.

And it meant that if he was taken away, they would have no way to find him.

He forced his voice out. "Get me back in my body," he managed to make it say.

"I already shut the Box off!" Lowell said.

Ryan dove across the van and hovered above his body. He thought he could see the terror in his body's face beneath him. "Turn it back on!"

Lowell flipped the master power, grabbed the paddles again. The Box was still in the low octaves. It would be minutes before it was ready.

Ryan sank into his body, felt it pull at him like a magnet, drawing him in. But he couldn't connect with it. He needed the jolt for that.

"Almost!" Lowell said. "Just a minute more!"

The van windows went suddenly dark. The lights of the city had gone out.

Another Blink had arrived.

Ryan looked at Lowell, who was kicking the Box, trying to make the charge meter rise faster. But Ryan knew it wasn't going to work, and he looked at Lowell and shook his head. There was nothing he could do.

And then Ryan was torn away.

He felt it like a blast of wind. At first it knocked him over, hurling him towards the side wall of the van. He twisted in the air, out of control on random currents. And then he was ripping apart and the whole world was tearing to pieces around him, stretching to astonishing lengths like putty and snapping apart in infinite places, whipping away out of sight behind him like he was riding on a bullet and leaving the whole world behind.

30

Ryan hurtled across a vast distance. Though it took no time, he felt the speed of his passage through immeasurable expanses of space. He was a bullet in the dark.

And then he stopped. Instantly. One microsecond he was moving, and the next he was not.

He opened the eyes he didn't have.

He was surrounded by faint light. But not daylight. It was dim, pale, shimmering, like moonlight reflected off shifting mirrors.

It was ghosts in the dark.

He couldn't count how many. One or two drifted past in front of him, another flitted in the corner of his eye, more floated in the distance. They floated around and apart from each other in a space that seemed to have no limits.

He was one among them. They milled and meandered, brushing past him as he floated in the blank space. They were nearly silent, only faint whispers passing between them. A few hushed murmurs brushed close past him and then faded behind him into the dark, never words he could make out.

He thought about Margie. Maybe she was here. Maybe she could explain... well, this. All of it.

He hunted for a direction to go. He wasn't sure if he was turning himself or just shifting his attention, but either way he was scanning his surroundings. And he gradually became aware of something. It wasn't new; it had been there since he arrived. But he hadn't noticed it until now. And as he focused on it, it grew in strength. After a few seconds it occupied all his attention like a minor toe itch that, once noticed, quickly becomes unbearable.

It was a sensation that something was subliminally calling to him. Beckoning him. Pulling him.

He wondered what to do about it. And then he got that it was *telling* him what to do about it and all he had to do was do it.

Just move, stupid.

So he did. He moved. It wasn't hard to determine which way he was being pulled. So he spun himself around until he was sure he was definitely facing the way that was somehow for some reason right. And he moved.

He drifted forwards through the ghosts as one of them. He felt insignificant among them, drawing no attention. And he was fine with that. There was a oneness to it. Somehow he and these people were not individuals, but unified. He didn't know where he was going but he knew he was going there.

What is this place? Is it even a place at all?

The realization came to him fast. It was clear now that Gwen had been absolutely right. He had arrived in a spaceless, timeless limbo, devoid of light and completely removed from the world he knew. It was an other other side, populated with countless ghosts. Their gathering formed a singular mass of energy. Perhaps this was the heart of the universe itself, the furnace from which all life energy sprung, and the ghosts were manifestations of it. Having escaped their mortal, material bounds they had returned to the wellspring. That was the only explanation. Once he figured it out and began to speculate what he was now a part of—indeed, had always unknowingly been a part of—it was awe-inspiring. And the pull he was feeling, irresistible now, must be towards whatever lay at the center. He didn't know what that would be, but surely it would be the greatest thing that had ever existed.

He passed a dishwasher.

That gave him a moment's pause.

It was at least a decade old, and well used. It leaned slightly to one side, like its adjustable feet were not adjusted properly. The ghosts drifted around it, not paying it much attention. But it was definitely there. He lingered in front of it for a while, pondering it cosmically.

The discovery seemed to warrant a better investigation of his surroundings. He discovered that the space was not quite as space-less as he had thought. The ghosts were not floating in limbo; they drifted across a smooth, featureless floor. He slid across it, and eventually came across a square column, holding up a ceiling twenty feet above that he hadn't been able to make out in the dark until now. There was a whole row of such columns, stretching off into the distance where the haze of ghosts were the only light.

And on every second column was a cardboard cutout of Abraham Lincoln.

He had his hat on, and that humble, reassuring smile. And he was giving a thumbs-up. A speech bubble attached to his head had words in it: "Take it from Honest Abe, all our appliances are haunting-free!"

Ryan was starting to feel that this was not the furnace of all universal energy. Instead, he thought it might be Abraham Lincoln's used appliance warehouse store. Probably the Dorchester location.

He confirmed it by noticing that the dishwasher was not alone. There were washers and dryers too. And mixers, blenders, and microwaves on a shelf against a wall. And more pictures of Lincoln. They were everywhere. On posters, on banners, on signs balanced on the appliances. And always in speech bubbles he was guaranteeing low prices, one-year warranties, and absolutely no hauntings.

The revelation surprised Ryan only mildly. He was so intent on getting where he wanted to be that he lacked the capacity for surprise. Whatever he was headed for, he somehow knew instinctively that it was the best place in the universe and he would be happy when he got there. And he thought that this source of pure joy, the center of the universe, must be just up ahead past the row of bar fridges.

He pressed on, feeling utterly at one with all the ghosts here. He was certain that he was heading in the right direction, but he didn't know *why* he was certain. He was merely moving from one side of a dark, dirty used appliance store to the other equally dark, equally dirty side. And yet he knew somehow that the side he was headed towards was definitely the better side. It was the much preferable side. It was the side full of junk that put the original side's junk somehow to shame. It was the side whose chipped concrete floor had much better chips than the chipped concrete floor at the other side. To the casual observer, one side of the place might have looked pretty much the same as the other. But he knew—and everyone he passed through knew—that the other side was far, far better.

He zeroed in on a corner where the ghosts were most densely packed. This had to be it. He quickened his pace, lifted his feet right off the floor and floated forwards in a way he hadn't even known he was capable of. The cloud of ghosts got denser as he advanced towards the corner but he didn't allow himself to slow.

And suddenly Roger Foster's ghost was in front of him, and he stopped. Seeing Roger was almost as surprising as seeing the first dishwasher.

Roger smiled at him, that piteous expression he had mastered long ago that simultaneously conveyed "I am deeply sorry for whatever ill has befallen you", and "I am running a business here, so let's move it along".

Ryan blurted: "Roger?"

Roger's smile thinned ever so slightly. Ryan didn't know if that meant recognition or annoyance, or some other reaction unique to Roger. "Is it your time?" Roger asked, dripping sympathy.

Ryan tried to see past Roger to the corner where all the ghosts were clumped. "My time for what?"

"Oh dear, I'm so sorry, it's a private viewing right now." He laced his hands together in front of him as though cradling a tiny hamster. "But we have a lovely vestibule where you can wait until the open viewing later. I'm so sorry." He extended a hand to indicate a space just to the right where a number of ghosts waited, looking impatient.

Ryan decided that there was no way he was going to be stopped. Particularly not by Roger, whom he felt he had good reason to dislike. So he strode ahead towards the corner, making only the faintest effort to get around Roger.

Roger pursued him, pleading his most demanding pleas. "So sorry, that's the wrong way. Please, if you would come this way. It won't be long."

Ryan raced forward through the crowd all the way into the corner, and looked down at what he was sure would be magnificent. He had never been here before, but he knew exactly where to look.

And there it was.

It was a toaster.

An old, yet somehow utterly perfect four-slicer. The brand name had been scraped off the side in a perfect way, leaving deep and flawless scratches in the chrome. It had a glorious bagel button, and the "shade" slider had been set—divinely, perfectly—to just slightly lighter than middle darkness. Its power cord was frayed in precisely the most perfect way at precisely the most perfect spot. Some of the burnt crumbs from its catcher tray had fallen out and formed a random but doubtlessly ideal pattern on the floor around it. And it was dented on the corner in a way that all things everywhere should be exactly dented, forever. It was perfection in toaster form. It was not just a toaster. It was The Toaster.

And yet despite how glorious it was, he almost gagged. "Ugh," he said out loud. "Toast."

Because toast was the bane of breakfast, the last desperate resort of the pitifully Froot Loop-less. Toast sucked.

And yet The Toaster was wondrous. This was confusing to him. His conscious understanding of it was giving him totally different information than his subliminal feelings about it. He was consciously very much aware that this was a broken toaster in a terrible second-hand store. And that its only function was applying brown to bread and rendering it into crunchy drywall. And yet, with all his heart, he believed it was the most beautiful thing he had ever seen.

"Isn't it the most beautiful thing you've ever seen?" a voice said.

It came from his right side. And at first he thought it was him, speaking his thought out loud. He was prepared to ignore himself and just keep looking at The Toaster.

But he turned just to check. And there she was.

31

Margie looked just like her physical self, except that he could see through her and she was glowing. He was consciously aware that he should be overjoyed to see her, because he had found her and everything was going to fine after all. But his joy was strangely muted. It felt secondary. It was there, but only in the background behind The Toaster and the fact of toast sucking.

"Margie?" It was a question, but not that he wanted her to confirm who she was, or that he had found her. What he wanted was for her to tell him about The Toaster. That was what mattered. That was *all* that mattered.

"You're here!" she said. "I knew you'd be here!" She floated close to him and smiled like he had never seen her smile, like she was delighted to be able to give him the best news he had ever heard and she couldn't wait for him to hear it. She even tried to take his hand. But of course she couldn't. So she just pretended that she had, and he played along by lifting his hand to follow hers. "What do you think?"

He understood without having to be told that she meant The Toaster. So he looked at it again. "It's incredible," he said. It was, and it wasn't.

He realized after a few seconds that he was gazing at it dumbly. He was embarrassed briefly, until he noticed that all the other ghosts around him were doing the same thing. He focused a little more and recognized some of them. Maybe most of them. Maybe *all* of them. Sitting cross-legged on the floor directly across from him and whispering softly to the toaster as though telling it all his darkest secrets, was Batman. Or rather, Mr. Tinsley in his Batman costume. He was freshest in Ryan's mind, having been a client only a few days before. But there were others he recognized too, whose names he hadn't even tried to retain. They were the missing ghosts, all thirty-nine who had disappeared in the first Blink. He had seen their faces before—some of them in Clinic files, and some in appointments with Margie. He even recalled helping with the extraction of some of them, like Mr. Tinsley. And now here they all were, together in this warehouse with him. He had found them. Or rather, he was lost *with* them. And he was okay with that.

No, better than that. He was happy about it.

Roger, still hovering nearby, seemed to sense his happiness and instantly moved in to ruin it. "I'm sorry," he said. "We really do need to keep the line moving. My sympathies. Such a trying time." In contrast to his smooth, apologetic tone he motioned briskly with both hands for them to move along.

Mr. Tinsley took one more look at The Toaster's sublime toasterness and then turned away, his cape billowing behind him, and strode off to make room for someone else. He didn't question Roger's instruction, and didn't appear annoyed by it. It seemed to be routine, like he was accustomed to just following Roger's direction on who could see The Toaster.

But it wasn't routine for Ryan. He didn't want to move. He had only just discovered the Toaster, and he wanted to enjoy it as long as he could. So he stayed, and Roger lingered off to his side, fretting. The curl in his lip said "I sympathize, and I understand", but the burning in his eyes said "If I had a meat hook right now, I'd drag you away with it".

Margie put her hand on Ryan's shoulder and slightly through it. "It's okay," she said. "Stay."

Roger simmered and carried on with directing Toaster traffic around them. He waved to the nearest ghosts waiting for a turn, ushering them forward and apologizing for Ryan. "So sorry for the inconsideration of some. What can one do?"

A tall figure emerged from the general cloud of ghosts, directing waves of greeting at everyone around him. The other ghosts gave him preferential treatment, clearing a space around him and making sure he had an unobstructed path to The Toaster. He acknowledged them, thanked them. He even nodded his thanks to Roger, who bowed slightly and backed away as he would from royalty. This arriving ghost carried with him an air of authority, which of course he would.

Because he was Abraham Lincoln.

Lincoln maneuvered himself creakily until he sat cross-legged on the floor. He gave the slightest nod to Ryan, and then he gazed. The Toaster had his full attention. As it had everyone's full attention.

Some part of Ryan's mind knew that he should be excited about this too. Lincoln was the one ghost who could perhaps clear his name, save the Clinic, and make him no longer a fugitive. And he had found him! He knew this was good. Yet he didn't care.

Because for reasons he couldn't figure out, all he wanted was The Toaster.

"Can I touch it?" he asked Margie.

She gave him an amused look. "That's the first thing I asked too. No, obviously, you can't. We're ghosts; none of us can touch anything. But you can sense it. Go ahead."

He checked to see if he'd be blocking Lincoln's view by moving in closer, but Lincoln just nodded encouragingly. He understood what Ryan wanted, and wasn't going to begrudge him it. So Ryan shifted closer, stretched out his arm, and let his ghostly fingers drift delicately down to the scuffed, dented chrome side of The Toaster. He wanted to see it move from the pressure of his hand. But of course it didn't. His fingers went easily through it and into the wondrous toasting chambers within. Yet he was sure he sensed its presence against him. His fingers were happy. He wanted the rest of him to be as happy as they were. Forever.

He definitely didn't want any toast, though. As nobody ever should. Because blech.

"Can I stay here?" he asked Margie. It was everything to him. All he needed and wanted and yet hated.

She laughed. "You don't really have a choice."

◇

So he stayed with it. And Margie too. And time soon became amorphous, meaningless, even forgotten. One moment blurred together with all the other moments until they became one big, fat moment. And even that big moment was small among all the bigger moments to come.

After some vague portion of time he was dimly aware of it being slightly brighter in the store, especially at the front where the windows were. So maybe it was daytime. But it didn't matter because it was dark at the back where The Toaster was, except for the reflections of the ghosts in its sublimely warped surface.

At first he was jealous of the other ghosts always trying to get at The Toaster too. He thought it should be just for him. He tried to push them back, which was predictably futile. He couldn't move other ghosts any more than he could move physical matter. But they wanted to be near The Toaster as much as he did, so they kept pressing in. And after a while he learned to accept their presence. Margie convinced him that they weren't trying to take The Toaster away from him; they could all share it. They had forever, after all, to spend with The Toaster in this perfect golden shrine. Or at least, they had until someone came and tore down the perfect golden shrine because of its obvious black mold and rodent infestation. But even if that happened, it would be in the shrouded distances of the future. They still had lots of time to spend with The Toaster and its divinely tarnished chrome.

The Toaster didn't talk much. Or at all, really. And yet Ryan soon felt like he had carried on extended, intimate, wordless conversations with it about countless subjects. And it undoubtedly knew more about all of those subjects than he did, so he spent much of that time just listening to it, hanging on every word it didn't say. He felt like sharing some of his secrets with it, but he couldn't think of any.

What he definitely *didn't* want, though, was to put any bread in it. Because that would result in toast.

Sometimes Roger insisted that they had to give the other ghosts a chance. Being an experienced funeral director, Roger had a way of keeping a solemn, formal occasion trucking right along. So Ryan divided his time between crouching next to The Toaster and meandering around the other side of the store talking with Margie about how great it had been a few minutes ago when he was over there with The Toaster. Margie concurred every time. And they started syncing up their time at The Toaster side of the warehouse so they would both have the same Toaster moments to talk about instead of different ones.

Out of curiosity, during a non-Toaster moment, Ryan managed to maneuver himself close to Lincoln in the crowd and introduce himself. Lincoln fortunately did not remember him from his loud, obnoxious yelp that night at the Orpheum. But still, the former president quickly accepted Ryan as a fellow admirer of The Toaster. They even shared a visit to The Toaster together as soon as they saw an opening. Ryan found that Lincoln talked about The Toaster on an entirely different level from everyone else. He had intuited things about it that others like Ryan and Margie could only imagine. He had divined, for example, the precise origin of the dent in its side and what that meant on a cosmic level. And he seemed to know the name of each shade on the sliding lever from dark to light, and how they represented the subtle gradations from good to evil. And, perhaps most stunningly, he knew where the burnt crumbs around it had originated. Ryan had assumed they had just fallen out of the little collector tray in the bottom, but Lincoln claimed to have other, far more profound explanations that he promised to share in good time. For now, he said they should learn to just enjoy being near The Toaster, and enlightenment would come later. He didn't seem to know what a toaster was actually for, which was unsurprising given that they hadn't existed when he was alive. But Ryan wondered if perhaps that was why Lincoln was able to appreciate it on a higher level.

Once, as the front of the store started to get dark again, Ryan tried to ask Lincoln about the Gettysburg Address. He felt stupid doing it, like there must be other less obvious things to bring up. And he felt stupid about the way he asked it, which was: "So... the Gettysburg Address, huh?" But this was Abraham Lincoln. He couldn't *not* ask about it. Lincoln chatted about it for a minute or so, but it seemed to make him tired. So their conversation quickly turned, in a surprisingly natural way, from the Gettysburg Address to the merits of a toaster versus a toaster oven. Lincoln had no working knowledge of either, so Ryan explained that toasters were clearly better, for numerous reasons from their smaller counter footprint to their easily understood user interface. That went on for a little while until they both decided to stop talking about it and go have another look at The Toaster instead. "Never you mind that little Virginia speech," Lincoln said, as they basked in The Toaster's aura. "It is long over, a temporal concern of mortal men. The Toaster is eternal. When folks talk of Lincoln in years to come, they must needs mention The Toaster in the same breath. That will be Lincoln's legacy."

Some walled-off part of Ryan's mind whispered quietly at him: *will it, though?* And yet he found Lincoln's point hard to argue with, because The Toaster was indeed pretty great. He could already remember more about it than he could about the Gettysburg Address. So maybe Lincoln had a point.

But always in Ryan's mind there was a hint of unrest. He was able to navigate around it for a while and keep his focus on The Toaster. But eventually his thoughts washed up on the unrest like a ship on an inevitable reef. And like that ship, he was forced to deal with the problem.

Toast sucks.

It was an incontrovertible fact, an immovable rock of truth. In a world where Count Chocula existed, why would anyone ever choose to eat slightly crisped bread?

So maybe, he started to think, *a dirty, broken toaster isn't actually as great as the Gettysburg Address. Or any of the other stuff Lincoln did.*
At first he dismissed the idea as ridiculous. Clearly The Toaster was the most important thing ever. Which was not to diminish Lincoln's other achievements in any way. Of course they were great too. Just not on the same level.
Or were they?
Finally the other ghosts cleared out of the way and he and Lincoln were able to step forward again. Lincoln nodded and waved Ryan ahead of him, a gracious offer that Ryan was happy to accept. He crouched and slid his hand back and forth through The Toaster. His palm felt somehow happier in the front left toasting chamber so he lingered there for a while. He thought he could see a tinge of rust on the top edge of the bottom right chamber, so he tried that too. He couldn't tell if that made his hand happier or less happy so he went back to the other chamber and then explored the crumbs at the bottom for a while. "Amazing," he said.
Wait. No it's not. Toast sucks.
He didn't like that the thought was making him less content, so he tried to argue with it. But he couldn't come up with an argument that would make it go away. He couldn't come up with any argument at all. So why was the toaster making him, and any part of him that came anywhere near it, so happy?
He started to wonder if Margie had ever had such doubts. She was smarter than him, so surely she would have considered The Toaster on its practical merits like he had. When he asked her, though, she got angry.
"What do you mean, 'doubts'?" she fumed. She had gone from perfectly content to piqued in a flash. And it was doubly unsettling because Margie hardly ever got

mad about anything. "Why would I have doubts? Look at it!"

They looked at it. They could see their faces reflected in it, except where it was scuffed. Which was most of it, so really they could only see their eyes. Or rather, three of their eyes. There was a deep rusted dent, almost a puncture, where one of Ryan's eyes would be reflected. But still, The Toaster was The Toaster, and it was pretty fantastic.

Until he pondered toast. And that led to pondering the dents, and the scuffs, and the rust. And that led to mentioning them. "It's kinda crap, though, isn't it?"

She immediately boiled over. He could see it. Steam was bursting through cracks in the armor plating of her composure. "Maybe if it was butter-flavored and had a caveman on it you'd be more respectful." She stood up and focused a scornful glare at him. "Just stay away from me for a while. And stay away from The Toaster while you're at it." She stormed off so hard she churned two other ghosts up into whorls of mist as she raged through them.

Ryan had never made her that angry before. Not at him. It gave him a feeling of dread in the pit of whatever passed for his stomach. And he still kind of wanted to look at The Toaster again.

But he also kind of didn't.

32

Ryan drifted away from Margie after that. He fought the urge to go gaze lovingly at The Toaster, and the almost-as-powerful urge to go apologize to Margie for saying something so offensive. He thought he might need to ask her forgiveness, or The Toaster's, or both. But he wasn't going to ask either of them right now. Instead, he decided to pace for a while. Pacing was good. Pacing would help him figure things out.

He went towards the front of the store, where the windows had gone fully dark again. But what day was it? How many days had passed? He could easily believe it was one, or a thousand, or any number in between.

Heading that way just made the pull of The Toaster more insistent, so he was forced to turn back. He found a microwave aisle where he was close enough to The Toaster that the tug wasn't overpowering, yet far enough that he had some room to pace apart from the other ghosts. And he tried to piece together what that small, vocal part of his mind was trying to tell the other parts of his mind in an insistent, nagging voice. Something about The Toaster being junk. It was clearly absurd, but he let himself think it anyway just to see where it went.

Think about the Box, he told himself. It seemed important. It seemed like it could explain some of this. *Yes. You know this. It's happened to you before.*

While the most frequently-used function of the Box was breaking the connections between ghosts and the things they were attached to, it could also be used to do the opposite. He knew because Roger, in one of his frequent evil moments, had once forced Ryan's ghost to haunt a snow globe and then thrown it in a landfill. It was not the most fun Ryan had ever had. For one thing, there had been a lot of diapers and bulldozers, sometimes unpleasantly interacting with each other.

But yes, that had to be it. The Box had attached him, and all these other ghosts, to The Toaster. That was why he so desperately wanted to be near it despite toast being so thoroughly awful.

But he also knew that artificially creating ghost attachments like that was unstable and dangerous. Breaking from the snow globe had nearly destroyed him. Indeed, according to Margie, it was the whole reason Ryan's ghost was in the disorderly, brink-of-disintegration state it was in. Or *had* been in, until he arrived here. As long as he'd been here, he hadn't felt like he was coming apart at all.

So could it be that his attachment to The Toaster was the reason he wasn't disintegrating right now? What would happen, then, if he broke from The Toaster?

"Ryan?" The voice came from far behind and above him somewhere. He turned, expecting to find Margie there. Maybe she would be calling him over to apologize. But why would she be up in the rafters? He certainly couldn't see her there. All he could see was a small group of ghosts behind him whispering among themselves, clearly about him. He could imagine that they were speculating why one of their number was pacing by himself rather than going to see The Toaster like he should be. He was prepared to ignore them, but also worried that their mutterings would get back to Margie before long. So he elected to find a more private spot to pace.

The warehouse was entirely open except for a walled-off area on one side with a door and a picture of Lincoln saying "Honest Abe proclaims Employees Only". The ghosts seemed disinterested in going near that area, given how far it was from The Toaster. So that's where he aimed.

He pushed himself through the door and into a narrow hall lined with sales offices, dark like the rest of the warehouse. He drifted ahead in search of a good pacing spot, his ghostly glow flowing down the walls and gleaming off metal picture frames hung between closed office doors. The hall was too short to allow regulation pacing distance, and too narrow to make U-turns in an effectively thoughtful manner. So he elected to look into the offices and see if one of them was big enough.

He caught his reflection in the glass of one of the framed pictures and paused to look at himself. He hadn't ever spent a lot of time looking at himself as a ghost, and was strangely pleased with how he looked. The transparency and the glow added a kind of youthful life to his face, which was strange given that he was effectively dead. He attempted to fix his never-fixable hair.

"Ryan, are you there?" A different voice, weirdly deeper, but again high overhead. And again he couldn't see who it was. He revolved in place, looking upwards.

But he stopped. Next to his reflection in the picture frame, he had caught a glimpse of the picture itself.

It was the front entrance of a warehouse store, presumably this one. And it was the grand opening. He could tell because of the big banner strung across the front of the store that said "Grand Opening". And behind the banner, attached to the wall above the front windows, were larger letters in a spectacularly boring font: "Lydecker Stuckey Refurbished Appliance Warehouse". That puzzled him. Was this not always Lincoln's store? A small group of store managers and employees posed beneath the banner, apparently having been instructed to smile like idiots and throw thumbs-ups to the camera.

But there was another picture hung right next to it. At first glance it appeared to be the same picture. The same warehouse, with a banner above and a whole bunch of thumbs below. But then he noticed that the name of the store had changed. It was certainly the same building, but the sign over the front now said "Four Score and Seven". Beneath that in a smaller but equally dull font it said "Guaranteed unhaunted appliances". And the banner was subtly different too, because in this picture the "grand opening" was now a "grand re-opening".

He looked deeper, and noticed that the group posed at the bottom in the second picture had some new additions. Right at the front was Abraham Lincoln's ghost himself, giving a thumbs-up. And somebody near him was holding a stovepipe top hat above Abe's ghostly head so it would almost appear that he was wearing it. The illusion worked. With the hat above him he was unmistakably Abraham Lincoln. It took a moment for Ryan to recognize the guy holding Lincoln's hat as well.

It was Roger Foster. Fully alive and wearing his thin undertaker smile.

Why would an appliance store need Roger? What could he possibly do—

He realized the answer before he finished thinking the question. *Unhaunting.*

The first picture's signage made no mention of the appliances being unhaunted. But the second picture's did. The picture with Roger and Lincoln in it.

Although the corridor was woefully inadequate for it, Ryan started pacing again. He began to construct a narrative in his mind, and found that it helped him think when he said it out loud.

"Okay, so somebody—Lydecker or Stuckey or whatever—opens a used appliance store. But sales aren't good because the appliances have ghosts attached. So what does he do? He goes to the Clinic and makes a deal with Roger. Roger says he'll unhaunt the appliances for a cut. The store buys used, haunted appliances for next to nothing, Roger unhaunts them, and they sell them for a huge profit."

But why Abraham Lincoln? Why a toaster?

Ryan paced faster. Lincoln had been talking about his Four Score and Seven stores at all his speaking engagements. He was on all the store chain's commercials and online ads too. It had been like that for a couple of years.

Ever since he had apparently, secretly come into the Clinic and been unhaunted from his hat.

Ryan could feel he was close. He thought out loud again. "So maybe appliance sales still aren't good enough. So somebody—probably Roger—has the idea that the store needs re-branding. Maybe—" He checked the picture. "—maybe 'Lydecker Stuckey' isn't such a great name. Maybe they need a celebrity, a mascot. Somebody people trust." He stopped pacing. This was all making a wildly improbable sort of sense, and it stunned him. "And then Honest Abe comes into the Clinic." He started pacing again, the narrative coming together quickly in his head now. "He's in town to throw out a pitch at a Sox game. And while he's here, could the Clinic please set him free of his hat? Roger says sure. And since he's a celebrity, Roger asks him if he'll shill for a bad used appliance store. Lincoln says no, why would he want to do that? He was president, changed history, all of that. What should he care about washers and dryers?" He stopped pacing again as the final piece fell into place. "So Roger *makes* him want to. He changes the code in the Box so when it detaches Lincoln from his hat, it also *attaches* him to some easily portable piece of the store. Like a toaster."

He remembered clearly what Margie had said in the exam room: *it's something I can't find that never got undone. So every ghost that got extracted after that was affected by it. It made them vulnerable somehow to the Blink, in a way that no other ghosts are.*

That had to be it. Roger had never taken the toaster part of the code out. So during their extractions, Ryan and all of the thirty-nine ghosts were left with a latent haunting that stayed hidden from them. Until the Blink somehow activated those hauntings, yanking them across the Earth to here. And now they were forced to love a toaster unconditionally on a molecular level. ˙

It was a theory. A crazy, implausible theory. Yet it accounted for the pictures on the wall, Roger's presence in them, Lincoln's endless sales pitching at his speeches, The Toaster... almost everything. But what if he was wrong? He needed to know for sure. He'd have to find a way to prove it.

"Yep," a man's voice said from down the hall.

Ryan spun around. A living man stood in the office door. Ryan recognized him as one of the people in the pictures. He was in the front of both of them, with the biggest smile and the biggest thumbs-up and the biggest beer gut. The original owner of the store, maybe? Lydecker? Or Stuckey? Maybe Lydecker-Stuckey. And now his beer gut was leaning against the door frame of the management office, talking to Ryan.

"Sorry?" Ryan asked.

"You were talking to yourself. And you were right. That's what happened. All of it."

"Oh," Ryan said, a little dazed.

"But you left out the part where all the ghosts disappear tonight, and nobody's appliances are haunted anymore, and my whole business model turns to crap."

"Oh," Ryan said again. "Right."

"Good for you, figuring it out," Ludecker-Stuckey said. "Now get out of here, and all your friends too. We're closing. Forever." And then he slipped his arms into a raincoat, pulled his office door closed, and trudged away down the hall.

Ryan thought about calling after him to ask questions, but was pretty sure Lydecker-Stuckey didn't feel like talking.

◇

Ryan hurried back into the main warehouse in search of Margie. He had to tell her all of this. Maybe if he told her, she'd know a way they could get free of The Toaster's bland, toasted tyranny. They could get back into their bodies and put all of this behind them. If she'd listen to him, and forgive him.

"Ryan, can you hear me?"

The voice again, high in the rafters over his left shoulder this time. He froze in place, spinning around and searching. But still, he couldn't see who it was. There was nobody in the shadows up there.

But the voice had sounded familiar this time. High-pitched, and trilling. Like...

Ryan, starting to like the thrill of figuring stuff out, realized who it was, and where it was coming from.

And he answered.

33

Lowell sat on the couch in Ryan and Margie's apartment watching a terrible talk show built around interviews with dead celebrities. He suspected it was called "Dead Famous", but that seemed too obvious even for network TV. He only kept watching it because he was curious if Sinatra's ghost was just going to talk the whole time or if he was going to sing.

Gwen, over in the kitchen, was starting to annoy him. Or rather, she had been annoying him all Thursday night and through Friday, and was now continuing to annoy him but in a new way. She was dangling her toy lantern and calling into the air things like: "Ryan, are you there?" or "Ryan, can you hear me?" She did it at various pitches, sometimes in a register even higher than her normally piercing voice, and sometimes trying to plumb the depths of the lowest octaves her limited range would allow. Maybe she thought if she found the right pitch her voice would transmit better across the ether, or whatever it was it transmitted across. It didn't make much difference to Lowell. All of her pitches were transmitting directly into the annoyance center of his brain.

"He's not answering. Because that doesn't work and is stupid. Can you just sit down or something." Lowell put his legs up on the couch as a signal that he didn't mean for her to sit next to him.

"At least I'm doing something. What are you doing?"

"I've done enough on this thing. It's time to hang it up. We tried to get Lincoln. It didn't work out. The big Blackout's in a couple of hours, so it's too late. Move on. I'll find another way to get business rolling after the big ghost-be-gone."

Gwen stormed over and shoved the couch with surprising force, trying to roll him off it. "This is still about business for you? Are you serious?"

"Why? What's it about for you?" They were looking for Abraham Lincoln so they could be famous psychics after Blackout 2. That's what they were doing. He had literally no idea what other thing she could mean. Was there buried treasure or a sick puppy or something else he had missed?

Gwen kicked the back of the couch, another failed attempt to roll him off of it. "We can still get Ryan and Margie back. If we can find them before tonight! You seriously don't care?"

He did, a little. He just wasn't optimistic about their chances of success. And it seemed like a lot of work only to have it fail. Plus he was annoyed at Gwen for what she was now doing, which was trying to appear more righteous than him. "Where did all this caring come from all of a sudden?" he shot back. "You don't care. You never cared about *me* when you were stealing my cases!"

He had apparently struck a nerve, because Gwen looked mortally offended. "I stole *your* cases? Who do you think Detective Blair used to give those cases to before you showed up with your out-of-body-experience shtick?"

Lowell admitted to himself he was a little surprised at that. "You worked with Blair before?"

She stormed around the kitchen counter in laps. Even the old ghosts at the kitchen table turned to watch her. "All the time! He used to call me ten times a year at least. Cold cases, missing persons, that kind of stuff. Then one day he told me he had a new guy even more tuned in to the other side. All of a sudden I had to work twice as hard for half as many cases. I almost lost my apartment, my car, my office. All because of you!"

Lowell found himself feeling uncharacteristically guilty. A little. A tinge. A hint of a smidgen. "It's not my fault I was better than you."

"Were you, though?"

"Totally."

"But were you, though? Really?"

"Stop it."

She returned to the couch and set her lantern on the back of it. "That's all in the past now, Lowell. Right now, we have to..." She cut off, staring at her lantern.

Lowell sat up, curious. "What?"

"Oh," Gwen said. "Oh wow." She snatched up the lantern and dangled it in the space between her and Lowell. She rotated it in the air, lifted it high and then lowered it between them again.

"What?" Lowell said again. "What is it?"

Gwen looked at him. And slowly, with obvious relish, the corners of her lips stretched out into what could only be a grin of some kind of victorious delight. For what reason, he had no idea. "I knew it," she said.

Lowell was flummoxed. He waited for her to say more. When she didn't, he turned his hands palm-up in a shrug of "what are you talking about?" and beckoned for her to go on.

She still didn't say anything. She just held the lantern close to her own sternum. Then, watching it closely, she moved it across the space from her all the way over to Lowell.

He clued in. And was immediately filled with the kind of existential horror he thought only people facing a firing squad could feel. "Oh no," he said.

"Oh yes," she said. "Right here." She swung the lantern across the space again, tracing a path between them from him to her. "I almost didn't see it. But I knew it!" She grinned with her tongue sticking out between her teeth a little, far too amused for Lowell's liking.

"There's no way," Lowell said. He mentally floundered, searching for any escape from this. He could feel himself turning red, and that just made it worse.

And then, a ray of desperate hope as he thought of something. "Well how do you know which direction it goes? How do you know it's not..." He swung his finger from her over to him.

Gwen's amusement vanished. Her face fell. She drew the lantern away and looked unsteady.

"Ha!" Lowell jeered, victorious.

"I have to sit down," Gwen said. And she did, on one of the stools at the kitchen counter.

Lowell had no idea where to go from here. He definitely didn't want to be around her anymore. He had to escape. The van was still outside. Maybe he'd go out and just take off. Maybe bring Shipp with him. They'd partner up and solve cases together and play good ghost-cop/bad ghost-cop. Lowell would obviously be the good one, which was fine. He could do that. Anything to give him something to think about other than what Gwen had just discovered, and why was she looking at him like that?

"Shut up," she said.

He was immediately even more annoyed. "I wasn't saying anything."

"You are now. Shut up." She looked away from him and up into the space between her and the ceiling. "Lydecker what?" She circled the living room, staring into the middle distance the whole time, listening to nothing at all. After a painfully long period of that she talked into the air. "Ryan, can you hear me?"

Oh no, Lowell thought. *This again.* Despite his annoyance he was slightly relieved, because it was better if she was talking at nothing instead of talking at him about... things.

Gwen straightened abruptly, looking startled. "Yes, I hear you! It's Gwen!" She laughed giddily. "You're answering! Nobody's ever answered before!"

Lowell started to wonder if maybe, just maybe, Gwen wasn't faking this. He had never seen her face do the bizarre things it was doing, so if she was faking, she was really good at it. He stood up from the couch and moved over to her, careful not to create a distraction.

She seemed to be listening to the air. He couldn't hear anything, but it certainly looked like she could. "What's it like on the other other side?" she asked into the air. "Is existence the same there as on this side? Does reality obey different rules?" She listened some more, and looked slightly disappointed. "A dishwasher? Where is it even plugged in? Or does the spiritual substrata of the universe power it?" Again she listened. "Slow down, Ryan. Where?"

After another moment of listening, her eyes snapped over to Lowell.

"Write this down," she ordered.

Lowell clicked his dry pen.

◇

They ran down the stairs and across the lawn to the van. And the whole way, Lowell tried to make sense of what Gwen was saying. "Wait, the other other side where ghosts go when they exit this mortal plane is a used appliance store in Dorchester? How does that work?"

"I don't know. Get out of my way!" She shoved him aside and rushed ahead towards the van.

Lowell paused on the lawn. All through the week the sky had been unusual. The solar explosions were playing havoc with the ionosphere or the stratosphere or whatever sphere it was that they played havoc with, so there had been auroras almost every night. Especially around the times of the Blinks, the sky had been alive with colors.

Tonight was more extreme. There was almost no dark left in the sky. It was all neon waves. Amber electric light from the streetlights mixed with the shimmering blue of the ghosts on the ground, and both rose together to meet the constantly shifting swirl of the aurora. And the power grid was clearly starting to feel the effect too, because even as Lowell watched, the streetlights faded and rose, faded and rose as brownouts rippled through the city.

The second Blackout was coming. And if all this was any indication, it was going to be a whopper.

Gwen arrived at the van first, and Shipp stood up off the back bumper and straightened his bathrobe to meet her. "Going somewhere?" he said.

"Shut up," Gwen said. She ripped the van door open. "Lowell, get in the van. We gotta go."

34

Ryan hunted through the store for Margie. He was thrilled from his deductions and needed to find her before Lowell and Gwen got here. But she was lost in the crowd of ghosts and it took him many precious minutes of searching.

He found her when Roger ushered her forward for her turn at The Toaster. She drifted out of the crowd and lay on the floor next to The Toaster with both her arms wrapped around it and her cheek up against its side, an enraptured look on her face. Ryan couldn't help but feel a little sour. She had never hugged him that way. But then again, he had apparently been more concerned about a box of cereal than about her, so...

Roger saw him approaching and failed to conceal a grimace of disdain. He recovered quickly, though, and blocked Ryan's path to The Toaster. "So sorry, sir," Roger said. "Would you mind waiting in the vestibule until some of the other viewers have paid their respects? I do apologize."

Ryan dodged around him, provoking some chafed grumbles from the ghosts waiting their turn. He could hear Roger already trying to appease them as he slid up to Margie.

"Hey," he said. "Let's go. Lowell and Gwen are coming. You don't know Gwen, but she's cool. No she's not. Doesn't matter. We can go back to the Clinic. Let's go!"

Margie looked at him and didn't move her cheek or her arms from The Toaster. She barely seemed to recognize him at all. "You're supposed to wait your turn." She turned away, maybe so that her other cheek could experience The Toaster too, and maybe just to not be looking at him anymore.

He could see this was going to take some persuasion. "No, listen. We can go. We don't have to stay with—" And then he looked at The Toaster, and he understood. She didn't want to go. He didn't want to go either, because The Toaster didn't want him to. He wasn't ready to say goodbye to it.

But yes he was. *Toast sucks.* He imagined slapping himself with a piece of dry toast, and that snapped him out of it.

Margie still wasn't looking at him. He didn't know how long Lowell and Gwen would take to get here, or how long he had until Blackout 2 hit. But he was fairly certain both were imminent. He had to persuade her now.

He tried a different tack, thinking maybe she could be convinced the same way he had. "So, I was wondering... do you want some toast?"

"No, I don't want any toast. Thank you." She still didn't look at him, or allow any feeling into her voice.

"Why not?"

"Because I'm a ghost, Ryan. I'm not capable of eating." She had him there, and it didn't allow for his follow up questions. But she went on. "And even if I was, it's unlikely I'd choose toast."

There it was. His opening. "Why?"

She turned back to look at him, clearly annoyed by what he was saying. "Are you getting at something?"

Roger, prodded on by the riled ghosts Ryan had cut in front of, approached from the side. Ryan could see he'd have to pick up the pace. "It's just that, since The Toaster is so great—which obviously it is, I'm not disputing that." It *was* great. He suppressed that, forced his mind past it. "But since it's so great, and it's really only for one thing, which is making toast... I thought maybe you might want some. Toast."

"Well I don't."

Ryan saw an opening, and went through it. "Don't you think that's weird?"

"Why?"

"Well, The Toaster makes toast. And The Toaster is great. So wouldn't toast from The Toaster be great? You like toast, right?"

She shrugged. "It's fine."

He had a reflexive, visceral reaction. "Ugh. Really? It's the worst." He caught himself. Now was not the time for his own preferences to slip in. Margie would respond only to objectivity and analysis. "I mean, if it comes from The Toaster, shouldn't it be better than just fine?"

Ryan glanced at the surrounding ghosts, nervous. Roger was at the front of the pack, watching both of them with an expression of barely contained offense on his face. Some of the others were whispering to each other, shifting, passing the word along.

Margie noticed too, and lowered her voice. "You shouldn't be talking about this."

"Isn't it worth thinking about, though? You don't even really like toast. I've never seen you eat it. So why do you like The Toaster? Have you thought about that at all? You're good at thinking. You do it all the time. I almost never do, and even I figured this out."

She unwound her arms from around The Toaster, and for a moment he thought he had already won. But after a few seconds of just looking at The Toaster she shifted to sit in front of it as though shielding it from him. Like he might try to kick it. "I don't need to. It's The Toaster."

"Yeah, but... it's a toaster. An old one. It looks broken. If you think about it, does it really matter in, like, the big scheme of things?" It physically hurt him to say these things. He felt an electric jolt, like a spark from a piece of metal snapping in two.

Careful, he thought. He remembered the box of Hubert, and how his connection to it had vanished entirely in a burst of explosive indifference. The same could happen here if he pushed too hard. And his connection to The Toaster was the only thing keeping him from flying apart right now. He had to tread lightly.

He allowed himself a loving gaze at The Toaster for a moment, and felt better. He realized he would have to walk the delicate balance of love and hate if he was going to make this work.

Margie wasn't looking at The Toaster anymore. She was looking at him, conflicted. "I don't understand." It was rare for Margie to not understand anything, so Ryan felt like he was getting through.

A reedy voice pierced out of the ghostly crowd. "Who is speaking such nonsense?"

Ryan turned just as Abraham Lincoln emerged from the cloud of ghosts. Lincoln was flanked by the superhero Mr. Tinsley off his right side and Roger off his left. Roger smirked triumphantly, and Tinsley gripped his utility belt and maintained a steely gaze, like he was prepared to apprehend Ryan if so commanded.

Lincoln towered over Ryan, his face stern. "What are we talking about here, son?"

Ryan gulped. Things had taken a decidedly challenging turn. Was he really prepared to engage in an oratorical duel with none other than Abraham Lincoln? About toast? He could only stammer: "Um... um..."

Lincoln looked past him to Margie. "It's alright, ma'am. You go back to what you were doing." He motioned towards Ryan. "Pay this one no mind."

Margie looked relieved. Lincoln had removed from her the burden of considering the intrinsic value of toast, which meant that Ryan had lost ground. He needed to get some of it back.

Looking at the faces of all the other ghosts, most of them horrified or offended but some obviously curious, it occurred to him that maybe, if he did this right, he could break all of them free. He could end The Toaster's reign of terror and let all these people go home. That would be good, wouldn't it? That's what Margie would do. She wouldn't let these people stay trapped here. It's why she had come here in the first place.

He stood and faced Lincoln as defiantly as he could. Which was hard, given that Lincoln had a solid 5 inches on him even without the hat. "Sir," he said. "All I'm saying is—"

"I heard what you were saying, son. Maybe you'd like to say it again. To me." He bent forward and Ryan was forced to lean back. Lincoln was looking almost straight down into Ryan's face.

Ryan gulped again. "Can I ask you a question, Mr. President? Would you eat two slices of bread for breakfast?"

Lincoln made a chewing motion with his jaw, like it helped him think. "I would not."

"Even if you put jam or something on them?"

"There is no man I know who would call such a thing breakfast."

"Right. So we've established that just adding jam to bread doesn't make it a breakfast."

"I would agree that we have. Now I presume you are proceeding towards some sort of point, son?" He hooked his hands into the lapels of his jacket and frowned, waiting.

Ryan tried to force his ghost to stretch taller so he could press his point and look like he had some control of this. Which he was not yet sure he did. "Okay. But for some reason, if you stick those slices of bread in the toaster first, that's breakfast? They get dryer and harder. They turn brown and chalky. I might even suggest that they're obviously *worse* than they were before. But for some reason that makes them a breakfast food?"

Lincoln lost a smidgen of his posture, and with it maybe half an inch of height. He cocked an eyebrow.

Ryan went for the kill. He pointed at The Toaster and circled it, ranting. "That's what this does. That's all it does. Why should a toaster matter to anyone when there are so many breakfast choices out there? There are Sugar Frootz, and Honeycombs, and Lucky Charms. Why would anyone, anywhere, *ever* eat toast?"

The crowd of ghosts gasped in unison, shocked to hear such a thing. And Lincoln's jaw chewed in long circles like a cow eating grass.

Ryan was jolted again, harder this time. He felt something snap, and it stung like he had broken a bone. He almost lost his balance, and felt invisible currents clawing at him to tear him apart.

But he raged against them, and thundered on. "I submit to you, sir..." He raised a finger and swung it around the crowd, accusing them all. "I submit to *all* of you that toast... sucks! This... this is not The Toaster. It's just a toaster! A bad one! Is there any one of you who really wants to be here? Don't you want to be home with your families and the things you actually love, and a wide selection of breakfast foods coated in processed sugar? I ask you, what is this... this 'toaster' good for?"

The ghosts were silent. They watched him with what he hoped was some form of awe. Even Lincoln appeared dumbstruck, and had taken a step back among the others.

Mr. Tinsley raised a bat-gloved hand. "Pop-tarts?"

Ryan hadn't thought of that. There were mutterings of agreement among the crowd. It took some of the wind out of Ryan's sails. He started to lose form again, but wrestled himself back together. "Yes, okay, Pop-tarts," he strained to say. "But please, we're all adults here. Let's limit our discussion to sugar frosted cereals."

"Frozen waffles?" a voice from the back said. Ryan couldn't see who it was, but he wanted them to shut up.

"Fine," he said reluctantly. "Those too. But please, who buys a toaster for frozen waffles?" It was a feeble defense, and the crowd wasn't buying it.

"And what's that chocolate spread called?" someone off to the right said. "The one with hazelnuts?"

The rest of the crowd agreed with that. He could feel them turning against him again. But it worked partially in his favor because he liked frozen waffles too, and as he imagined toasting them he felt some of his form come back together. It gave him new energy.

"I agree with the gentleman from Boston," Lincoln said. He stepped forward from the crowd and turned to face them. "Listen to the young man. I have never felt entirely sure about this toaster. And perhaps it is for good reason. We have much to think about."

The ghosts considered him in silent incredulity for a moment. And then they encircled him, clamoring for more information, demanding explanation. Lincoln led the crowd away from The Toaster, leaving Ryan and Margie alone. Perhaps he could convince them; he had a reputation for doing things like that. But it was out of Ryan's hands now.

And dimly, he saw a ripple go through Margie. Her knees buckled and he instinctively ran to her side, trying to catch her. She passed right through his arms, and he felt everything that was Margie pass through him as she fell. He felt her relief, and her gratitude, and a whole host of feelings for the Clinic and how much she wanted to get back there. And nothing, absolutely nothing, that had anything to do with toast.

He crouched next to her, wanting but unable to help her up. When she looked up at him, she appeared annoyed. He was pretty sure it was not with him, but with herself.

"Well," she said, "this has been a waste of time. What did you do to my Clinic?"

He had a moment of joy. He had freed her.

But that led quickly to another electric jolt as his final connection to The Toaster snapped. The jolt traveled through him, ripping him apart as it went.

And then the floor around him lit up. And the shelves, and appliances, and ceiling. The whole warehouse was flooded with rising light. At first Ryan though that somebody had flipped on the store lights. But a quick look at the ceiling proved him wrong. The light wasn't coming from above. It was coming from the front window.

Ryan fought some small measure of awareness back, and saw a pair of headlights coming up fast, straight at the store window. One of the headlights flickered dimly as it approached, and Ryan immediately recognized it: *It's the House Call Wagon.*

He heard the crash and saw the front window of the store disintegrate. And then the jolt tore him apart, and the dark flowed over him.

35

Ryan's nose itched. Just a little, but it was annoying him. So he scratched it.

Wait, I have an itch? That was his first thought. His second thought went bigger-picture. *Wait, I have a nose?* He tried smelling with it and found that yes, indeed, he did. He could smell gasoline and smoke and the flesh on the back of his scalp roasting. It concerned him that the mix smelled slightly delicious.

So he was back in his body. It was not entirely pleasant given all the various itches and pains that he now had to cope with, but he was still grateful.

"He moved!" It was Gwen's unmistakable squeaky balloon voice, much too close to him. This time, instead of being disembodied, the voice was actually connected to Gwen. Ryan opened his eyes to see the pink lantern dangling inches from his face. "How many lights do you see?" Gwen said. "I'll turn it up." She cranked the little knob at the bottom, which broke off in her fingers. She irritably tried to screw it back on. "Piece of crap."

"Just one," he croaked.

"Good! You can still count, at least to one. That's a good sign." She swung the lantern away from him.

He could see the van roof swaying side to side. He felt the hammock tangled around his limbs. So he was still in the House Call Wagon, and it was moving. From the violence of its swerving, he deduced that it could only be Lowell driving.

"Wooooo!" It was from the front. Yep, Lowell was driving.

Ryan summoned what strength he could to turn his head sideways and look at the other hammock. Surely by now they had put Margie back in her body too, and this whole nightmare was over. He frantically wanted to see her.

The other hammock was empty. Her body was gone. He couldn't decide if that was good or bad. Bad because he couldn't see her but good because maybe she was up and walking around?

He was so focused on the hammock that he barely noticed the ghosts. But once he noticed them, it was hard to stop noticing them.

Because they were everywhere. The van was loaded with them, a wall-to-wall mass of ghostly forms. And not just on the inside. Every window, too, was filled with faces and limbs, all moving around and over and through each other like some horrible, morphing mutant monster. Ryan expected that, seen from the outside, the van looked like a small storm cloud hurtling through the city. They shifted independently, each coping differently with the van's momentum, so every time it sped up or slowed down the whole vaporous crowd churned anew.

Ryan, still disoriented, could recognize some of them. They were the ghosts from the appliance store. All of them, it seemed. All crammed into and on and around the van. Which was now careening down a city street.

"Ryan! Good!"

That wasn't Gwen's voice. It was a better voice. The one he wanted to hear most.

Margie appeared from the back of the van, doing her best to dodge around the ten or twelve ghosts stacked in her way. She scrambled over to him and he had never been so relieved so see anything, ever. He stretched out his arms to her, unable to find words.

But she was all business. If there were going to be hugs and happiness they would have to wait until later. "Are you suffering any ill effects? Describe everything."

"I'm..." He hunted for a detailed way to describe the various pains and discomforts and imbalances he was feeling. "...fine?"

"Good. We'll do a scan when we get there, and verify that you've fully reconnected. Your hair is still on fire, by the way. I'm going to have to fix that one day."

So that was what he was smelling. He swatted it out. "What's happening?"

Margie was already looking away from him. "Mrs. Rhodes?" She rushed towards the back, where one of the ghosts was losing her grip on the van. It was an elderly woman, and she appeared dazed, disoriented. Her feet were sinking into the floor and she was drifting towards the back, unable to match the van's momentum. Worse than that, the particles that made up her form seemed to be coming apart, slipping off of each other and pouring down over her like an avalanche. "Mrs. Rhodes!" Margie barked sharply.

Mrs. Rhodes snapped back to awareness, and her particles swirled back into place. Life returned to her eyes and she looked at Margie. "Oh!" she said. Her feet emerged from the floor and locked onto the floor of the van. "I'm sorry," the old woman said. She hardly seemed to know where she was. "I was somewhere else for a moment."

Ryan managed to stand up. "What's wrong with her?"

"It's wrong with all of them," Margie said. "The Blackout hasn't even hit yet but the buildup of energy is already affecting them."

"Why? What's wrong with them?"

"The artificial connection to The Toaster destabilized them. The Blinks weren't strong enough to destroy them, but the Blackout almost certainly will be. We have to get them back to the Clinic and into their bodies. Those should act as shields just like yours has."

"What happens if we don't?"

Margie paused, looked around at the ghost faces. Some of them were looking back at her. Others were fighting to stay conscious, or keep their shape. Lincoln moved among the ghosts in the van, reassuring them, then climbed through onto the roof to talk to the ones outside. But even he seemed blurry, out of focus. He was recognizable only by the size of his form; his face was a featureless mass.

Margie shook her head. "We will."

◇

The further across the city they went, the more the effects of the encroaching Blackout became obvious. Rolling brownouts flickered across the city in waves, sometimes casting entire blocks into darkness and then lighting them up seconds later, sometimes only at half intensity. The streetlights along the major arteries kept blinking off and then flickering on again as though they couldn't decide if it was night or day. And twice they saw electric transformers explode, once just a few feet in front of them at the side of the road, the explosion tracing searing paths through the air in tendrils of burning plasma. The city's electric grid was staggering under the assault from the sun.

More distressing, though, was the flickering of the ghosts in the streets. One second the van would be careening through a sea of them, whipping past the windows like waiting passengers on a crowded train platform. The next second they'd be gone, vanished into darkness. And still another second later they'd be back as though they had never been gone. It didn't appear to bother the ghosts themselves at all, but it was painful on the eyes of the living. Every time it happened Lowell momentarily lost control of the van as the light level in front of him precipitously dropped and then blasted up again.

The one advantage the impending Blackout provided was that traffic was mercifully thin. Most people seemed to have decided to spend the Blackout at home with the ghosts they might not see again until they were ghosts themselves. So Lowell was able to navigate all the way to the Clinic with hardly a pause. Even the traffic lights, some of them flickering on and off, seemed disinterested in delaying them.

Gwen kept a running countdown the whole way on how much time they had until the Blackout was predicted to hit in full force. It succeeded in intensifying Ryan's stress level at a steady rate. By the time they approached the Clinic's block, Gwen's quavering voice announced that they had only twelve minutes left, and Ryan wasn't sure his blood pressure would let him survive to the end of the twelve.

Lowell was the first to bring up the question on everybody's mind. "How are we going to get in?"

Ryan dared to be optimistic. "Maybe Prewitt's done at the Clinic. Maybe they're all gone." He doubted it, but it felt good to say it.

Lowell slowed as they drew close to the last curve of Mass Ave before the Clinic. Ryan squinted ahead, looking for any sign of flashing lights from the government cars, or road barricades, or patrolling agents. But there was nothing aside from the ghosts in the street. Ryan allowed himself another touch of optimism.

They cleared the trees and the Clinic swung into view. Dark and abandoned. Only a few disinterested ghosts in the street.

"Hey," Ryan said. "It looks okay!"

"Pull in the back, Lowell," Margie said.

Lowell nodded, and accelerated.

And then slammed on the brake.

Orange lights spun, blinding them, as government cars sped out onto Mass Ave, seemingly from nowhere, and skidded into a circle around the van, quickly boxing them in.

36

"We have you surrounded!" Prewitt said through a megaphone.

Ryan squinted through the windshield to see where Prewitt was in the darkness. Prewitt's utter lack of defining characteristics would have made him hard to recognize even standing a foot away in daylight wearing a name tag. Here, in the chaos of darkness and cars and government agents doing government agent-y things, he was practically invisible. Ryan spotted him, crouched and shielding himself behind an open car door as though he expected Ryan and Margie to attempt a blaze-of-glory moment.

Prewitt held his megaphone around the end of the door. "Or at least, I *assume* we have you surrounded. Do I have a lot of ghost agents with me? Are they surrounding you?"

Ryan's eyes were adjusting, and he could see at least five or six dark figures of living government agents among the cars, all of them armed. And there were at least as many ghostly agents filling in the gaps. They were, as usual, unarmed and totally incapable of putting up any resistance to living people at all. But still, it could be said that they had the van surrounded. "Yes!" he called back. Margie shot him a look for co-operating. He didn't know why he kept doing that.

"Good!" Prewitt said. "I was hoping we did. Seems like the best way to go about this, right?"

Ryan looked behind him. Most of the ghosts were crammed into the very back of the van. He wasn't sure they were aware of what was going on, because they didn't seem aware of much at all. Most of them had lost their details and become vague, blob-like versions of themselves. But they were holding on, and waiting to be told what to do.

Gwen tapped her wrist and mouthed "eleven minutes!"

Ryan turned back. Prewitt still hadn't moved out from behind his car door. He was motioning for some of his nearest agents to move in, and the dim shapes of those agents emerged from behind their vehicles and started to close in on the van.

Ryan looked at Margie, hoping she'd give him a signal what to do. But she wasn't looking at him, instead focusing on the spot where Prewitt was cowering. She was remarkably calm, especially given how not-calm Ryan felt. He wondered why he seemed to be the only one here sweating.

"This is all going very well so far, isn't it?" Prewitt said through the megaphone. "I'm glad. Honestly, I like you people. It would have been a shame if I'd had to have you shot instead of putting you in a federal prison forever. I'm sure we can all agree, this was the marginally better outcome."

The agents were halfway across the gap to the van. Ryan recognized one of them as the Lego-goateed guard from the parking lot. He hoped that the man bore no grudge from having been almost run down.

Margie leaned across the passenger set to yell out the window. "Prewitt! We found Lincoln. He's fine! He's right here!"

Gwen tried to stick her head around the seat and yell out the window as well. "I found him! Madame Gwendolyn! Say it on the news!"

Prewitt said nothing for a moment. The two agents coming across the gap paused and looked back towards the Director for instructions. But Prewitt raised the megaphone again. "Lying won't work," he said. The megaphone screeched a brief blast of feedback. "And frankly, it offends me that you would lie when I'm being so understanding."

Margie leaned further towards the window. "He's right here! We can bring him out! He's not gone!"

"I don't believe you!"

Margie waved Lincoln forward out of the crowd. "Mr. President, could you come up here."

Lincoln appeared even hazier than before. For a moment Ryan couldn't even recognize him. But the president concentrated and the detail in his features returned. He gave Margie a nod, and she led him to the front.

Understanding the situation, Lincoln didn't stop at the dashboard, but walked straight ahead through it and through the engine until he was standing in front of the van in the street. He held the lapels of his jacket and nodded benevolently at the agents around him. He looked about as Lincoln-like as it was possible to look. Once again, Ryan wished Lincoln had died with his hat on.

The agents coming at the van gave each other questioning looks and then turned back to Prewitt. Lego Goatee spoke up. "They're not lying, sir. He's there."

Prewitt grimaced in frustration. "I don't care!"

The agents appeared as surprised and confused as Ryan felt.

"I've been in charge of this agency for nearly two years now," Prewitt ranted. "Two years! And do you know what's on my list of achievements?"

"Nothing," Shipp said from inside the van behind them. He stepped through the mass of ghosts and strode all the way to the front to stand between Margie and Ryan. His face was hardened, and he tied up his robe.

"Nothing!" Prewitt bellowed into the megaphone.

"We know!" Margie said. "Shipp already told us!"

"Tell Shipp to shut up! The answer is nothing! And after tonight, the Bureau of Ghost Affairs will be redundant! No more ghosts, no more ghost affairs, no more bureau! I refuse to end my tenure at the top of this department with no legacy, no achievements to my name! I'm not going back to food inspection!" He threw the megaphone down angrily. It made a crack and a blast of shrill feedback as it struck the pavement. "And now I've broken that! That's also on you people! I'm arresting you! Arrest them!"

The agents advanced, uncertain, on the van.

Ryan again looked to Margie for some hint of what to do. But she was doing the same, looking at him. They silently confirmed to each other that neither had an answer.

Shipp leaped forward through the hood of the van and stopped beside Lincoln. He pointed a commanding finger at the agents. "Slow down. Half pace. That's an order."

The agents heard him, and looked even more uncertain. But they slowed their advance.

"What's he doing?" Lowell whispered. Nobody knew.

"What's happening?" Prewitt called from among the cars. Deprived of his megaphone he had to cup his hands around his mouth. "Why are you going so slow?" Shipp turned around to face Ryan and Margie. "You people in the van, Ryan and the doctor one. Exit through the rear doors. Take all of the ghosts and go directly back to the next corner using the van as cover. Then circle down the side street to the back entrance of the Clinic." He turned back to the agents. "Nobody will interfere with them. Is that clear?"

They nodded, and appeared grateful to have someone giving them something easy to do.

"You can go faster than that!" Prewitt called to the agents, totally unaware that Shipp was with them. "Arrests are usually fast!"

Shipp turned back to the van. "You other two, the crazy ones, you're staying here. We're going to buy them some time." He strode back through the engine block and into the van.

Lowell asked the obvious. "How?"

Shipp sat in the passenger seat. "You're taking me hostage."

Lowell and Gwen looked equally shocked. It was Lowell who broke first. Specifically, he broke into a Christmas morning grin. "Oh ho ho yeah! Now you're talking!" He jammed his head out the window. "Call off your goons! We've got your man Shipp and we'll hurt him if we have to!"

Prewitt frowned. He turned to the agent nearest him. "Can they do that? Can they hurt a ghost?" He sighed. "Fine. Does anybody know anything about hostage negotiating? I'm hopeless at it."

Shipp turned to Ryan and Margie. "What are you waiting for?"

Ryan thought he should probably thank Shipp. But Margie didn't give him the chance. She plunged through the ghosts and threw open the back doors of the van.

37

Ryan and Margie jogged along the basement corridor with the cloud of gradually deteriorating ghosts flooding the space behind them.

The overhead lights blinked off and the ghosts behind them vanished, leaving them in the total darkness of yet another brownout.

Margie's voice came out of the dark ahead of Ryan, a resolute whisper: "Don't stop!"

He could hear her footfalls, still jogging in front of him. So he put out his free hand and ran it along the wall for guidance, and jogged after her.

The darkness dragged on. It felt like it was lasting too long to be another brownout, and panic rose in his gut.

"Is this the Blackout?" he whispered. "Did it come early?"

He could only hear Margie's breathing and footfalls in reply.

Then the lights flickered on with glassy *snap-pops,* and suddenly the air around Ryan was thick with ghosts again. A dozen ghostly faces materialized around him.

He could see Lincoln among them, urging the others on. "This way! Stay with our friends!"

Ryan squinted to see through them and keep running straight. He could barely make out Margie's shape ahead of him.

"The Blackout is getting close," Margie said between ragged breaths. "A few minutes maybe."

Ryan tried to stay focused and figure out the task at hand. All he had were questions. "Some of these ghosts have been out of their bodies for years. Will they still be able to get back in?"

"They don't have to stay in permanently," Margie said from ahead of him. "Just long enough to get through the Blackout. The bodies should hold them that long."

There was a bigger question that had been gnawing at Ryan for a while now, but which he had suppressed for fear of finding out the answer. He couldn't wait any longer. "How will we have time to get them all—"

"We will," Margie said. It was a flat statement, and implicit in it was a refusal to even consider any other possibility.

Ryan considered other possibilities for her. If Margie was right, they had a few minutes at most. And nearly forty ghosts to put into bodies. The Box took at least a minute or two to charge up, after which it could be used twice before needing to recharge fully again. It took virtually no math before Ryan could see that their task was impossible. Margie had to know that, didn't she?

"We can't do it," he said.

"There's the Box in the exam room and two spares in storage, if they haven't been confiscated," Margie said. She got the words out in sharp bursts of breath between long running strides. "Early prototypes, but they can do this. We'll swap between them. Charge two while using one. We won't move the bodies. Leave them in their cabinets, proceed row by row, we can get through two, maybe three in a minute. There's time."

Ryan wrestled with the numbers, trying to figure out if she was right, or just optimistic. But the light of the storage facility loomed up around the corner ahead and he ran out of time to think about it.

Ryan's other big remaining fear was that Prewitt would have left some of his people on guard in the basement, just in case. But the storage facility was empty. It appeared untouched. All the slide-out body cabinets were closed, and nobody stood guard over them. It seemed Prewitt didn't give Ryan and Margie enough credit to think they might actually get this far.

Margie didn't stop. She pointed back at Ryan as she kept running through, headed across towards the hall and the exam room. "I'll get the Boxes," she said. "You open the drawers. You know the names. Get as many of the original bodies out in the open as you can!"

Ryan didn't want to be left alone, but Margie didn't wait for him to respond. She disappeared into the shadows of the corridor and he could hear her fast footsteps thumping away, echoing off the pipes.

Ryan stopped. The mass of ghosts engulfed him, and for a few moments he couldn't see anything but glowing fog. He spun in place, disoriented.

"Everyone, please, may I have your attention." The voice was Roger's. He emerged from the crowd and took up a position outside the general mass. "I'm terribly sorry, I know this is very difficult, and we've had a lot of excitement. But could I trouble you to all line up in the corridor? Quietly please. I do apologize. It is a trying day for us all. Thank you."

And the ghosts, conditioned by days of listening to Roger's direction at The Toaster, obeyed. They filtered into the hall and jostled to form a line, with Roger nodding to them at the front and Lincoln waving them through at the back.

It was the first time Ryan had ever liked Roger. At all.

With the ghosts out of the way, he turned his attention to the storage facility computer. It had direct access to the database of what body lay in what drawer, and he knew if he hurried he could have the whole list accessible in seconds. He tapped the screen, and as the interface popped up he ran through the names of all the toaster-obsessed ghosts in his mind. Lincoln, obviously, would not have his body stored here. Ryan would just have to find a random one for him. It would eventually reject him and spit out his ghost again, but it would last long enough to ride out the storm. But first, he would find the names he knew.

Tinsley. Ryan started to type.

He got as far as the N, and the lights blinked out again.

The ghosts vanished. And the monitor, like the room, went black.

Ryan let out a guttural caveman noise. It bounced around the pipes and off the cabinet doors and came back at him from all directions. For a moment he felt like he was about to be mobbed in the dark by a colony of ill-tempered primates.

To his relief, the lights flickered back on just a few seconds later. The ghosts reappeared and resumed lining up. And the monitor came back to life.

"Loading..."

It stayed that way for a long time, the little ellipsis at the end of the word constantly cycling from one dot to two to three, back to one. Ryan danced in place.

The word disappeared, and was replaced by another word. "Connecting..."

If Ryan had been wearing a watch, he knew he would be looking at it and confirming for himself that this was not going to work. There simply wasn't time. And the power was certain to go off again. He needed a new plan.

And a new plan was obvious. It came to him so quickly he assumed it must be stupid. They needed thirty-nine bodies. But they didn't necessarily have to be the *right* thirty-nine bodies. Any body at all would shield a ghost long enough to get them through the Blackout.

So all he had to do was pick thirty-nine bodies at random. All of these ghosts could be mixed and matched into whatever bodies he could find, and they'd survive.

He abandoned the computer, which had proceeded on from "Connecting..." to the even less helpful "Indexing..." And he scrambled to the closest row of drawers.

He knew from experience how heavy they were. The door hinges were old and worn, so it took effort to get them open. And the drawers inside required almost his full body weight to get out. Doing this thirty-nine times was going to be a workout.

He stretched his arms and cracked his fingers and opened the first cabinet. Without even checking the body inside he grabbed the handle and leaned his full weight backwards.

The drawer came hurtling out with little resistance, and Ryan was flung backwards and jerked to a stop so abruptly that it nearly tore his fingers out at the knuckle.

Stunned, he checked inside the drawer. It was empty. No body.

About a third of the drawers in the facility were always empty. They hadn't done enough extractions to fill them all yet. So it was bad luck that he had opened an empty one, but not really surprising. Fairly consistent with how the rest of his week had gone, really.

He tore open the next cabinet and pulled that drawer out, a little more cautiously

Empty.

He shifted to the next row and pulled one of those open. And another.

His tension intensified as he grabbed every cabinet door he could see, ripping them all open, pulling out the drawers.

All empty. Not a single body.

The realization of what that meant took its time drilling into his mind because he was so resistant to it, so unwilling to let it be a thing. But it was a thing. A thing that he was now going to have to tell Margie. And Margie would not like that thing.

By the time she returned, rolling two Boxes on their carts ahead of her and pulling a cart full of car batteries behind her, Ryan was sitting on the floor with his back against the cabinets, holding his forehead in his hands. He wanted this not to be true, but it was.

With all the empty drawers hanging open, it was obvious. But he said it anyway.

"Prewitt took the bodies," he said. "They're all gone."

38

Margie walked, zombie-like, from cabinet to cabinet. She looked into each open and empty one and pulled open a few more herself, as though hoping Ryan had overlooked a stray body in one of them. But he hadn't.

Ryan sat on the floor in the corner and watched her. He could feel all energy and will draining out of him. He was in his body and yet still felt like he was once again coming apart into tiny pieces. They had come this far with only minutes to spare, and now there was nothing they could do.

Margie gave up opening the cabinets and let her back slide down the wall until she was sitting next to him. Both of them hugged their knees. Lincoln and Roger watched them from the hall at the front of the ghost line, sensing that there was a problem. Ryan thought Roger must already know what the problem was, but he wasn't saying anything. Not yet.

The lights blinked off, this time for barely long enough to let darkness fall, and then flashed on again. The light directly over Ryan and Margie continued to flicker and buzz, casting them in an irregular strobe that they lacked the will to move out of. They said nothing for what felt like a long time.

Ryan looked over as the ghosts in the hall vanished briefly and then reappeared. He wondered if they understood what was about to happen. He remembered with frightening clarity the feeling of approaching obliteration. A year ago he had spent days in near-certainty that he was going to disintegrate. It was a time spent in constant dread, always trying to decide: *if these are my last moments, what do I do with them?* He wouldn't wish that feeling on anyone.

This time he was lucky. This time he felt pretty secure he'd be safe. His body had three times proven a resilient shield against whatever forces the sun was lobbing at the Earth. But these people were fully exposed. Thirty-nine ghosts—thirty-nine *people*—were about to be destroyed forever. He didn't think he could watch that. But he also didn't think he could run away.

He looked to Margie. She was brilliant. She always had ideas. She'd have an idea any second now and everything would be fine. He watched her eyes study the data feed that constantly scrolled through her mind and waited for her to settle on something.

She sat up from the wall. He watched her replay an idea again and again in her mind, maybe rearranging steps, perfecting it. She turned to him. "I need your help," she said.

Ryan jumped up. "Anything," he said. And he meant it. He was fully in bottom-of-the-Frosted-Flakes-box mode.

She looked past him at the ghosts in the hall. Roger had perked up a little, perhaps sensing that Margie had thought of a way to save him. He wasn't about to interrupt her if she was doing that.

She turned back to Ryan. "I need you to..." She studied his face. He shifted on his feet, restless, as she looked at him. And he saw a flicker in her eyes that he thought signaled she had decided something. "I need you to use the Box," she said.

"I can do that." While filling in for her illegally in the supposedly-closed Clinic he had gotten pretty good at using the Box. Whatever she needed him to do this time, he felt confident he could do it. "Who are we using it on?"

The power flickered off, stayed dark for a second, and then snapped back on. When the light hit her again, she was taking off her lab coat. "Me," she said.

He searched the corners of his mind for some theory about what her plan was. But those corners of his mind were filled with little more than dust bunnies. He would have to just ask. "Why?"

She pulled one of the empty cabinets in the bottom row open and slid the drawer out. "These ghosts need to be in a body to shield them from the Blackout. So you're going to put them in one." She climbed into the cabinet and lay down, using it like an exam table.

Ryan thought he had figured out what she meant, but the idea seemed insane to him. He couldn't be right. "All of them? In you?"

"That's right."

"That's nuts."

"No it's not. Cases of multiple ghost inhabitation are fairly common. You yourself had Sye inhabiting you for days and didn't even know it. A study in Tokyo discovered a subject with fifteen ghosts all bonded to his cortex, sharing animation and cerebral functions."

"And he was okay?"

She frowned. "Well, no. He was unconscious much of the time and eventually escaped the lab and fell into a volcano, possibly on purpose. But still, it's technically feasible. Turn on the Box."

Ryan didn't go anywhere near the Box. He shook his head. "That was fifteen. This is thirty-nine."

"Yes. I know. We don't have time to talk about this. Turn on the Box."

He still didn't move. He looked again at the ghosts in the hall. Lincoln was trying to help Mrs. Rhodes, whose arms were coming apart and falling into a pile at her feet like sand. Lincoln himself was clearly struggling just to keep his form while still attempting to calm her. All of the ghosts, in fact, seemed to be in distress. And all of them kept looking over at him and Margie.

The lights flickered vaguely, and crackled.

"Ryan," Margie said. She was level, assured. Everything he couldn't be. "No time. Power up the Box please." She rested her head on the floor of the cabinet and closed her eyes. The decision was made.

Ryan hated this idea. But it was apparently the only idea.

So he left her, rolled one of the Boxes over, and connected it to the batteries. He started the charge and watched the meter creeping upwards.

"You don't need the spider," she said. "This is a general application, non-targeted. Just the paddles. One hundred percent, single-stage."

Ryan picked up the paddles from the cart. His mind screamed at him. *No no no no no no.* "You're going to be okay, right? I mean, this isn't going to hurt you or rip your ghost apart or something, is it?"

She didn't open her eyes. "It's never been done before, so I can't say that. It's definitely extremely dangerous. There are many things that could go wrong. It might even be impossible."

Ryan chuckled. "You could say you'll be fine. Just to make me feel better."

She smiled softly. "I never do anything just to make you feel better." She reached up and slapped his cheek lightly. "Bring them in. Have them get as close to me as they can. You're going to open a door for them, but it won't stay open for long and they all have to go through it at once. One discharge only."

Ryan motioned to Roger, who nodded in reply. He waved to the other ghosts. "Could I trouble you all to come this way, please. I know you're all uncomfortable, but could we move forward please, thank you. Faster, please. Faster, you fools!" He instantly regretted it and regained his composure. "Terribly sorry about that. Difficult day for us all."

The whole crowd hurried into the room and over to the open cabinet. They stood around Margie, uncertain what to do.

"Get in close," she said. "You're going to have to bunch together."

The lights flashed off and on and the ghosts vanished and re-appeared three times as they squeezed together, overlapping each other, all thirty-nine of them in a fog around the cabinet. Ryan tried to stay outside of them, but still felt the chill of them passing through him, and their fear. Mostly their fear.

Margie closed her eyes again. She looked serene, resolved. *Fine* with this. He didn't know how she could be. He wasn't fine with it at all. There was so much that could go wrong. Doing this could mean never seeing her again. It could mean she'd never recover. It could mean she'd jump into a volcano. It could mean she'd never get back into her body that he'd just fought so hard to keep her in.

He flexed and un-flexed his fingers around the paddles. "I don't know if I can do this," he said.

"You have to. There isn't time to talk about it. Do it now."

As if to underscore her point, the lights blinked bright, and then went out.

And stayed out.

Ryan breathed fast while his eyes adjusted to the glow of the ghosts. Were the lights going to come back on, or was it—

"It's the Blackout," Margie said. She was still miraculously calm. She squeezed her eyes closed. "It's now or never, Ryan."

She was right. It was now or never. The moment hung frozen.

She wasn't going to let these people be annihilated. Not when she'd dedicated her life to helping them. And he couldn't either. But he also wasn't going to let Margie get hurt.

There was one way to achieve both.

He pressed one of the paddles to his own chest, and the other to the back of his head.

Margie opened her eyes and saw what he was doing right before he stepped on the pedal. She tried to leap out of the cabinet at him, reaching for him.

He was amazed how calm he was as he pressed down with his foot and sent fire blasting through his body. He felt the room pitch fully sideways and all his senses explode.

Thirty-nine ghosts passed through him and into his body at once and he didn't fight against them, but welcomed them all, invited them, made room for them. He floated up and out to give them space as the world plummeted away and cast its deep shadow across him.

39

The standoff in the street was not even close to resolved.

Lowell had presented a list of demands to set Shipp free including a helicopter to the airport, a charter flight to the Cayman Islands, and a crate of snack cakes, preferably Yodels. Prewitt was making calls, but seemed to think his superiors wouldn't move on the Yodels.

Then the darkness hit.

The streetlights went out first. Then the buildings. And when they didn't come back on, everybody knew it was time.

"This is it," Lowell said. "Here we go."

Lowell leaned forward to watch and Gwen slid into the space between the seats to join him as a wave of darkness spread across the ground, like the night sky was leaking through the swirling aurora and flooding across the Earth.

Electric lights blinked out ahead of the onrushing wave that left no lamp alight in its wake. But that wasn't the most stunning part.

What most struck Lowell was the ghosts vanishing, one after another, as though swept under a black blanket spreading fast across the ground. The ghosts didn't seem aware of it. None of them panicked or tried to outrun it. Maybe, as he had seen at the Common, they couldn't even tell it was happening. Maybe things wouldn't change all that much for them.

But to Lowell's eyes, and probably to the eyes of every living person in the world, the wave left in its wake the utter darkness of a hundred billion brilliant lights going out.

"Oh wow," Gwen said. She put a hand on Lowell's shoulder, and he let her.

Ahead of them in the street, Prewitt, oblivious to what was happening, shook his cell phone. "Hello? Hello? I've lost service. Does anyone have service?" Then he seemed to clue in to the Blackout, and went silent. He stood and gazed around him at the uncommonly dark city.

Lowell turned to Shipp in the passenger seat. He was still there, his disappearance delayed somehow. He gazed out the window, puzzled. "It's happening?" he said.

Lowell nodded. "Sorry, man. It's happening." He felt a little sorry for the guy. He wasn't that bad in the end.

"Hey," Gwen said, "you wanna tell us what's in the van that you're haunting? We can leave it somewhere for you. Somewhere you want to be."

Shipp shrugged. "That's nice of you," he said. "It's—" And then, with the slightest of flickers, he vanished.

They both watched the empty space for a while.

"I'll ask him later," Lowell said. "Maybe we'll hang out."

"Cool."

The city was utterly black, absolutely quiet. Lowell sat with Gwen and absorbed the unfamiliar darkness.

There was movement in the street ahead. Prewitt emerged from between the cars. He rotated himself in the middle of the road, trying to look in all directions at once.

"What's he doing?" Lowell asked. Gwen had no answer. They watched.

Prewitt scrambled up the hood of the nearest car, and from there onto the roof. He revolved slowly, transfixed by something that lay in all directions around him. He whooped in amazement. "I see them!" he said. "I see dead people!"

Lowell wasn't surprised. He wondered if anything would surprise him ever again.

"Looks like we got some new competition," he said.

40

Lowell yawned. He had been up all night waiting for the lights to come on. And he couldn't remember, but he thought he had been up the whole night before as well. So he felt like he had good justification for yawning.

It didn't help that he was bored. He sat on the floor in a dark corner of the Clinic's ugliest, coldest room and watched Margie and Gwen keep doing what they had been doing since the lights had flashed back on just before dawn. That was several hours ago now, and he was sick of it.

Ryan's body lay in one of the slabs pulled out of the wall cabinets, and Margie leaned over it with some kind of scanner thing that looked like she'd made it out of a car battery tester and bent binder clips. As she swept it up and down Ryan's body, Gwen kept swinging her toy lantern and listening to the air.

Lowell yawned again, and wished he had a breakfast burrito. Or maybe some toast. No, a breakfast burrito.

Margie stopped her sweep and held the scanner in place. Even from a distance Lowell could see the little needle on it dancing. "There's another emerging," she said.

Gwen sprung over to her and dangled the lantern just above the scanner. "Is somebody there?" she said into the air. "Speak to us!" They waited. Lowell had seen this process repeat so many times now that it had lost all meaning for him. He wanted sausage in his burrito.

"I'm getting an L," Gwen said, tapping her teeth with a finger. "Or an A." She listened some more. Despite her success so far, Lowell couldn't shake the feeling that she was faking. He couldn't shake some other feelings too but those were for another time. "No, it's an L," Gwen went on. "Lancer? Lobo?"

"Those aren't names," Lowell inserted.

"They could be," Gwen shot back.

"Lester?" Margie said.

"Yes! Lester. Definitely Lester."

Margie noted that on a chart she had hung from one of the cabinet handles.

Lowell was slightly relieved. Lester Massey was apparently fine, and would likely soon be back to the top floor of the former Robbie and Bobbie's Bar, invisibly this time. He could sit where he wanted and not bother the residents. It had all worked out pretty well. Lowell made a mental note to inform Massey's daughter, and then forgot it.

Margie shut her scanner off and straightened. "That's it," she said. "That's thirty-nine. They're all out. All intact." She wheeled The Box away from the cabinet and yanked its cable free of the stack of car batteries. She was trying to look clinical and professional, but even Lowell with his limited intuitive abilities could see that she was struggling.

Gwen looked into Ryan's motionless face with amazement. "He saved all of them. I wouldn't have thought he had it in him. But he did."

Specifically, he had thirty-nine of them in him, Lowell thought.

"Do you think he's still in there?" Gwen asked.

Ryan hadn't moved at all. Lowell suspected he might be dead. And if he was dead, then his ghost was out. And Ryan's ghost couldn't survive outside his body for long; he had made that clear many times. But Lowell wasn't going to say it because Margie already knew it.

Margie stepped closer to Ryan. "I don't know. I don't know *where* he is. It's possible he was destroyed by the procedure. It's possible the Blackout obliterated him. It's possible he just stayed out of his body too long and disintegrated." She clenched her eyes briefly closed, held them that way, then forced them open again. "I don't know. He had nothing to anchor him or shield him. No permanent connection." She lowered her voice, and looked at Ryan piteously. "Nothing real." She shook it off again and looked back to Gwen. "You're still not getting anything on your..." She pointed at Gwen's lantern.

Gwen hoisted it again and held it over Ryan's body. The little pink light was feeble after so much use, but she squinted hard and swung it. And something about what it was doing intrigued her. "Wait a second," she said.

Margie looked at her sharply. "What?"

Gwen swung the lantern away from Ryan's body and over close to Margie. She dangled it there, squinting. Margie, more tense than Lowell had ever seen her, wrung her hands. "What?"

Gwen pushed the lantern closer to Margie, almost up against her. "There's something..." She held it there.

Margie's eyes lit up, hopeful.

Then the little pink light flickered and died. Gwen lowered the lamp again, frustrated. "Piece of crap. And these are new batteries." Gwen threw her head back and spoke to the ceiling. "Ryan! Are you there?"

She listened. They all did. Lowell didn't know why, because nobody but Gwen would hear a response and he wasn't even completely sure that *she* could.

The silence dragged out long. Gwen shook her head. "Nothing," she said.

Margie put her hand on Ryan's arm and stood over him for a long while. Long enough that Lowell started to feel awkward and wanted to go upstairs. He motioned with his head to Gwen that he was going to leave, and she signaled with a point at the floor that she was going to stay.

Lowell shuffled towards the hall.

"If you see Ethan and Ewan," Margie said quietly, "send them down. I need them to get him hooked up for storage."

So she was going to keep Ryan's body alive, just in case she could put him back in it. Lowell thought it was probably faint hope. Ryan was gone. But better to be safe, he supposed. He nodded and headed for the stairs.

◇

Lowell went out the Clinic front door to get a touch of sun, hoping maybe it would wake him up and substitute somehow for the burrito he hadn't yet had.

It was strange seeing the world empty of ghosts. Ordinarily he'd have to dodge around dozens of them just to get from the front entrance to the sidewalk. But now he just walked in a straight line, seeing and feeling none of them. He knew he must have passed through them. They were there, and they could see him. But he couldn't see them. Nobody could. It was going to take some getting used to. And in a weird way, he wasn't sure he liked it.

The press had showed up and were in mid-interview out on the sidewalk. Five or six tired-looking reporters who had probably been out covering the Blackout 2 story all night now held out microphones towards Director Prewitt, who was grinning like a fool. Lowell leaned against a planter and watched.

Prewitt kept pointing at the air beside him. "You seriously can't see him? Really? It's President Lincoln. Right here. Say something, Mr. President!" He paused for a few seconds, then looked to the reporters for acknowledgment. "See? Who else but Abraham Lincoln would say something so wise and perceptive. Thank you, sir. You've given us all something to think about."

The reporters blinked at him. One of them snapped a picture.

"Anyway, you can thank the good people of the Federal Bureau of Ghost Affairs, East Division for bringing him back to use safe and sound. Definitely a department that needs to stay active and not decommissioned, don't you think? Are there any more questions?"

All of the reporters stuck their hands up, but Lowell didn't hang around to hear what questions they would ask. Prewitt taking all the credit made him feel slightly sick, and the sun hadn't perked him up at all. He was going to steal a quick nap and then go find some breakfast. Or lunch, depending on how long that nap turned out to be.

He went inside to his office and briefly considered sleeping in his desk chair. But he feared that Roger might be sitting invisibly in it. Plus the dentist chair was more comfortable. So he lay down and it took him only minutes to fall asleep despite his stomach rumbling.

A minute after that he jumped down off the chair, leaving his body reclined in it. He stretched his ghostly limbs, and pondered what he'd do while his body got some rest. Maybe go to the Common, watch the British troops march. He wondered if they'd keep doing that when nobody alive could see them.

On his way out he looked over at his desk, and stopped. He had been right about not sitting in his chair. But Roger wasn't in it.

Ryan was.

"Finally," Ryan said.

Lowell wasn't surprised. Because, again, nothing surprised him anymore. "They're looking for you downstairs," he said.

"I know. I've been yelling at Gwen for an hour. Does she literally not hear you unless you spell your name first?"

"Apparently."

Ryan shook his head, annoyed. "I'm not spelling. That's stupid."

"I agree."

"Will you tell them I'm still here?"

"Sure. When I wake up." He looked at his body in the chair. It rolled over on its side. "It could be a while. You like American Revolution stuff? There's this thing at the Common."

Ryan shook his head. "I can't leave."

"Why not?"

"I don't know." He studied the Clinic around him, as though hunting for something that might be holding him here. "I just can't."

Lowell's body rolled too far and tumbled off the chair. It hit the floor with a heavy *thump*, and echoes of the pain were still bouncing through it when it woke up and Lowell's ghost snapped back into it.

He picked himself up and squeezed his nose, worried it was sprained. "Never mind," he said through his hand. "I'll go tell them."

Remember to leave a review on Amazon.
Reviews make authors happy!

Acknowledgements

All thanks to my wife, Nancy.
For reading the first book.
For helping me write the second one.
And for everything before, after, and in between.

About the Author

If you've ever turned on a television and are not picky, you've probably seen something written by DM Sinclair. He's written more than a hundred hours of that stuff, and will happily take the blame even for the shows he didn't write. Later he switched to writing books because he thought it might be nice. It isn't, though. Nevertheless, he plans to keep writing as long as he is alive. After that, he intends to visit Australia. Like many Canadians, he lives in Canada

You can connect with him on:

🌐 http://dmsinclair.com

🐦 https://twitter.com/D_M_Sinclair

📘 https://www.facebook.com/dmsinclairauthor

Subscribe to DM Sinclair's newsletter:

✉ http://dmsinclair.com/index.php/newsletter

Or just email him at:
author@dmsinclair.com

Made in the USA
Coppell, TX
08 January 2023

10738950R00198